The Doctor of Thessaly

The Doctor of Thessaly

Anne Zouroudi

B L O O M S B U R Y

LONDON · BERLIN · NEW YORK

First published in Great Britain 2009

Copyright © 2009 by Anne Zouroudi

Map on p. vii © John Gilkes 2009

The moral right of the author has been asserted

Bloomsbury Publishing, London, Berlin and New York

36 Soho Square, London W1D 3QY

A CIP catalogue record for this book is available from the British Library

ISBN 978 0 7475 9882 4
10 9 8 7 6 5 4 3 2 1

Typeset by Hewer Text UK Ltd, Edinburgh
Printed in Great Britain by Clays Ltd, St Ives plc

The paper this book is printed on is certified by the © 1996 Forest Stewardship
Council A.C. (FSC). It is ancient-forest friendly. The printer holds
FSC chain of custody SGS-COC-2061

Mixed Sources
Product group from well-managed
forests and other controlled sources
www.fsc.org Cert no. SGS-COC-2061
© 1996 Forest Stewardship Council
FSC

www.bloomsbury.com/annezouroudi

For CP
Acta est fabula, plaudite!

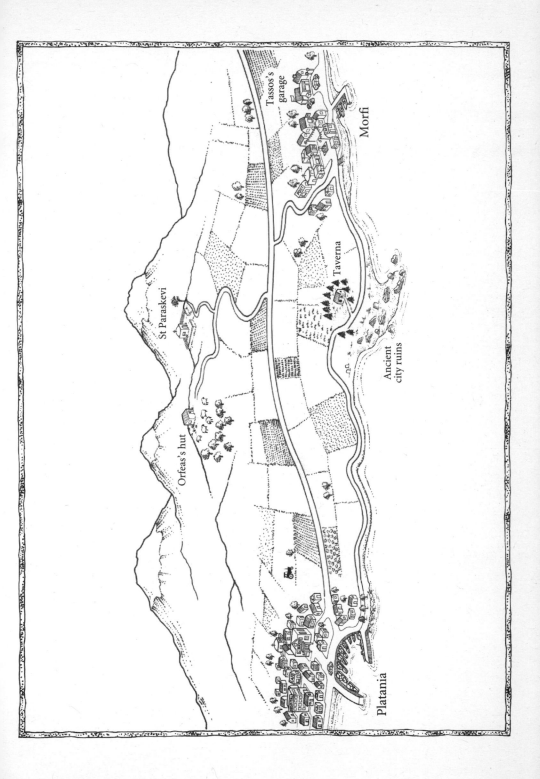

DRAMATIS PERSONAE

Hermes Diaktoros – an investigator from Athens
Chrissa Kaligi – a bride-to-be
Noula Kaligi – her unmarried sister
Aunt Yorgia – the sisters' aunt
Adonis Anapodos – a simpleton
Evangelia (Eva) – owner of a *kafenion*
Dr Louis Chabrol – a French doctor
Tassos – a car mechanic
Litsa – his wife
Christos – their teenage son
Dr Dinos – a retired doctor
Angelos Petridis – the town's new mayor
Orfeas – a mountain-man and shepherd
Apostolis – a postmaster
Vangelis – a pharmacist
Lambis – a grocer
Stamatis Semertzakis – the government minister for Public Works
Arsenios – assistant to the minister

... There within
she saw that Envy was intent upon
a meal of viper flesh, the meat that fed
her vice ... And when she saw the splendid goddess dressed
in gleaming armour, Envy moaned: her face
contracted as she sighed. That face is wan,
that body shriveled; and her gaze is not
direct; her teeth are filled with filth and rot;
her breast is green with gall, and poison coats
her tongue. She never smiles except when some
sad sight brings her delight; she is denied
sweet sleep, for she is too preoccupied,
forever vigilant; when men succeed,
she is displeased – success means her defeat.
She gnaws at others and at her own self –
her never-ending, self-inflicted hell ...

Ovid, *Metamorphoses*, Book 2
(Translated by Alan Mandelbaum)

One

One by one, peal by peal, the joyful church bells fell silent. First, word reached the chapel of St Anna's; from there, the message passed to St Sotiris's, where the ringer looped the bell-rope on its hook and set off to her daughter's for more news. Long before the time agreed, the bells stopped at St George's on the coast road and at Holy Trinity in the foothills, though for a while, the bell at distant St Paraskevi's still rang out, its elderly ringer not noticing, in her enthusiasm and her deafness, that all the others were quiet. So they found a bicycle and told the oldest boy to travel quickly; and midway through a celebratory peal, that bell too faltered in its rhythm, and was still.

Across the fields, the buff slopes of the mountains were growing dim. Small waves broke harmlessly on the town beach, and the dark sea stretched towards a sky already pale with evening. The mildness of the afternoon was gone, and a cold breeze raised ripples which ran like shivers across the water.

From the beach head, a woman was making for the sea. The heels of her satin shoes caught between the stones, turning her ankles; but she went determinedly on, carrying the hem of her white gown above her feet, whilst behind,

I

the long train of her dress dragged like a trawl-net, hooking debris left by the high spring tides: brittle kelp and the cap of a beer bottle, the bleached, ovoid bone of a squid, liquorice smears of marine oil.

Close to the sea, the stones were small, becoming shingle at the water's edge, and beneath the water, sand. As she followed the water-line, her heels sank deep into the shingle, discolouring the shoes with damp. Where three flat rocks stood out from the shallows, she stopped and looked back up the beach, along the road.

No one was there. No one followed.

She turned back to the empty sea. The last good light of day lit her face, picking out the crow's feet where powdered foundation had set in lines; the trails of mascara-dirtied tears marked her cheeks. In her hands – where raised veins and slender bones stood prominent, and the first brown stains of liver-spots had bloomed – she held two garlands of fake flowers: orange blossoms twisted around paper-covered wire, joined by a length of white ribbon – *stefani*, the headdresses of a bride and groom.

As hard as she could throw, she cast the garlands away from her on to the sea, expecting them to float on the deep water and drift away to the horizon; but her throw was weak, and the *stefani* landed in the shallows, where the water quickly turned the delicate flowers ash-grey. The garlands sank, their white ribbon flickering briefly on the surface. Settling on the seabed, their circular shape was lost, shifting and distorted by the water.

Along the road, the street-lamps were lit. Still no one came.

Sinking down on the shingle, she kicked off her satin shoes; and pulling her knees up to her chest, burying her face in the soft skirts of her wedding dress, she wept.

*   *   *

2

The women gathered at the house (nieces and aunts, cousins, second cousins, neighbours and acquaintances) were reluctant to leave. They didn't begrudge the care they had taken over clothes and coiffure, the time and money they had wasted; but the aborted wedding was a drama to which they were witnesses, and it seemed harsh, to them, to be asked to leave the scene. They went slowly, muttering to each other behind diamond-ringed hands, carrying their gifts – still wrapped – in their arms. To Noula, they said nothing; there was no form of words for this occasion.

Noula shut them out, forcing home the bolt on the apartment door. On the *salone* floor, by the cane-bottomed chairs where they had sat, the musicians' empty glasses stood beside the whisky bottle they had drained before they left. The plates for the walnut cookies held nothing but crumbs; the roasted peanuts and the pumpkin seeds were all gone, their cracked shells scattered by children across the rugs and into the room's far corners. A silver tray was still half-filled with long-stemmed glasses of melon liqueur; the tall, ribbon-trimmed candles the pageboys should have carried were abandoned in the window alcove. After the chatter, the laughter and the music, the silence of the room seemed profound.

The room must be put back to how it was before. Chrissa had taken liberties, moving the sofa, changing the tablecloths, rearranging the coffee service in the cabinet.

But all could be quite easily restored. Noula surveyed the work to be done, and smiled.

In the doorway, Aunt Yorgia pulled on a jacket over her black dress. The loose flesh of her upper arms trembled; on the skin of her bony chest, a gold crucifix glittered. With each year, Noula was growing into her likeness; in both

3

her and Chrissa, the legacy of that generation's women was manifesting: frown-lines and jowls, thread veins and thin lips. The make-up Chrissa had lent Noula had worked no magic, and Chrissa had been right about the greyness in her hair. Perhaps, as Chrissa said, she should have coloured it. But what did it matter, now? Dyeing out the grey had not, in the end, saved Chrissa.

'I paid the musicians,' said Aunt Yorgia. 'I gave them half.'

'I'll give you the money.' Noula's purse lay on the dresser, beneath the mirror; pulling out banknotes, she turned from her reflection in the glass. 'There's enough there for a taxi. You'll find Panayiotis in the square.'

'If there's a blessing in this, it's that your mother didn't live to see it, God rest her.' With three fingertips, Yorgia made the triple cross over her breast, then took the money Noula held out to her. 'The shame of it would have finished her, for sure. You should get those good clothes off now, and go and find your sister.'

Noula spread her arms to take in the room.

'How can I leave this mess? There's a week's work to be done here, and I'll get no help from Chrissa. She doesn't need me running after her. She'll come home when she's ready.'

'With things as they've turned out, she'll never want to come home,' said Yorgia sharply, 'and in her position, neither would you. You go and find her, as your mother would want. Fetch her home, and take good care of her. Be a sister to her, until all this blows over.'

'But where's her home to be, Aunt? Up here, alone, or downstairs in the old place, with me?'

Yorgia picked a length of cotton from the shoulder of her jacket.

'If you can manage to be civil with each other, I should say downstairs, with you,' she said. 'Your father paid for this apartment as a dowry.'

'As my dowry.'

'As your dowry, because he expected you to be first to marry. As there's still been no marriage, we'll keep the dowry ready until there is. Now go and fetch her. There's only a few minutes before dark. Take her something warm to put on over that dress. It's cold, now the sun's gone down. And you be kind to her, Noula. Your sister's been dealt a hard blow, and we'll all be made to feel it. Things will be difficult for us all, but we'll keep our heads high. Ach, *Panayia!*' She put her hand to her cheek, remembering. 'No one's told the taverna we won't be coming! I'll go; I'll tell the taxi to go round by there. They'll have to be paid, of course. I'll tell them you'll call in, in due course.'

'Me? Why should I go?'

'Because,' said Aunt Yorgia, 'it would be cruel to make your sister suffer the embarrassment of paying for a wedding breakfast she never got to eat. Don't let them charge you anything for wine. They won't have opened any yet, no matter what they say.'

She stepped across to Noula, and placing her hands on Noula's shoulders, kissed her on both cheeks. Noula smelled the sweetness of old cosmetics, of lipstick and loose powder, the citrus of eau de Cologne. 'Now go and fetch your sister. Bring her straight home and put her to bed. And make her some camomile tea; it'll help her sleep. Be kind, Noula. I'll come and see how she is tomorrow. Your uncle will bring me over in the morning.'

The apartment door banged shut. Aunt Yorgia's court shoes clattered down the outside stairs and away down the side street, fading into the dusk.

5

Noula moved to the *salone* window. The outlook was commonplace, on to a street she had known a lifetime, yet this elevated angle gave it novelty. From here, she could see over the neighbour's wall into Dmitra's kitchen, and even to the upper windows of the buildings around the square. Downstairs, where they had always lived, the view was dull, of high walls and their own garden.

She switched on a table lamp she had chosen years ago, and in its light, gazed round the objects that had so long been hers: the soft-cushioned sofa with its matching armchair, the unused china displayed in the cabinet, the Turkish rug woven in burgundy and cream, the lace cloths and doilies relatives had made for her. As the oldest, all this was intended for her – except no suitor had ever come. So when the doctor had asked for Chrissa, Noula was expected to step back and hand her sister everything.

But not now.

In the bedroom, the bed – her bed – was made with embroidered white linens, and on the coverlet, the local girls had formed a heart in sugared almonds. Noula took the almond from the heart's tip and putting it in her mouth, bit down on the hard, pink coating. No one had listened to her view that, at Chrissa's age, fertility rites were pointless. The girls had gone through all the rites regardless, scattering handfuls of uncooked rice between the sheets; the grains they had let fall cracked beneath Noula's feet.

Opening the wardrobe, she ran a hand through Chrissa's clothes, hung where her own should be: Chrissa's best dress, Chrissa's skirts and blouses, Chrissa's two pairs of shoes placed carefully together, as if Chrissa had been playing house arranging them. On the shelves, she found a cardigan of black wool, and put it aside to take to her sister.

There was nothing of his in the wardrobe, but by the bed was a suitcase battered with use. Pricked by curiosity, she

6

crouched beside it: what had the faithless doctor left behind? A guilty glance to window and door confirmed no one would see, and so she slipped the catches, and raised the suitcase lid.

A scent she didn't know came off his clothes, a man's scent, earthy but intriguing. One by one, she lifted out the shirts, the sweaters and the ties, and beneath the trousers found his underpants, large sizes in plain cotton. There were vests, and a washbag with a razor, soap, cologne and ointment used for rheumatism; and, at the very bottom and well concealed, a large, manila envelope, unsealed and unaddressed.

With careful fingers, she extracted the envelope from under his belongings, and without hesitation, withdrew the folded papers it contained.

They were letters of some length, whose opening pages bore the coats of arms of official offices. But the language and the alphabet were foreign, and Noula could make out nothing but the years of their writing: last year, and the year before.

Outside, a motorbike roared past, its rider calling a greeting to someone walking by.

Replacing the letters in the envelope, she repacked the suitcase as best she could, fastening its latches as she closed it.

The letters and their envelope, she kept.

Switching off the lamp which had been hers, she pulled the *salone* door closed behind her, locked it and pocketed the key. Downstairs, she hid the envelope in a kitchen drawer, and set off to look for Chrissa.

But the suitcase in the bedroom stayed in her mind; for why would the doctor, disappearing, leave most of what he owned behind him?

Two

The hound under the bed scratched at its fleas, rattling the iron bedstead with its haunches. Adonis Anapodos – Adonis Wrong-Way-Round – pushed the blankets from his face, and growled down at the dog – *Give over, Vasso*; but through the window, the sky was growing light, and so Adonis clambered grumbling from the bed, pushing the dog away when it rose to lick his hand.

There were no rugs on the floors and the unswept tiles were gritty to his feet. So early in the year, the house's old stone walls still held damp, and as he picked up from the bed-foot the clothes he had worn yesterday, they gave off the earthiness of mildew. He pulled the crumpled trousers over underpants he had slept in for several days, and took his time to match each fly button to its hole; with his shirt he did the same, except where buttons were missing. The pattern on his sweater was marred by snags where thorns had caught it; Adonis made sure the sweater label was to the back, because it often entertained the men to submit him to their inspection, and if anything about him was *anapodo*, they'd punish him with ridicule and ear-cuffing.

His woollen socks were stuffed inside his boots, and as he unballed the first, a smell rose from it, similar to the foreign cheese in Lambis's shop. Indifferent to the socks' stink, he pulled them on, and by his mother's system (a rough 'r' marked inside the right boot's tongue matched his right hand where, on his little finger, he wore a silver ring), he got his boots correct. By concentrating, he managed both his laces, and calling to the hound to follow him, he went outside.

In the cold dawn, the chickens were already scratching in the dirt. As Adonis fastened Vasso to his chain, the white rooster on the coop roof stretched its throat and crowed.

Between the house wall and a patch of flourishing thistles, Adonis rocked his old Vespa from its stand. Sliding the key into the ignition, he free-wheeled down the short track to the road, where, steering carefully around the potholes, he fired the engine.

In the town square, no one was open for business. Above the grocer's shop, a light shone behind drawn curtains; the green cross over the pharmacy was lit, though the windows behind their iron grilles were dark. The shutters at the *kafenion* were barred and the door was closed, but someone was there, waiting to be served: at a pavement table sat a stranger.

Adonis, riding by, stared at the man – a big man, perhaps even fat, whose curly, greying hair was a little too long, and whose glasses gave him an air of academia. Beneath a beige trench-coat, he wore a suit without a tie; beside him lay a holdall of green leather. In Eva's uncomfortable chair he seemed relaxed, drawing on a freshly lit cigarette, one foot crossed over the other; and it was the stranger's feet that drew Adonis's eyes. The fat man was wearing tennis shoes – old-fashioned, canvas shoes, pristinely white.

Outside the pharmacy, red-painted barriers surrounded mounds of rubble and a hole in the road. Swerving to avoid the workings, Adonis switched on his indicator to signal left.

9

Making the turn towards the mountains, he glanced back at the stranger, who smiled as if Adonis were an old friend and raised his hand in greeting.

As the old Vespa laboured on towards St Paraskevi's, the morning's first sunlight broke the line between sea and sky. Away down the hillsides, beyond the cultivated fields of the plain, the coast road followed the line of the beach as far as the port, then disappeared amongst the streets and houses of the town. The ascent was long, increased by twists and loops in the mountain road, and lacking power in his small engine, Adonis leaned forward over the scooter's handlebars in the hope of persuading it to higher speed; but his progress remained slow, and as he reached the right-hand bend where the weather-worn sign pointed the way to the chapel, the bell of Holy Trinity far below was already striking seven.

The unpaved track was rough, scattered with loose stones and rutted by trucks spinning their wheels in the mud of a wet winter; but the incline was gentle, and the long grasses which flourished on the slopes were coloured with the flowers of spring: powder-blue blooms of wild chicory, tall hollyhocks and purple lupins, fresh white margaritas.

The grazing where Adonis kept his flock lay beyond St Paraskevi's, but as the little church came into view, he slowed the scooter to a walking pace. Beneath a conical roof, the round and ancient walls were no taller than a man, the whitewashed courtyard walls a few stones higher. Above the arch of the courtyard gate hung a single bell, its rope tied on a rusting, cast-iron hook.

Adonis made frequent promises to his mother to take the time each day to light the chapel lamps, though often – like today – he forgot matches. Those in the chapel were damp, their pink tips soft as chalk when they were struck.

But his conscience pricked; so, riding as slowly as he could, he whispered his apologies to the saint, and making several crosses over his heart, promised he would visit her tomorrow.

He changed gear and, accelerating, prepared to ride by.

But St Paraskevi, it seemed, rejected his excuses. High over the courtyard wall flew a missile, which, missing his head by very little, landed heavily on the track ahead of him.

Startled, Adonis braked, the scooter sputtering gravel as he did so; but the scooter's brakes were as poor as its tyres were bald, and before he came to a stop, the missile was behind him. He had, however, seen the object clearly. The saint had tried to hit him with a shoe.

Switching off the engine, he pulled the scooter back on to its stand and walked the few paces to where the shoe lay. Cautiously, he bent to pick it up. It was a man's shoe, well worn and unremarkable, except for a few splashes of white on the brown leather, like spilt milk. Frowning, he turned it over, wondering at its message; but as he did so, a hoarse voice called from inside the chapel courtyard.

'Help!'

Holding the shoe before him, Adonis crept to the courtyard wall, stepping up as close to it as the sharp-thorned thistles allowed. He listened. The shout was not repeated, but, above the rustling of the wind in the grass and the rattle of bells from his nearby flock, a voice was muttering. He strained to catch the words, but the language was not Greek, and he understood nothing of its meaning. The speaker's misery, though, was plain, and, still hidden safe behind the wall, Adonis dared to call out.

'Is anyone there?'

The muttering stopped.

'Here!' called the voice. 'I'm here! Hurry!'

The chapel gate was closed. Reaching in through the ornate ironwork, Adonis found the bolt, wriggled it back and stepped over the threshold.

The chapel showed the past winter's neglect, with storm-blown leaves and pine needles unswept amongst dirt and lime-shards flaked from the walls. Untouched as yet by the rising sun, the courtyard shadows were dark, and the place was chilled from the fall of recent rain.

Between chapel and wall, a man lay quite still on a stone bench, covering his eyes with the flat of his hand. His plump belly rose up above his trousers. One of his feet was missing a shoe.

'Are you there?'

The man's voice was rasping, as if his throat were sore; as he spoke, his hand remained over his eyes. In curiosity, Adonis approached him.

'*Kyrie? Kyrie*, are you all right? Do you need a doctor? I have my scooter. I think I could find the doctor.'

A sad smile touched the man's mouth.

'Am I so changed, then?' he asked. 'Friend, I *am* the doctor.'

Adonis looked again at the man, considering his stature and his clothing.

'I knew straight away it was you, *kyrie*,' he lied; and then, anxious not to give offence, he corrected his form of address. 'Forgive me. *Yiatre.*'

'Who are you?' asked the doctor. His Greek was excellent, but his accent was a foreigner's, with the strange pronunciation of northern countries. 'What's your name?'

'Adonis. They call me Adonis Anapodos.'

'Then I know you, by sight.' The doctor gave a bitter laugh. 'By memory, now. Listen to me, Adonis. You must fetch me some water. As quick as you can, fetch plenty of water.'

Adonis placed the shoe by the doctor's stockinged foot.

'Gladly,' he said. 'Right away.'

On the far side of the chapel, outside the old refectory and kitchen, an aluminium pail strung on rope stood on the well wall. As he raised the well's iron cover, the hinges squealed with lack of use; once opened, a smell of ferns and water rose from far below.

Adonis lowered the bucket, flicking the rope as the pail touched the water's surface, tilting it so it would fill; hauling it heavy from the well, he stood it on the wall, and considered the problem of how to take the water to the doctor. The bucket was tied to the cover-hinge, and the knot was complex, and tight; without a knife to cut the rope, the bucket could not be freed.

He looked around. The door to the kitchen was behind him. Clicking open the latch, he went inside.

The kitchen was dank, and musty; heavy cobwebs covered the small window, obscuring the light. Adonis sniffed. He knew this room. If bad weather ever caught him, he took shelter here, and often in summer he refilled his bottle at the well, and sat a while at the table to drink where it was cool – and today, beneath the faint and usual scents of old woodsmoke and incense, there was something unusual.

The long, pine table – dulled with the bleach and scrubbing of zealous women – held scores of plates and cups and the great fire-blackened pans for boiling and frying on feast days. Today, alongside them was a tartan-patterned Thermos flask, its cracked cup standing beside it. Picking up the flask, Adonis opened it, and the out-of-place smell, the scent of coffee, intensified. He glanced into the cup, which, though empty, had been recently used, and, anxious to be tidy in St Paraskevi's house, replaced the cup over the flask's cap.

Below the window, mounted on plinths of bricks, was a stone trough drilled through to drain water, and under the drain-hole stood a yellow bucket. He took the bucket, and a china cup from the table, and at the well filled the yellow bucket from the metal pail.

Returning to where the doctor lay, he found him exactly the same, his eyes still covered.

'Are you there?' asked the doctor, uncertainly. His voice was weak. 'I shouted for hours, but no one came.'

'I'm here,' said Adonis. 'I got water. And a cup.' He dipped the cup into the water; but as he did so, the doctor waved it away with his free hand.

'My eyes,' he said. 'The water's for my eyes.' Slowly, he raised himself to sit. 'Put my hand to it. Show me where it is.'

Adonis placed the bucket by the doctor's feet, and guided his free hand to its rim.

'Here, *yiatre*,' he said. 'It's here. I can fetch more, if you need it.'

'It hurts to bend,' said the doctor. 'Better put it up here.' He patted the stone bench beside him, and Adonis lifted up the bucket, placing the doctor's hand on its rim once again.

'Hold it steady,' said the doctor.

He put his free hand in the water, and, taking the other at last from his eyes, placed it too in the bucket.

Astonished, Adonis stared at the doctor's face. His eyes were milky pale and featureless, with no distinction between white and iris, or iris and pupil, as if some artist had rubbed out their drawn-in details; the skin of his lids and below his eyes was raw and red, wet and weeping. The bridge of his nose, the low part of his brow and his cheekbones seemed to have no skin at all, as if someone had held a blow-torch to his face – except for his eyes, which seemed, in their whiteness, frozen.

In shock, Adonis crossed himself.

'*Yiatre*,' he said. '*Panayia mou*.'

14

The doctor turned his face towards Adonis, and his eyes – like stone, like marble – seemed as compelling and beguiling as the damning eyes of Medusa.

Adonis shuddered.

'Is it bad?' asked the doctor.

Adonis, confounded, was reluctant to give his honest opinion.

'What do you mean, *yiatre*?' he asked, cautiously.

'My face,' said the doctor. 'Is it bad?'

Adonis moved close to the doctor, and, fighting his revulsion, studied his face, rocking his own head from side to side as he considered.

'Quite bad, in places,' he said, truthfully. 'In others, not so bad.'

The doctor turned his stone eyes away, and Adonis was glad. Bending his head, filling his cupped hands from the bucket, the doctor lowered his face to the water; as the water dribbled back into the bucket, he scooped out more, tenderly bathing his eyes and his damaged skin.

After a while, he stopped.

'The pain is bad,' he said. 'Do you see my bag?'

Adonis looked about them. There was no bag.

'No,' he said. 'It isn't here.'

'He took it, then.'

'Who, *yiatre*?'

'Whoever did this to me. Still, there'll be something in the saddlebag. I want you to go to my motorbike …'

'There's no motorbike,' interrupted Adonis. 'Only my scooter.'

'It must be there,' insisted the doctor. 'I didn't hear it go. Go and look for my bike, and bring me whatever you find in the saddlebag. And hurry – though it makes little difference now, how fast we are. The damage is all done.'

He bent again to bathe his face. Adonis hurried through the chapel gate to where his scooter stood on the track, and looked around. Behind the chapel, where the land began its descent down to the plain, the weeds and grasses had been flattened into an indistinct trail around the outer wall. There, thrown on its side, lay a silver motorbike, and dropped on top of it, a black leather bag. Adonis grabbed the bag, and ran back to the doctor.

'I've got your bag,' he said. 'Your bike is round the back. It's fallen over. I think it might be broken.'

'Open the bag,' said the doctor.

Adonis did so, revealing inside a confusion of objects he didn't recognise: a stethoscope, paper-wrapped packets, strange scissors, needles and thread.

'Look at the bottom,' said the doctor. His face was wet; his stone eyes stared ahead. 'You'll find syringes. I need one of those. You can read, can't you?'

Adonis hesitated.

'Not well, *yiatre*,' he said. 'I didn't spend long at school.'

'You must find me some vials – little bottles, Adonis – that hold liquid the colour of honey. There are some in there that look like water. Not those. Find me the honey-coloured bottles. Take your time.'

Adonis hunted carefully through the bag. The doctor sat, apparently calm; but his fingers held each other tightly, and he pressed his thumbs together, as if this helped him to control the pain.

'I've found them.'

'Good lad, good lad. Now listen to me very carefully; you'll need to do everything just as I tell you.'

As Adonis prepared the injection, the doctor rolled up his sleeve to expose his upper arm, and when Adonis was ready, he pointed to a spot in the crook of his elbow. Before sinking the needle into the flesh, Adonis offered a prayer to St Paraskevi. As the needle went in, the doctor flinched.

'Press the plunger slowly, Adonis,' he said, 'and then we're done.'

As Adonis withdrew the needle, the doctor's red eyelids closed over his marble eyes. For a time, he was silent.

'Better,' he said, at last. 'Much better. Now, are you a good driver on that scooter of yours?'

'I think so, *yiatre*.'

'Then you must take me down to the town, somewhere they have a phone. When we get there, you must tell them that I need an ambulance urgently. Can you do that?'

'Gladly, *yiatre*.'

'Good lad, good lad. First take my bag, and hide it with my motorbike. We'll send someone to fetch them in due course. When you've done that, come and take my hand. You'll have to lead the way; you have the only pair of eyes to see where we are going.'

Three

Evangelia's constant boast was that she never cut her hair, but this was a lie. On the first day of every second month, she used the dressmaking shears to trim the ends, to a line as straight as possible above her buttocks.

This morning, she rose within ten minutes of the alarm clock's ring, and sat before the mirror to count one hundred brushstrokes. With them complete, her hair was sleek and straight, and twisting it at the base of her skull, she secured it with sharp pins in a tight knot. From a jar whose label showed a long-stemmed rose, she rubbed rose-scented cream into her face, concentrating on the crow's-feet around her eyes and the slack skin of her neck. Picking up a gold-cased lipstick, she applied red to her lips, baring her bad teeth to the mirror to check for smears. She'd done the best she could; still her reflection was disheartening. Teasing matted, grey hair from its bristles, she laid the brush back on the dusty dressing table, in its place between the hand-mirror and the comb. There seemed to be too much hair in her hand, and she leaned towards the mirror, touching the bald place above her temple uneasily, but to her relief, it had grown no larger.

Loneliness had led her into unconventional habits: muttering her thoughts as she left the chair, she unfastened the window over the outhouse roof to drop the hair lost to the brush on to the tiles. She thought the birds might draw its strands to build their nests; but month after month, year after year, the birds never came.

She turned out the bedroom light. As she made her way downstairs to the *kafenion*, her breath was laboured and wheezing.

The shutters were closed, and the *kafenion* was dark. A tap dripped water into the porcelain sink. Groping for a socket, she threw its switch, and the glass-fronted fridge began to hum, though its light flickered on and off until she thumped its side, rattling the bottles of beer and retsina on its shelves. Overnight, as usual, a pool of water had formed around the base, and something, somewhere, smelled rancid.

In a cage hanging over the counter's end, Mimi the cockatoo was silent. Evangelia tugged at a corner of the cage's covering shawl, and the white bird slowly withdrew her head from beneath her wing, blinking as the sulphur-yellow feathers on her head rose in a crest.

Evangelia poked a fingertip through the cage bars, waggling it to attract the bird's attention.

'*Kali mera sou*,' she said. '*Kali mera*, Mimi. Say "Mimi", *agapi mou*. Wish your mama a *kali mera*.'

But the bird was nervous, and turned away her head, edging her clawed feet along its perch.

Evangelia held the shawl up high, matching corner to corner to fold it. Worked by gypsies, its embroidered peonies were bright on the antique silk, but the fringe was loose and uneven, and there was a bad tear on one edge. For a moment, she swayed her hips, thinking of the days she had worn it dancing. There was no dancing now; the memories were sweet, the present bitter, and, disheartened, she dropped the shawl unfolded on a chair.

Crossing heavy-footed to the windows, she swung back the left-hand shutters, letting the early daylight brighten the room. Lifting the bar from the door, she turned the iron key and kicked the wooden door-stop into place. At the right-hand window, as the shutters opened, the crown of a man's head showed above the sill.

A stranger was waiting.

She took the unwashed ashtrays from the shelf, and went outside.

At his table, the fat man was writing a postcard. A paper bag held a collection of local views – the precarious monasteries at Meteora, a headless statue of Artemis, the snow-covered peaks of Mount Olympus – but the card he had chosen showed a donkey in a hat. His handwriting was small, but very clear, the letters carefully printed so a child could read them.

As Evangelia approached, the fat man laid down his fountain pen, and smiled.

'*Kali mera*,' he said.

Evangelia returned his smile, in a way that she intended to be winning.

'*Kali mera sas*,' she said. 'What can I get you?'

'Greek coffee, no sugar, if you please,' said the fat man. 'In fact, make it a double. I was here well before dawn, and I've had little sleep.'

'I never open before seven,' she said, as if he had offered a criticism. 'There's no call for coffee here, before seven.'

She laid an ashtray on his table, and turned away to distribute the rest. He watched her bend to reach the furthest tables, the hem of her shift-dress lifting to show the heavy thighs above her stocking tops; as her foot came off the ground to reach still further, he saw the hole worn through the sole of her fur-trimmed slipper.

The butts of three cigarettes he had already smoked were ground out by his feet, and he picked them up and placed them in the ashtray. As she made coffee, he signed his name on the postcard he was writing, and, replacing the gold-trimmed cap, tucked the pen into the inside of his jacket. He slipped the written postcard back into the paper bag, and covering a yawn with his hand, looked around the square. Between the lamp-posts, blue-and-white bunting – triangles of the national flag – flapped in the breeze. Around a fountain so new the builders' shovels still leaned against its basin, tubs of young plants were coming into flower. Inside the *kafenion*, over the clatter of crockery and spoons, he heard Evangelia swear and the slap of her hand on the counter; a young cat with a chicken neck in its mouth slunk out, and away.

When Evangelia brought the fat man's coffee, she took a chair beside him at the table. Across the square, a red-eyed grocer carried out a box of oranges, and dropped it on a bench at the store front. Ripping a flap from the box, he took a marker from behind his ear, and wrote '800dr' on the cardboard; laying the price on the fruit, he went back inside the shop.

'That's 50 drachmas more than yesterday,' said Evangelia. 'The older his stock is, the more expensive it gets.' She eyed the postcards in their paper bag. 'You're a tourist, are you, *kyrie*? You've wandered off the usual track, to be touring here.'

The fat man held out his hand.

'Forgive me,' he said. 'I haven't introduced myself. I am Hermes Diaktoros, of Athens.'

She didn't take the fat man's hand, but watched as the grocer dropped a crate of cauliflowers beside the oranges. Kneading a shoulder as if it pained him, he sighed, and disappeared again through the shop doorway.

'Three days old, those cauliflowers are now,' said Evangelia. 'Whoever does he expect to buy them? You're a long way from home, if you're from Athens. Is your family not with you? Where's your wife?'

'My travelling is all business, not pleasure,' said the fat man. 'And I never married. But I'm writing to my family. My grandson likes to know where I have been.'

At the implication of children outside marriage, she pursed her lips in disapproval, but the fat man took no notice.

'I spend too long away,' he said. 'The little ones change so quickly. But there's always business to attend to.'

'Is it business that brings you here?'

'Business finds me everywhere I go,' he said, 'and I've an inkling there might be work here. But I stopped because I've a problem with my car. I'm hoping the town might supply me with a competent mechanic.'

'Oh yes, we've a mechanic,' she said. 'That's one thing we can supply.' Her eyes ran over him, and for a moment rested on his shoes. 'But I was sure that, smartly dressed as you are, you'd come for the wedding.'

'Wedding?' asked the fat man. 'No, indeed. I know of no wedding.'

He lifted his cup, and allowed the drops from its base to fall back into the coffee Evangelia had spilled in the saucer. He tasted the coffee; it was too weak to have flavour, and already growing cold.

'I was invited myself, of course,' she said, 'but I didn't plan to go. I'm tied to this place, night and day. I'm a woman alone, and there's not much help for a woman with no husband; just the half-wit, from time to time. Everything that's to be done, is done by me. I wanted to go, of course; the break would have been welcome. But I was glad, in the end, I'd made no effort. What a farce it turned out to be!' She leaned close to him so her shoulder touched his own, and as she went on speaking, he caught the unpleasantness of her breath. '*Because the groom didn't come, and the wedding never took place!* He thought better of it, I suppose; she's no spring chicken, after all. But even so, it's hard to bear such disgrace. Better never to have been asked than to be jilted on your wedding day! How she'll hold her head up again, I don't know.'

The fat man seemed thoughtful.

'Poor woman,' he said.

Reaching into his coat pocket, he withdrew a pack of cigarettes – a box in the old-fashioned style, whose lid bore the head and naked shoulders of a 1940s starlet with softly permed, platinum hair curled around a coy smile. Beneath the maker's name ran a slogan in an antique hand: 'The cigarette for the man who knows a real smoke'. Producing a slim, gold lighter, he knocked the tip of a cigarette on the table, lit it, and laid the cigarettes and the lighter beside his cup.

Across the square, the grocer hauled out a sack of onions. An elderly woman, bent-backed and bow-legged, made her slow way towards the alley where the bakery was opening its doors, and Evangelia called out a greeting.

'No word, nothing,' she went on, still close to the fat man. 'His wedding suit hung ready, the band playing, bells all ringing, and no groom. Have you ever heard of such a thing? Without a word, he's vanished. And her – they say she's devastated.'

'And is this ungentlemanly fellow a local man?'

She tipped her chin and tutted, as if his suggestion were absurd.

'Not local, no,' she said. 'Not even Greek. A foreigner, a Frenchman. But an educated man, a doctor, and a good doctor, in fact. I'm under him myself. I suffer with my health, *kyrie*, though I suppose you'd never know to look at me.' The fat man's eyebrows lifted, just a little. Everything about Evangelia seemed hopeless and neglected; like a wilting plant whose season had passed, she seemed to droop, and the skin of her face, the corners of her mouth, the badly fitting clothes, the stockings wrinkled at the knees, all sagged. The fat man sipped his cold coffee, and drawing on his cigarette, let her go on. 'The doctor has said to me many times, Eva (he calls me Eva, and I allow his familiarity – he's a professional man, after all) – Eva, he says, it's a wonder how you carry on. My joints are swollen, and my lungs are weak. Winter is bitter, here; every year, I expect the cold to kill me. Sometimes, I struggle to make it down the stairs. Dr Louis tells me I have thin blood. He gives me medication. Take these, he says, and these and these and these … When I object, he presses me. I must take them, he says, or I won't see fifty. I'm well over forty now, *kyrie*, though perhaps you wouldn't guess.'

The fat man gave a small smile, and sipped again at his coffee.

'The town will be wanting a new doctor, I suppose,' he said. 'I don't imagine this Dr Louis will be welcomed back, if he shows his face.'

Evangelia frowned.

'Why wouldn't he be welcomed?' she asked. 'Good doctors are hard to come by, outside the city.'

'Does the bride have no father, then? No brothers to protect her honour?'

'There are no men left in the Kaligi family. Chrissa's father is long dead, and there are no brothers, only a sister. At her age, she was lucky to be asked, especially by a doctor. The sister – Noula, they call her – is older, and still a spinster, the obstacle in Chrissa's way. The father always said he'd see the elder married first, and after he went, the mother stuck by

24

his wishes. But she passed away recently – she suffered, poor woman, though Dr Louis did what he could for her. It was at the mother's bedside that they met. It was in poor taste, of course, but I suppose she saw a last chance, and led him on. They're no beauties in that family; there are some who say they weren't fathered by a man but by a mule. When other girls were marrying, they were passed over, though there was another suitor for Chrissa for a while. But there's other ways to win a man than by a pretty face, and I suppose she dipped into that box of tricks every woman has at her disposal … She'll have been thinking her chance had come again. Don't get me wrong, *kyrie* – he's not a handsome man, not tall either, nor young. But qualified, and well paid, and well respected. It seems he thought better of it anyway, in the end.'

From the baker's alley, the elderly woman made her slow way towards the grocer's, carrying a paper-wrapped loaf in a string bag. At the grocer's, she stopped to examine the cauliflowers, and immediately the grocer was at her side. The old woman chose the smallest, and the grocer slipped it smiling into her bag; the old woman offered him her open purse, and he dipped into it, still smiling as he helped himself to coins.

'And her half-blind,' said Evangelia, shaking her head. 'You'd think he'd be ashamed.'

The fat man frowned.

'Indeed,' he said, quietly. He knocked ash from the tip of his cigarette, and drank the last of his unsatisfactory coffee.

'Tell me,' he said, indicating the bunting, 'is there some festival planned?'

She laughed, derisively.

'We have a new broom in town,' she said, 'a mayor who thinks new drains are the answer to all our prayers.'

25

'Not all prayers, naturally,' said the fat man. 'Yet bad drains can make life miserable.' He sniffed; the morning air was scented with damp grass, salt water, fresh bread. 'But I smell nothing untoward.'

'This town suffered for decades with its drains,' she said. 'I remember as a girl we didn't need drains. Each house had a cesspit of its own. I remember my grandfather digging one, and how afraid he was I'd fall in it. But I was in no danger, *kyrie*; I kept well away. Those pits were deep and dark, and I knew what was going in there. You'll know the old system, of course: lime on the walls, some water and a sheep carcass thrown in, then seal it up and let nature do its work. The rot that eats the carcass will eat anything that man – or woman – can throw at it. My grandfather used to say that water from a cesspit properly made should be sweet enough to drink, though I never saw him try. Then someone came and gave us some improvements. Mains drainage, they said, was healthier and better for us all. But did they do the job right? Of course they didn't! All leaking pipes and blockages – in summer, you couldn't open the windows for the stink. It's better now, of course. But the price we've paid! Digging and drilling, noise and dust! Chaos: we've had weeks of chaos. See?' As she pointed to the barriers around the hole outside the pharmacy, and a similar one beside the post-office door, the fat man looked in puzzlement around the deserted square. 'Traffic diversions, water cut off for hours. But our new mayor's a young man, and the young have big ideas. He's wholly responsible. If you want to complain, that's where the blame lies.'

'But why the bunting?'

She gave a mysterious smile.

'We're expecting a visitor,' she said. 'A minister from Athens. A dignitary. A VIP, from the department that gave the mayor the grants for these – improvements. There'll be ribbon cutting, and a plaque to be unveiled. They're bringing in the press – TV, and newspapers. And the mayor, of course, to shake the minister's hand.'

The fat man took a last draw on his cigarette and, leaning forward to the ashtray, stubbed it out.

'I should like to see that,' he said.

'If you're going to be staying, I can offer you a room,' she said, eagerly. 'It isn't much, but if I air the bed to get the damp out, you'll be comfortable enough. I'd have to make a charge, of course. A man like yourself'd be wanting hot water, and it costs so much to heat. Two thousand a night, including breakfast.'

The fat man shook his head.

'Your offer is very kind,' he said, 'but I don't expect to stay. And if I did, I couldn't impose on you. I'm sure there's a *pension* here that is well prepared to receive guests.'

She smiled, wide enough to show her discoloured teeth.

'No *pension*. No visitors,' she said. 'And you'll be no burden, unless you've a mind to be. It's just a bed, and a little hot water. There's no shower, but I can fill a bath for you in the yard, or in the kitchen, if you feel the cold.'

Across the square, the grocer, red-faced with effort, dragged a sack of potatoes from his shop. Hauling the sack into place beside the onions, he rolled back the hessian to display the potatoes, and picked out a mud-dried tuber to inspect a weevil-hole. The damage was fresh and obvious, and so he rummaged in the sack to make room, and hid the infested potato deep amongst the healthier ones.

The fat man glanced at the gold watch on his wrist, and judged there was still a while to wait until the mechanic might be expected at his work; he wondered what kind of living the man made in this small place where, at an hour when country folk were certainly stirring, there was no sign of traffic on the streets.

Then, from the far side of the square, an engine broke the quiet of the morning, and the battered scooter that had passed the fat man some time earlier came into view. Its driver was the same – a young man with the slipped mouth of a simpleton – but now he had a passenger on his pillion, a plump man who clasped the driver's waist with one arm, and covered his own eyes with the other, as if in horror at the younger man's bad driving. Yet the young man rode carefully, avoiding the worst of the square's bumps and dips.

Seeing the fat man, Evangelia and the grocer, the young man began to shout.

'Help! Call an ambulance! The doctor is injured!'

The fat man and the grocer merely stared; but Evangelia rose slowly from her chair.

'The doctor,' she whispered. 'Here he is, at last!'

The scooter stopped before the *kafenion*'s tables. The man riding pillion placed his feet down on the cobbles – one foot, the fat man noticed, was missing a shoe – and sat motionless and silent, his arm across his face. The fat man, in curiosity, stood and approached; the grocer began to cross the square towards them.

'What is it, *kalé*?' called out Evangelia to the driver. 'Adonis, what's happened?'

Agitation, it seemed, prevented Adonis from speaking; instead he shook his head, and placed his hand over his eyes in mimicry of the doctor. But in a few heavy strides, Evangelia reached him, and taking his shoulder in a tight grip, shook him.

'Spit it out, fool!' she said. 'What has happened?'

'He's blinded!' cried Adonis, flinching. Like a cowering

28

dog, he turned his face from her. 'He says we have to call an ambulance!'

'*Panayia mou*!' Evangelia pulled at Adonis's sweater. 'Out of the way, fool!'

Adonis climbed off his scooter, and moved a little way off, where he stood biting the knuckles of one hand. Crossing herself, Evangelia stared at the unmoving doctor, until the fat man, frowning, touched her shoulder.

'Go, quickly, and call them,' he said. 'Dial 111. This is an emergency.'

She left them, and the fat man moved to the doctor's side. The doctor's clothes were marked with splashes of white; around his mouth and jaw, the skin was raw and weeping. The grocer joined the fat man; as he leaned across to see the doctor's face, the air filled with the smell of onions.

'What's happening?' asked the grocer. 'What's going on?'

The fat man held up his hand to silence him.

'You don't know me, *yiatre*,' he said to the doctor, 'but I have a little knowledge of first aid. Will you let me see your injury? Perhaps I can be of help, before the ambulance arrives.'

The doctor's lips twitched as if attempting a smile, but the smile was cut off by pain.

'I'm sure it isn't pretty, friend,' he said, his Greek inflected with a foreign accent. 'If there are ladies present, or children, I suggest you ask them to move away.'

'There's no one here,' said the fat man. 'Please, let me see.'

The doctor lowered his hand, revealing his blank eyes. The grocer grew pale; he crossed himself, and opened his mouth to speak, but the fat man signalled again to him for silence. Leaning closer, he studied the doctor's face.

'Some chemical,' he said, quietly. 'Who did this to you?'

29

'I don't know,' said the doctor. 'I didn't see him. Does the damage look bad? I couldn't get to water. I'm afraid the burn's gone deep.'

Gently, the fat man laid a hand on the doctor's back; the grocer's expression was of dismay.

'Your colleagues at the hospital will know what to do,' said the fat man. 'Are you in pain?'

'Not so bad, now. With the young man's help, I gave myself some morphine. I'm comfortable, at least.'

'Can you walk?' asked the fat man. 'Just a short way, to a chair.'

'I'm sure so, yes.'

'Take my arm, then. Grocer, be so good as to keep the lady out of the way. There's no need for hysterics or too much fuss. *Yiatre*, I believe you have a fiancée. Should she be brought?'

Cautiously, the doctor shook his head.

'Don't tell her yet,' he said. 'I don't want her to see me in this state. Send someone to tell her when I've gone.'

As the ambulance pulled away, the small crowd in the square began to disperse, the men taking seats in the *kafenion*, the women moving to the baker's and the grocer's to share the news.

As Evangelia served coffee at the next table, the fat man touched her on the arm.

'Regarding your accommodation,' he said. 'I believe I shall be delaying my departure for a while. So if you'll prepare that room for me, I shall accept your offer of lodging after all.'

Four

The fat man crossed the square and made his way along the side street where he had left his car. Beneath the overhanging branches of a pomegranate tree a small boat stood, stripped and sanded, on wooden blocks; an empty paint tin lay under the hull, a dried-out paintbrush by the upturned crate used as the painter's seat, but of the painter, there was no sign. A woman threw back the shutters of an upstairs room and watched the fat man curiously as he passed. Looking up, he smiled, and called out *kali mera*; but the woman gave no answer, and stepped back in silence from the window, out of sight.

His car was an aged Mercedes, grand in the style favoured by statesmen and industrialists, its cream paintwork unmarked except for a little mud spattered around the wheel arches. As he opened the door, the car released its scent of polished leather and the perfume of ripe apples from a well-filled paper bag lying on the passenger seat. He slipped behind the silver-symbolled steering wheel and placed his holdall in the footwell, then, making himself comfortable in the red leather seat, turned the key in the ignition.

The engine, quiet and reliable, came to life; but immediately it did so, the wipers scraped across the windscreen, squealing on the dry glass and returning noisily to their resting place. The fat man frowned. For a short while, he waited; the wipers remained still. A minute passed, and he moved the automatic gearstick into drive; but as the gearbox engaged, the wipers squealed again across the screen.

Tight-lipped, the fat man pushed a button to squirt water on to the windscreen, but the water-tank was empty and only a dribble emerged. Releasing the handbrake, he moved off down the side street, and, as he reached its end, the wipers passed before his eyes again.

Heading for the outskirts, the fat man drove slowly through the town. It was a place that might have been attractive: the old buildings had architectural interest, the setting between sea and hills had charm. But care was lacking; there seemed no pride taken in the upkeep of the houses, and there were no showpieces amongst the neglected gardens. By contrast, public works in progress showed small improvements everywhere: the collapsed wall around a churchyard was half rebuilt, fresh concrete showed where a road had been repaired, a new basketball hoop stood in the high-school yard.

Beyond the sign which marked the town's end, the road dipped and turned in a tight loop, forming an oval of land which was almost an island. Here, the garage stood. Two old-fashioned pumps bore the EKO logo; the forecourt ran back to a workshop where the ground was black with oily dirt, and around the carcasses of vehicles stripped to the bone – cars, trucks and motorbikes – lay the litter of their maintenance: grease cans, cables and springs, tyres and hub-caps, spanners, spark plugs, exhausts in rusty lengths. At a short distance was a single-storey house, and between the house and its privy was grassland, where a line held the washing of three generations, and a tethered goat nibbled at a crust of hard bread.

The fat man pulled up alongside the petrol pumps and considered the oil-soaked dirt in front of the workshop. Reaching down to his holdall, he took out a parcel loosely wrapped in newspaper, and removed from it a pair of rubber galoshes. Folding the newspaper for re-use, he slipped the galoshes over his pristine tennis shoes, and stepped out of the car.

Inside the workshop, the sound of hammering was loud. Between workbenches chaotic with tools, lubricants and rags, a little Fiat was raised on ramps, its underside lit by a caged light bulb on a long length of flex; and from beneath the Fiat, two legs protruded. A selection of the car's components lay under its rear bumper.

The hammering stopped, and was replaced after a moment by a ratchet quickly worked. A bolt dropped to the floor and rolled towards the fat man's galoshed feet; from under the car, a hand patted the ground, feeling for the bolt like a blind man.

The fat man cleared his throat, and with his toe, moved the bolt towards the hand. The hand became still, and there was silence; then a voice called, 'Tomorrow! I told you tomorrow!'

The fat man's eyebrows lifted as he smiled.

'Forgive me, mechanic,' he said, 'but you told me no such thing. I have yet to commission any work from you.'

On his back on a low trolley, the mechanic slid from beneath the car. His forehead was streaked in lines where dirty fingertips had pushed his blond hair from his eyes; the hems of his filthy trousers were laced into military boots. On his muscled torso, he wore nothing but an oil-smeared vest; feeling the morning's chill on his behalf, the fat man shivered.

The mechanic looked the fat man up and down, taking in his suit, his raincoat and his galoshes.

33

'*Kali mera sas*,' he said. He reached for the Fiat's door-handle and pulled himself to his feet, wiping his hands on a rag tucked into his belt. 'Forgive me. I was expecting someone else.'

'And I suspect you are not disappointed that I am not he.'

The mechanic's eyes narrowed, as if he were baffled by the fat man's beautifully enunciated Greek, and he tilted up his chin, assessing him. His profile was handsome, but there were lines of middle age around his eyes and ridges of bad temper on his forehead.

'Can I help you?' he asked.

The fat man had noticed the grime on the mechanic's hands, and did not offer his own.

'I am Hermes Diaktoros, of Athens,' he said, 'and I have a small problem with my car. The windscreen wipers have developed a mind of their own, and I would like them restored to my control, rather than having them operate on their own whim.'

The mechanic crossed to the workshop door and looked out at the fat man's car.

'That yours?' he asked. 'Merc, is it?'

'That's the car in question. Actually, it belongs to my cousin.'

'Let's see what we can find.'

He led the way to the Mercedes; reaching it, he opened the driver's door and peered in at the walnut-veneered dashboard.

'You don't see many of these,' he said. 'What year is it – fifty, fifty-two?'

'I couldn't say,' said the fat man, 'except it's elderly. My cousin's owned it from new.'

Pointing an oily fingertip at the odometer, the mechanic gave a low whistle.

'There's some mileage on it,' he said. 'What's he done, driven it round the world?'

'He likes to travel.'

'So how come it looks so good?' He stepped back to view the bodywork. 'It could have come from the dealer's yesterday.'

'The car is his pride and joy, and he is a cautious driver. He works hard to keep it in perfect condition, and that is how I must return it to him. So this fault, although minor, must be fixed. It's not a big job, I'm sure.'

'It'll be wiring.'

'So can you take care of it?'

'Pick it up tomorrow afternoon.'

The fat man smiled.

'I realise you're busy,' he said, 'but I was hoping you could take a look at it now.'

'Now?'

'If you could. Of course I'd be prepared to pay a little extra.'

The mechanic hesitated, and glanced towards the Fiat in the workshop.

'I think,' said the fat man, 'a 25 per cent premium would be fair.'

The mechanic held out his hand for the key.

'You can wait up at the house,' he said. 'Tell Litsa I said it was OK.'

The fat man removed his holdall from the footwell, and leaving three apples on the seat, picked up the bag of fruit.

As he walked up to the house, the goat paused in its chewing and watched him with its devil's eyes. The kitchen door was open, but the house was quiet. A linnet in a bamboo cage was silent in the window. The fat man knocked, and waiting on the threshold, watched the mechanic move the

35

Mercedes to the workshop. The linnet dipped its beak into its feeding bowl, scattering seed but eating nothing. The fat man knocked again, but there was no response; and so he sat down on the step, and choosing the reddest apple from the bag, bit into it.

The apple was down to the core when a woman entered the kitchen, fastening the ties of an apron. Short and slight, she was like so many housewives he had met: weary and work-worn, unremarkable and undervalued, her face tight with strain.

The fat man stood, and tossed the apple core to the goat. The woman, preoccupied, began to place clean cutlery in a drawer. At his greeting, she turned to him, startled.

'May I help you?'

The fat man smiled.

'Forgive me,' he said. 'I didn't intend to surprise you. I'm Hermes Diaktoros, of Athens. Your husband is working on my car, and gave his permission for me to wait here.'

She did not return his smile, nor offer any words of welcome, but indicated a chair at the kitchen table.

'Come in, then,' she said. 'Do you want coffee?'

Sitting, he laid the bag of apples on the table and his holdall at his feet.

'Thank you,' he said. 'No sugar, if you please.'

She lit a burner on the stove, and filled a *kafebriko* at the tap.

'You know,' he said, as she spooned coffee from a jar, 'when I was talking to your husband, I didn't ask his name.'

Her back was to him; she gave her answer to the wall.

'Tassos. They call him Tassos.'

'And you, he said, are Litsa. It's a pretty name.'

The compliment brought no response. She put the *kafebriko* on the flame, and turned it high to hurry the coffee's boiling.

Through the window, the fat man watched the mechanic raise the Mercedes's bonnet. Litsa took a cup and saucer from the dresser, and filled a glass with water at the sink, and as the coffee's froth rose, filled the cup. Opening a tin painted with roses, she cut two slices from a home-baked cake, and laying them on separate plates, placed one before the fat man with a fork and a napkin, coffee and water. She carried the second plate to the house door.

'If you'll excuse me,' she said, 'I have to see to my mother.'

She left him. The fat man sipped the excellent coffee; the cream-filled sponge cake was moist and sweet. Outside, a truck laden with straw bales turned off the road and pulled up alongside the Mercedes. The mechanic called out a greeting to its driver and laid down his pliers. Somewhere inside the house, a woman's voice murmured. As the men outside talked on, the mechanic lit a cigarette.

Finishing his cake, the fat man looked with interest around the kitchen. All was ordered and well kept: the floor was swept and mopped, the work surfaces wiped clean; the salad greens in the colander were freshly picked, and washed. On the dresser, a set of silver frames held family photographs: a boy and girl together, the boy with front teeth missing; a younger, prettier Litsa smiling down at a swaddled baby; a sepia print of a woman taken in profile.

Outside, the men's conversation ended in laughter. The mechanic sent the truck on its way with a slap to the rear, as if it were livestock; stalks of straw blew off the bales and settled golden on the oil-black dirt. The mechanic took up his pliers and bent again beneath the Mercedes's bonnet.

Litsa returned to the kitchen. The cake on its plate was only half-eaten.

'I'm sorry to leave you alone,' she said, 'but my mother's care is demanding.'

'Is she unwell?'

'Stroke. The first one, we thought she'd recover from; the second nearly finished her. Sometimes I think it would have been better if it had. She has no movement to speak of, and no speech. She relies on me for everything – feeding, dressing, cleaning … Lives change, don't they? As she cared for me, as a child, I now care for her.'

'I'm sorry. It must be very hard for you. You have your own children too, I suppose?'

'A boy and a girl, both at high school. Christos will be leaving soon. I wanted him to go to university, study for a profession, but he has no interest. He's going to help his father in the workshop.'

She opened a cupboard beneath the sink and scraped the uneaten cake into a bucket already half filled with table scraps. She rinsed the plate under the tap, then stood, arms folded, looking out of the window, her eyes on the road where it disappeared around the bend. The silence between them grew long, as if she had forgotten the fat man's presence. When eventually she put her question, it was not out of interest in his answer, but a means of dispelling awkwardness.

'So what brings you here, *kyrie*?'

'Business,' he said. 'I travel a lot, in my work.'

'And what line are you in?'

'I'm with the justice department.'

'That's a good job. I wanted Christos to be a legal man. But does your family not miss you, when you're travelling?'

'I'm not a family man.'

She regarded him now with curiosity.

'That's a shame,' she said. 'You look to me like a man who'd be a good father.'

He smiled, apologetically.

'Without wishing to offend your sensibilities,' he said, 'I didn't say I'm not a father; only that I'm not a family man.'

'Divorced?'

'Never married.'

She seemed not disapproving, but philosophical.

'It's the modern way,' she said. 'Each to their own.'

'It was the ancient way, too,' he said. 'Not all modern practices were invented yesterday. My children are grown now. I see them, from time to time.'

'You didn't ever want to settle down?'

For a moment, he considered the attractions of the setting – the domestic order of the kitchen, the home-baked cake, the photographs on the dresser, the old woman cared for in her illness – and he was slow to answer.

'Sometimes,' he said. 'But if I am truthful, freedom suits me very well.'

She wasn't listening; instead, she watched the mechanic lower the Mercedes's bonnet and let it drop the last few inches to secure the catch.

'I think your car is ready,' she said.

'Excellent.' He pushed the bag of apples across the table. 'I'd like to offer you these. They're from my father's orchard; he says they are the finest in all Greece, and makes great claims for their restorative properties. Certainly, their flavour is exceptional. They're excellent for invalids. Your mother might enjoy them, if you bake them soft with honey and some cinnamon. The English have a saying, you know: an apple a day keeps the doctor away. They may be right.'

'They're right in this case.'

Walking through the open door, the mechanic dropped the Mercedes's key on the table. The prints of his boot-soles were dark on the marble tiles. Reaching into the paper bag, he picked out an apple, sniffed it, and took a large bite.

'Very nice,' he said, chewing. 'Wife, coffee.'

In silence, Litsa took an old newspaper from a stack beneath the sink and crossed to her husband; as he raised his backside, allowing her to spread the paper across his chair-seat, he winked at the fat man, and smiled. Glancing beneath the table, she saw his boots and the line of dirty footprints to the door.

'For God's sake,' she said. 'I've just washed this floor.'

'For God's sake,' he said. 'It's just a bit of mud.'

'It's oil, and you know it. How many times do I have to ask you?'

The argument was stale; she abandoned it, and lit the burner at the stove. She held up the *kafebriko* to the fat man, offering him a second cup.

'If it's no trouble,' he said. 'Your coffee's very good. The coffee I had this morning was, I'm afraid, a little disappointing.'

The mechanic took another bite of his apple.

'Where was that?' he asked.

'The *kafenion* in the square.'

The mechanic laughed.

'Evangelia's. Her coffee's horse piss. And don't, for God's sake, think of eating there. Her food's worse than her coffee.'

'I'll bear that in mind,' said the fat man. 'Though I'm committed to a bed there for tonight, at least.'

The mechanic laughed again.

'Drink plenty of brandy before bedtime, that's my advice,' he said. 'Knock yourself senseless. The bed'll be alive with vermin.'

Litsa turned from the stove, where the smell of good coffee was rising once more.

40

'Tassos,' she said, 'don't be unkind. The woman has to make a living.'

'Let her make an honest living, then; she'd find it would serve her better. Thin coffee and bad food draw no customers. For half a teaspoon of coffee powder, she keeps the whole town from her door.'

'She has her regulars,' said his wife.

'And when they're dead, what then? She's plenty salted away, anyway, I'll bet. She needs no pity from you.'

The coffee was rising to the boil; as Litsa opened the cake tin, the fat man touched his plate in anticipation.

The mechanic bit for the last time into his apple, and spoke as he chewed, pointing with his apple core to the bag of apples.

'Your English saying's not wrong,' he said. 'I've just been hearing all about our doctor, and he'll be keeping away for a while. You'll be interested in this, wife.' Litsa's back was to him as she cut more cake, and she seemed not to be listening, so Tassos looked instead at the fat man. 'My wife and the doctor are close,' he said. He gave an unkind smile and held up two fingers, crossed. 'Like that, *kyrie*. Like that. Isn't it true, wife, that we see a lot of the doctor at this house? We see an awful lot of him. Or used to. We'll not be seeing so much now.'

Litsa turned from the sink, red-faced: with anger or embarrassment was impossible to say.

'He comes to see my mother,' she said, 'as you well know. Here.'

She slammed down cake and coffee before the men. The mechanic dug a fork into his cake and placed a piece in his mouth, again chewing open-mouthed as he spoke.

'Your mother's no attraction, is she?' he said. His eyes were back on the fat man. 'Something brings him here, *kyrie*.

41

Something brings him here more often than it should. But he won't be visiting for a while. Someone's taken against him, is what I hear. He's blinded: some chemical thrown in his face. So his absence from his wedding is explained, after all. Seems someone didn't like the man, my love. Not everyone thought the same of him as you.'

'I think no more of him than of any tradesman,' she said. 'How is he?'

'In hospital, and likely to remain so for a while.'

'So who'll care for Mother?'

'She'll be no worse off without him. She wasn't dancing *shiftatelli* in his care, was she? Not that I saw.'

Litsa was silent, though to the fat man, it seemed her shoulders were more stooped, as if some extra weight had been added to her burden.

The fat man ate the last of his cake, and finished his coffee.

'I must be going,' he said. 'What do I owe you?'

The mechanic named a price; the fat man took out a pigskin wallet and counted a number of notes on to the table. The mechanic left one there and slipped the remainder into his pocket.

'It's all fixed,' he said. 'You'll have no more trouble there.'

The fat man picked up his holdall and took his key from the table. To Litsa, he offered a small bow.

'My thanks,' he said, 'for your hospitality.'

Tassos also stood, and offered a grimy hand, which the fat man took with reluctance.

The mechanic followed the fat man to the door.

'There's money on the table, wife,' he said, over his shoulder. 'Fetch me a paper when you go out.'

'If you'd like a lift to the square,' said the fat man to Litsa, politely, 'I'd be glad to wait and drive you.'

Lowering her eyes, she shook her head.

'My son'll take her, if she doesn't want to walk,' said Tassos. 'I taught my wife to accept no lifts from strangers.' He held out his arm to guide the fat man through the door. 'After you, *kyrie*. It'll be my pleasure to see you to your car.'

Five

Outside, the morning was full light, but inside, the stone-built cabin was as dim as evening, brightened only where small stones and dried, cementing mud had fallen from the walls, creating holes to let in spots of sun. When the wind blew, the corrugated iron roof – lashed down with rope and weighted with rocks – sang like the haunting dead, rattling its own percussion. There was no glass in the windows to keep out draughts, but shutters of hammered planks set on rusty hinges; the door – fetched from an abandoned house in the town – was a poor fit, held to (when he was here) by a single hook, and by a rock pushed up against it when he wasn't.

He hadn't lit the fire; last night's ashes were grey dust in the grate, the last heat and smoke long carried away by the wind. The blankets of the camp bed were unstraightened; the pillow was yellow with age and hard with matted chicken feathers, their points prickly through the unbleached calico cover. On the wooden table – an elegant, antique piece ruined with watermarks, cigarette burns and candle grease – the flame of a single candle flickered in the draughts; beside it lay an empty tin of sardines and a fork, the last of a stale loaf, and in a bottle, a few measures of the fiery *tsipouro* he distilled himself.

Outside, a lamb bleated; a tethered dog barked.

Seated at the table, leaning on his elbows, he studied a photograph. His beard was growing long, his hair the same; silver and grey ran through the black of both. His trousers were tied over boots whose leather was cracked and caked with drying mud; over his shirt and sweater, he wore a sheepskin jerkin, so rough cut and shabby, it seemed he'd stripped it from the sheep's back and fitted it directly to his own.

The photograph had lost its regular shape; around its edges, the paper was scorched, with scallops of it burned away. In the picture was a woman, seated on a wall; but the picture was not new, and though the woman in the photograph was young, in life she would be twenty years older now.

With red-rimmed eyes, he stared at her. Then, almost carelessly, he held a damaged corner of the photograph close to the candle, until smoke rose and the scorching spread; but before it caught, he whisked it from the flame, blowing to put out the glow of almost burning.

Outside, the dog barked again.

He pulled out a drawer set in the table; the wood was swollen from the damp, and, sticking, didn't open easily. Except for a box of matches, the drawer was empty; he laid the photograph face-down inside, and pushed it to.

Taking a swig from the bottle of spirit, he blew out the candle; and throwing open the badly fitting door, went out to berate the barking dog.

Six

The post office reeked of gloss paint; entering, the fat man caught his arm on the doorpost and glanced down to make sure there was no wet paint on his sleeve. Some effort, it seemed, had been expended on improvements. The painters' tools – ladders, paint cans and dustsheets – were still stacked in a corner; the skirting boards and window frames were newly brilliant white, and the walls wore a mint-green emulsion, a little patchy where they'd missed the second coat.

But fresh paint had worked no magic on the place, and the dinginess of decades of neglect was seeping through. Inadequate light shone through the north-facing windows, so the low-wattage lights were always on, turning the daylight yellow and creating shadows that fresh paint failed to lift. The outdated public-announcement posters had been pinned back on the walls; the *poste restante* pigeonholes stood where they had always stood, with the same uncollected letters left in the same dusty slots – several for a German who had gone home a year ago, some for a Cypriot now deceased, a few the postman had failed to deliver, addressed to people he had never heard of. In the umbrella stand, a forgotten bamboo-handled umbrella remained forgotten; the side table where

46

customers filled out forms had the same beer mat folded under one leg to stop it wobbling and the same non-working biro chained to its top; the dog-eared information leaflets were back in their pinewood rack; and on the back wall, the handwritten sign that had always been there advised customers to check their change before leaving.

Behind the counter, the postmaster held a lighted cigarette between his lips. He was short and very thin; his grey moustache was stained with nicotine from the smoke he exhaled down his nostrils with each breath. A missing button on his shirt showed the neckline of a woollen vest and curls of grizzled chest-hair creeping over it; hands hidden in the pockets of a bottle-green cardigan, he watched over the top of silver-framed glasses as the fat man approached, sprightly and smiling.

The fat man lifted his holdall on to the counter, placing it next to a large parcel already left there; the parcel and the holdall together filled the workspace. With exaggerated impatience, the postmaster shifted the parcel a little to the right, and the fat man's holdall a little to the left, clearing himself enough room to place his hands.

'*Kali mera*,' said the fat man, still smiling.

The ash on the postmaster's cigarette – already of such length, it drooped like a wilting flower – grew as he exhaled. The cleared counter top was covered in flecks of ash; the ashtray at the counter's end was overflowing.

'*Kali mera sas*,' said the postmaster. To keep his cigarette in place, he spoke with tightly clamped lips, like a ventriloquist; but the slight movement of his mouth dislodged the length of ash, which dropped to the counter. In annoyance, he swept it away, on to the black-and-white tiled floor.

The fat man opened his mouth to speak, but before he could do so, the postmaster held up a hand to stop him.

'Would you mind, *kyrie*,' he said, 'doing me a favour? My back is bad, and this damp weather we've had makes the problem worse. Would you move this wretched parcel over there, out of the way? The damn thing's been here all morning, taking up the whole damned office.'

'Gladly.' The fat man lifted the parcel easily, and carried it over to the side table, where it covered the pen on its chain.

'Another delivery for the mayor,' said the postmaster. 'God knows what's in this one. He seems intent on wasting every cent in the public coffers. God saves money and the devil spends it.'

'I've seen the improvements around the town,' said the fat man. 'Your mayor's a busy man. Surely it's not a waste of money when it's spent for the good of all?'

The postmaster drew deeply on his cigarette, and removing it very briefly from his mouth, leaned towards the fat man, looking at him intently over the top of his glasses.

'Flowers,' he said. 'Do you think that's a good way to spend money, on flowers? We have flowers by the thousand in the mountains, and he's wasting public money on plants.'

'The only flowers I've seen are at the fountain,' said the fat man, 'and I have to say, to an outsider's eye, they look most attractive.'

'But at what price?'

'A few drachmas only, surely?'

'Pah!'

The postmaster's cigarette had burned down almost to the filter. Taking the butt from his mouth, he ground it out in the overflowing ashtray. Out of habit, he still spoke from between tight lips; his voice was raw, roughened by smoke.

'May I help you with something?' he asked.

'Indeed you may,' said the fat man. From his raincoat pocket, he withdrew his paper bag of postcards, and removed two

48

already written and addressed. Then, unzipping his holdall, he took out a parcel wrapped in brown paper and laid both parcel and postcards on the counter. 'I wish to mail these.'

Ignoring the donkey in the hat, the postmaster turned the second postcard – the rock-top monasteries at Meteora, spectacular in a sunset – towards him.

'Meteora,' he said, bitterly. 'Where the foreigners travel in droves. There's nothing for tourists in a place like this. You'll find us all cabbages and cotton. A few sights like these, and we'd be laughing.'

From the pocket of his cardigan, he took a pack of cheap Greek cigarettes, lit one and placed it burning between his lips. Turning his attention to the fat man's small parcel, he moved his glasses up his nose to read the address, tapping on the name of its destination with a nicotine-yellowed fingertip.

'This where you're from?' he asked.

'I have a house there.'

'So what brings you here?' The postmaster placed the parcel on the scales and read off its weight, then ran his stained finger down the wall chart listing inland postal rates. 'You're just over.' He named the price of postage. 'Is it business? Do you want a receipt? Are you a government man, by any chance? You look as if you could be, to me.'

'I'm not a government man, no. But I do work for the authorities.'

'North or south?'

'My work takes me all over.'

The postmaster blew a long stream of smoke down his nose and looked at the fat man with suspicion.

'You're not from the tax office, are you?'

The fat man smiled.

'No,' he said, 'I am no tax man. The parcel is just a curiosity, something of interest I found on my travels.'

The postmaster gave a snort of laughter.

'If you like curiosities, you'll find we have more than our share of those here! And all living and breathing and walking the earth! All possible strangenesses of mankind, they're gathered here, in one small town. Keep your eyes open! We won't disappoint you there!'

The fat man smiled politely, and handed the postmaster a note from his wallet. The postmaster removed the cigarette from his mouth, and flicking off the ash from its tip, laid it on the edge of the ashtray. In a drawer beneath the counter, he placed the fat man's banknote under a clip and picked out a large number of coins, counting aloud as he did so. Closing the drawer, he laid a handful of change before the fat man.

'My apologies,' he said. 'I've no small notes.'

The fat man glanced at his change, then looked at the postmaster, who replaced his cigarette in his mouth, eyes narrowed against the sting of its smoke.

The fat man smiled.

'Petty theft,' he said.

A touch of colour came to the postmaster's cheeks, and he frowned.

'I'm joking, of course,' said the fat man. 'But I think you'll find my change is thirty drachmas short.' Spreading the coins across the counter, he sorted the coins with a fingertip into small piles, putting like with like, and having done so, counted them aloud. 'You see?' he said. 'You owe me another thirty drachmas.'

Obsequiously, the postmaster bowed his head, and took thirty drachmas from his drawer.

'Forgive me,' he said. 'My fault entirely.'

'Oh, I forgive you this small mistake,' said the fat man. 'But if mistakes became a habit, and the habit harboured intent, then the authorities would take a dim view. Thirty drachmas here and there might add up, over years, to a nice little sum.'

The postmaster slammed the cash drawer shut.

'An honest mistake,' he said.

'Indeed,' said the fat man, 'indeed. Will my parcel go today?'

'This afternoon, if the van's not delayed.'

'That's good. I wouldn't like the contents to deteriorate.'

The postmaster looked at the parcel with renewed interest, and seemed on the point of putting another question; but behind them, the street door was opened by a young man, who stood a few moments under the portico, calling out his side of a conversation with someone who remained unseen.

'Don't let me down!' he said, allowing the door to close. 'Tomorrow, for sure!'

He took a step towards the postmaster, then seemed to be overtaken by a thought and stopped, patting the side pockets of his leather jacket. Obviously feeling what he sought there, he took another step, only to stop again, raise his eyes to the ceiling as he thought again, and turn to leave.

The postmaster gave a slow smile, and touched the fat man's arm.

'Here's your chance,' he said, very quietly, 'to meet our spendthrift.' Raising his voice, he called out to the young man.

'Mr Mayor, *kali mera sas*,' he said. 'Don't be leaving without picking up your mail.'

With his cigarette burning at the corner of his mouth, he jerked his head towards the table where the fat man had placed the large parcel.

'It's here,' said the young man to himself, 'thank God.'

He crossed to the table, and laid a hand on the parcel as if about to pick it up; but then he seemed to change his mind, and instead turned to the postmaster, his mouth open to speak.

But the postmaster spoke first.

'This gentleman's from out of town,' he said. 'He's been admiring your flowers.'

The fat man held out his hand.

'Mr Mayor,' he said, 'it's a pleasure to meet you. Hermes Diaktoros, of Athens. I have admired not only your flowers but all your projects. A man of drive and vision such as yourself is quite a rarity.'

The mayor took the fat man's hand. Close up, he was older than he had at first seemed, and his face was developing lines of strain; but his physique was strong, and his expression open, so he seemed to the fat man both likeable and attractive.

'Thank you,' he said. 'They call me Angelos, Angelos Petridis. And I am only doing my best. I love this town; it's my ambition to see it flourish.' He glanced at his watch. 'I'm running late,' he said to the postmaster. 'I might have to leave the parcel till tomorrow.'

'You can't leave it there,' said the postmaster disagreeably. 'People use that table. This office isn't big enough for great parcels like that to be left for your convenience. What's in it, anyway? What have you been spending our money on this time?'

'It's a plaque,' said the mayor, 'to commemorate the minister's visit. It's going on the fountain, to remind us of the day our betters in the capital took notice of us.'

The postmaster shook his head, as if in despair; the fat man smiled broadly.

'What an excellent idea,' he said, 'to encourage civic pride. Perhaps I can assist you, if you'll allow me. Shall I deliver it to the town hall? I have plenty of time, and you, apparently, don't.'

The mayor smiled, and the smile removed the stress-lines from his face, showing him to be somewhat younger than he had seemed – young enough, in fact, still to be called a youth.

'I'd be very grateful,' he said. 'There's so much to organise for the minister's visit. I have a meeting with the police to discuss security, and I'm already late.'

'Consider it done,' said the fat man.

The mayor left them. The postmaster watched him go, narrowing his eyes like a predator as his cigarette burned low.

'How refreshing,' said the fat man, 'to see such commitment and optimism. I think your mayor could have a bright future ahead of him – a political career would suit him, don't you think? You must all be very proud.'

'Optimism has its place, and so do improvements,' said the postmaster. 'But we've managed without either for many years. Still, young wood makes a hot fire. He'll burn himself out before long. I'll welcome the day; then we can all get back to normal.'

'You surprise me,' said the fat man. 'Does this town not deserve to be improved? Is the mayor the only one who cares for it at all?'

The postmaster turned away and placed the fat man's parcel in a mail-sack which held little else. He took the burned-down cigarette from his mouth, and stubbed it out in the ashtray.

'A place like this,' he said, 'the pace of life is steady.'

'Steady, or stagnant? In my experience, a good dose of change can make a world of difference. The ministerial visit he mentioned – that's quite a coup he's pulled off there, bringing a government official to a place as small as this. Usually they require a larger audience for their appearances.'

A smile touched the postmaster's lips.

'Ah yes,' he said. 'Stamatis Semertzakis, from the Ministry of Public Works. As you suggest, a great event for us, who see so little excitement.' Feigning deference, he tipped his head; his tone was sarcastic. 'He's coming to see how our good mayor has been spending his department's money; in short, he's coming to inspect the plumbing. It will be a great event: they're having a parade of schoolchildren, and a banquet at the town hall for a privileged few. There'll be TV cameras and newspaper men; no doubt they'll be covering the great unveiling of the plaque. If you're just passing through, you'll be sorry to miss all the fun.'

The fat man smiled.

'As it turns out, I shall still be here. And I'm looking forward immensely to the festivities. What an excellent boost for the town! You'll be expecting an upturn in trade, no doubt, as a consequence of the publicity.'

The postmaster took his cigarettes from his cardigan pocket.

'Publicity may be good or bad,' he said.

The fat man picked up his holdall, and crossed to the table for the mayor's parcel.

'Not in the ad men's books,' he said. 'What they would say is, there's no such thing as bad publicity.'

Seven

That day, at its end, held more of winter than spring. The low sun was hidden by cloud, and the light had reached that moment of dusk where, though adequate to see by, its luminosity was lost. The absence of light turned all colours drab; it stole the greenness from the grasses and thistles, the purple from the spiked blooms of the lupins, the sugar pink from the petals of the cyclamen, and made everything monochrome, camouflaging all true variations.

Adonis Anapodos had returned to the chapel of St Paraskevi, because his mother had made him; he was to light the lamps for the poor doctor's sake, as she had said.

Inside the chapel, his offertory candle cast dark shadows on the walls, making his own shadow monstrous as he carried the oil-lamp to the icons. Created for candlelight in rich reds and gold, the images of the saint seemed to move as he stood before each in turn, making the triple cross and kissing the glass which covered them (though his obeisance, he noticed, did not brighten their dismal faces). As he honoured the icons on the chapel's right side, wondering at the origins of the beaten-silver offerings tied to them – an arm, a nappied baby, a man in a trilby hat – he felt the saint's other eyes on him, waiting for an error in the ritual, or disapproving of his starting on the right and not the left. Shadows hid the corners of the chapel; behind the altar screen was darkness, and once his eyes had strayed there, the certainty of someone hiding there began to grow.

Mid-cross, he stopped and stood quite still, holding his breath to listen for the breathing of another; but the place remained silent in the way of lonely places. Rebuking himself for his own stupidity, he moved down the line to the next St Paraskevi.

But as he lifted the lamp to invoke blessings for her, outside, across the courtyard, beyond mistaking the chapel gate squealed; and although he heard no footfall, the fading light falling through the dirty window changed, so he knew someone was out there, crossing the courtyard stones.

And for a moment, the chapel grew still dimmer as a figure passed across the half-open door. Adonis turned, expecting someone to enter; but there was no hand on the latch, only a return to the stillness that the movement had disturbed, as if a breath of wind had passed, and no more than that.

More than ever, the saint's images seemed not kindly but conspiring. Unmoving, he waited, knowing anyone here would know that he was here too – the open door, the lamplight gave him away – and yet no one had shown themselves. He began to doubt himself (the gate's squeal, the figure he thought he'd seen – had they been real?), for who would come here and not first enter the chapel to honour the saint?

He placed the lamp in the sandbox where the one candle he had lit dripped creamy wax, its thin form bending in its own heat. Crossing to the doorway, concealing himself behind the heavy door, he put his eye to the hinged edge and looked out into the courtyard. His view through the crack between wood and wall was restricted; but though he saw no one, the courtyard gate was not how he had left it, but ajar.

Adonis considered the distance between chapel door and gate; he had almost done his duty here and could avoid sinister company by making a run for it, jumping on to his scooter and riding away. But the scooter was temperamental and might easily let him down, and so he decided it would be better to make himself known, to be overt about his presence. With this in mind, still hidden behind the chapel door, he called out.

'Is anyone there?'

He listened to a silence which was deepened by the dropping of the wind; and the silence lasted until he was convinced the visitor was supernatural and his calling out had frightened it away. But as he was asking himself whether this was good or bad, someone passed the chapel window and came into the range of his restricted view.

He knew the visitor; he recognised the stature of the man, his raincoat, his unusual white shoes. And yet Adonis was still afraid, because he had no idea where the man came from or what his business was in town; and when strange events happened – and the blinding of the doctor was certainly strange – it seemed quite possible that a stranger might be responsible.

He regretted, now, that he had called out, and drew himself back into the space behind the chapel door and looked across to one of the icons; but there was no help in the empty, painted face. He crossed himself, and closing his own eyes tight like the most naive of children hiding, he waited, breathing as low and as quietly as he could.

Whilst he stood, eyes shut, it seemed to him that nothing moved; but a gentle click close by surprised him into opening his eyes.

The fat man stood before him, a gold lighter in his hand burning with a steady, blue-based flame.

'*Kali spera*, Adonis.' The fat man's expression was serious, and Adonis found no comfort in being addressed by his own familiar name. 'I'm glad to find you here.'

From the racks beneath the sandbox, the fat man took a slender candle and applied his lighter to the wick. The string burned away quickly, disappearing in a wisp of smoke, and with the excess gone, the flame grew steady. He held the candle close to his face, and moth-like, Adonis's eyes were drawn there. The light of the flame gave empty depths to the fat man's eyes, and Adonis thought of the pool in the mountain cavern where his cousin worked in summer. There, the tourists sailed on boats and the boatmen told them the water's depth could not be measured, that the pool went down and down right to the earth's core; and as the boatmen shipped their oars and let the boats drift, the tourists would go quiet and shift their handbags and their cameras to safe places on the bottom boards and pull their children close. But Adonis knew the secret of that pool. The truth was, the water was only three feet deep, and it was the light – or lack of it – that made it bottomless: lack of light and the visitors' own belief, because, told that the pool was bottomless, they saw what they expected. And Adonis told himself that what he saw now was nothing frightening: not empty eyes like the doctor's had been, but everyday eyes made otherwise by tricks of light.

The fat man smiled, and moving the flame away from his face, held it instead to each wall in turn, casting more shadows on the saint's many faces.

'Just pictures, nothing more,' he said. 'It's the habit of Orthodoxy to venerate pictures. The saints, you know – some were extraordinary people, of course, but many in life were quite ordinary and got pushed into sainthood by martyrdom. Some suffered extraordinarily unpleasant deaths. Does that make them worthy of a halo? It's a very rare man who deserves other men's worship. Why are you here?'

The question was unexpected, and asking it, the fat man looked hard at Adonis. His sternness made Adonis nervous, and nerves often made him stammer; and so, although he wished to answer, he didn't dare, because he knew the words would be misshapen and malformed, hard-set and clinging to his tongue like barnacles, refusing to take flight like the free birds they should be.

The fat man was patient, not pressing for his answer; but when Adonis eventually managed to speak, the words that came were irrelevant.

'You're supposed to make an offering for the candle,' he said.

The fat man smiled.

'You mean, pay cash,' he said. 'Here. Let me show you something.'

He crouched, and touched the old stones which made the chapel floor. Holding the candle close, he ran a fingertip along a line carved in the stone.

'Look,' he said. 'Here. And here.' The lines were unmistakable but faint, worn away by centuries of feet. 'Do you see this inscription? That lady on the walls is an interloper, an intruder. She and her servants have no more than squatters' rights. This place belongs to someone else; there's a much older claim than theirs.'

Fascinated, Adonis crouched beside the fat man to read the ancient lettering. When he spoke again, his stammer was forgotten.

'What does it say?' he asked. 'Whose building is it really?'

'Hard to say, for certain,' said the fat man. 'There's an "A" there. Apollo, Asclepius, Aphrodite. Someone, anyway, with better credentials than your Johnny-come-lately nun.'

He laughed. 'Don't tell your mother I said so. She'd have me shot as a heretic. It was she who sent you here, no doubt, to light the lamps and do the honours.'

Adonis traced the lettering with his fingertips as the fat man had done, trying to make sense of what was there; but there seemed no sense to be made.

'They're just fragments,' said the fat man, standing, 'perhaps relaid from some temple which once stood here.'

Still crouching, Adonis said, 'She tells me to come every day, but I don't.'

The fat man waited for him to continue, but when Adonis said no more, the fat man spoke instead.

'This place has an atmosphere, hasn't it?' he said, looking around them. 'I expect it makes you afraid.'

Adonis stood.

'Mother says too many things frighten me,' he said.

'What are you afraid of?'

'Dogs. They bite. The sea, when it's rough. And I don't like the dark much.'

'Are you afraid of me?'

'No.' As he answered, Adonis lowered his eyes, and the fat man laughed, knowing it was a lie.

'No need to be afraid of me,' he said, 'not if you tell the truth. It'll be dark soon. Let's step outside, and you can show me where you found the doctor.'

With no deference to the icons and no cross-making, he twisted his candle to stand upright in the sandbox. Leading the way outside, he crossed the courtyard to the wall which faced the sunset, and stepped easily up on to the stone bench to look over it; but except for the first lights of the town down by the sea, there was little to see in the dusk.

'I'm too late for the view,' he said. 'No matter; another time. Where, exactly, did you find him?'

He climbed down, and followed Adonis around the chapel's far side. Again, the fat man stepped up on to the stone bench, and looked out over the chapel's surroundings. There was only the rutted track and the scrubland running down to it – nothing, it seemed, to interest him.

'Did you come to light the lamps this morning?' Still standing on the bench, he was imposing, perhaps intimidating; and, as if aware of this, he jumped down on to the courtyard before Adonis answered.

Anxious to be truthful, Adonis shook his head.

'No,' he said. A little ashamed, he avoided the fat man's eyes. 'My mother told me to light them, but I decided not to. I was late. And I don't like this place. People say bad things of it.'

'You mean ghosts,' said the fat man. 'Creations of people's imaginations. A ghost story's so much more romantic than a creaking floorboard or a draught on the back of the neck. They build the stories on memories; they take a grain of truth, and let it grow to the size of an orange. The human mind distorts what it remembers. But these stones –' he tapped his foot '– might be different. They might remember things without embroidering. They might have memories, I think.'

'Do you think so? How could they?'

The fat man laughed.

'You're right – how could they? But if they could …' He laid a large hand on Adonis's shoulder. The hand was warm, unaffected by the evening's chill, but its weight was uncomfortable to Adonis because he was unused to being touched. 'The stones would tell us tales, if they could. And they'd tell the truth, for sure; rocks would never dissemble. My job would be very much easier if stones could talk. But since they can't, I must rely on you – and do you know, Adonis, I trust you in the same way I would trust a rock.

61

You are a truthful lad, it seems to me; so tell me, if you weren't going to stop and light the lamps this morning, what changed your mind?'

Adonis shrugged at the obviousness of his answer.

'His shoe. He threw his shoe over the wall. It landed in front of me and made me jump.'

The fat man laughed. A gust of evening's breeze lifted his coat, and taking his hand from Adonis's shoulder he thrust both hands into the raincoat's pockets to keep it flat against his thighs. Adonis felt suddenly cold; for warmth, he wrapped his arms around himself, like a straitjacket.

'That was ingenious,' said the fat man. 'Our doctor is a clever man. So you stopped, and you helped him.'

'I fetched him water first. He asked me to.'

'Good lad. Show me where from.'

Adonis led him around the chapel, and pointed to the well.

'There. I found a bucket in the kitchen.'

'Which is where?'

'Through there.'

He pointed to the battered kitchen door. The fat man glanced at it briefly, then looked around and frowned.

'Where is the bucket now? Did you return it to its place?'

Adonis, too, looked around.

'I don't remember. I don't think so. I think I left it there, where he was lying.'

The fat man seemed thoughtful.

'What did you do next?'

'He bathed his eyes, then asked me for his bag. He wanted medicine. He needed an injection. I did it for him.' His pride showed in his voice; but the fat man's thoughts had moved on.

'Where was his bag?'

'Outside the gate. Left there with his bike.'

'Show me.'

Adonis led the way to the gate, and through it pointed to where bag and bike had been.

'The bike's not there now,' he said.

Again, the fat man frowned.

'Neither is the bag,' he said.

Returning to the kitchen, the fat man clicked open the latch and went inside, sniffing at the damp and glancing up at the ceiling's cobwebs. Beneath the stone sink stood the empty yellow bucket.

From the doorway, Adonis looked on uncertainly.

The fat man pointed to the bucket.

'Did you put this back here, Adonis?'

'I don't think so, no. The doctor needed help. He wanted me to phone for an ambulance. There wasn't time.'

'There wasn't time,' echoed the fat man. 'Of course there wasn't time. Someone has been here, and tidied up. Tidied up, and helped themselves to his motorbike.'

'The bike had fallen over, or someone threw it down. I told the doctor; I thought it would be damaged. It was a good bike, powerful, but I took him on my moped. I've had no practice, riding a bike like that. So we went on my moped. It didn't matter. We had to go slowly anyway, because he was in pain.' He, too, sniffed, realising something was different from the last time he was here. 'Coffee,' he said. 'It smelled of coffee. There was a flask. It's not here now. It was on the table, there.'

The fat man looked to where he pointed, and once more at the empty, yellow bucket.

'Who has been here? Who else might have been here, Adonis?'

'I don't know. I don't want to get anyone into trouble.'

'There'll be no trouble for anyone who deserves none, you have my word on that. But someone has been here, and may have seen something which will help me find the doctor's attacker. Maybe the same someone knows the whereabouts of the doctor's motorbike.'

'It was a Yamaha, 500cc, a silver one. I'm going to have a bike like that one day. I'll bet a bike like that could do two hundred easy, wouldn't you?'

'I expect it could; more, probably. You want a bike like that, Adonis, but I don't think you came up here and took it, did you?' Vigorously, Adonis shook his head. 'But it seems that someone else did. You know the difference between right and wrong; you know it's wrong to steal. But someone else doesn't know the difference quite as well as you do. Someone seems to have just come and helped themselves.'

'He wouldn't do that.'

'Who wouldn't?'

'I don't want to get anyone into trouble.'

'There'll be no trouble that isn't warranted. And of course I would never mention your name. You have my word on that.'

'He wouldn't take it anyway,' insisted Adonis, 'but he does come here, sometimes. He comes for water, like me, or for shade, or to get out of the rain. He never lights the candles, though.'

'Who is he?'

'They call him Orfeas. He's a shepherd. He's got more sheep than me.'

'And where will I find him?'

'He has a house in town – it was his mother's house. But don't look for him there. He prefers his mountain place; he has a cabin. I'd like a cabin like that, for summer at least. You can live wild, with the animals. But mother says she's not dragging up there every day to feed me.'

'You can't blame her for that. And it's a lonely life, up there in the mountains. The life's too quiet for most; those that choose it generally have good reasons. Come on, it's time to go. You won't want to ride down in the dark.'

'I don't. The lights on my scooter aren't very good.'

'Follow me, if you like. I've kept you here; I'll see you get back safely.'

Somewhere, an owl screeched. As Adonis pulled the chapel gate closed behind them, the bell over their heads moved in the rising wind and the clapper touched its side, giving the ghost of a ring.

'There are storms to the north,' said the fat man to himself, 'but not for us. No storms for us, just yet. Fetch your scooter, Adonis, and follow me to the road. I didn't bring my car up this rough track.'

The fat man led the way, walking quickly along the track in the direction of the road; and on his moped, Adonis rolled along beside him, weaving amongst the stones to keep his balance, staying close to the fat man to keep the shades away.

Eight

When the fat man reached the town, darkness had fallen. Reversing the Mercedes up to the kerb he'd parked at that morning, he locked the car and made his way along the side street to the square. The evening was cold; the house doors were closed, the windows lit by lamplight and the flickering images of television.

At the *kafenion*, the fat man closed the door behind him as he entered, and called out *kali spera* to Evangelia, who stood below the birdcage at the counter's end, trying to provoke the cockatoo's interest in a dish of sunflower seeds. Around a table, four men were laughing; but as the fat man laid down his holdall and removed his raincoat, their laughter died away. There was beer and whisky on their table, which was littered with the empty pods of broad beans; a saucer of salt was dinted where the men had dipped their shelled beans.

Two of the men, the fat man knew. The grocer looked his way with bloodshot eyes, then returned his attention to his glass of beer, whilst the postmaster, leaning over an ashtray already half full of butts, drew on a burned-down cigarette and blew the smoke out down his nostrils. A third man ran a hand through his thinning hair, patting its long strands into place over a prominent bald spot. The fourth – somewhat older than the others, almost elderly – had dressed with care: a watch chain dangled from the breast-pocket of his European tweed suit, and there was a shine on the leather of his outmoded shoes.

The fat man looked from one man to another. The man with thinning hair split open a bean-pod with his thumb, and tossed the raw beans into his mouth, one by one, as if performing a party trick. As the postmaster stubbed out his cigarette, the elderly man picked up a briarwood pipe and knocked its bowl against the leg of his chair until black ash dropped on to the floor tiles.

'*Kali spera sas*,' said the fat man.

The men at the table did not respond. Evangelia dropped a sunflower seed on to the floor of the birdcage, and beckoned to the fat man with both hands.

'*Kali spera, kyrie*,' she said. 'Come in. Come in and sit.' She waddled towards him, pulling down her dress over her wide backside, re-fastening a cardigan button which had popped open over her stomach. 'Here, sit.' Her plump hand touched the back of a chair at an empty table. 'What'll you have?'

'I wonder,' said the fat man, 'if there's anything to eat?'

She considered; her expression was doubtful.

'I've nothing in,' she said, 'and the shop's already closed.' She inclined her head towards the grocer, whose eyes stayed on his glass. 'I've eggs, and cheese, if you want an omelette.'

'That would do very well,' said the fat man. 'And ouzo, with a little water.'

In no hurry, she crossed to the men's table and cleared it of empty bean pods. Behind the counter, she unscrewed the cap off a dusty bottle and poured a long measure of ouzo into a tumbler.

The four men now sat in silence. The fat man folded his arms and smiled across at the postmaster, who, disconcerted, reached for a fresh cigarette.

The silence persisted. Evangelia ran a little water into the ouzo, turning it from clear to milky pale, and placed the tumbler on the counter. The fat man rose from his seat to fetch it; back at his table, he took a sip and gave a nod of satisfaction.

'Excellent,' he said. 'Forgive me, gentlemen, for interrupting your conversation. Perhaps you'll allow me to buy you a drink, by way of apology.' The postmaster paused in putting a lighter to his cigarette; the elderly man reached into his pocket for his tobacco. 'Evangelia! Put drinks on my bill for these gentlemen.'

The grocer raised his half-empty beer glass to the fat man.

'Thank you, friend,' he said. 'Your health.'

'And yours,' said the fat man, placing his own cigarettes and gold lighter on the table. Then, holding out first his right foot, then his left, he inspected his shoes by the light of the unshaded bulb above him, and, unzipping his holdall, took out a bottle of shoe-whitener. As the four men watched bemused, he shook the bottle, removed the cap and dabbed whitener first on one shoe, then the other, until, satisfied his footwear was at its best, he re-capped the bottle, tucked it into his bag, zipped up the bag and leaned back in his chair to take another swallow of ouzo.

Evangelia had been breaking eggs into a bowl, and the fat man's performance had stolen her attention. Now she pointed with a fork towards the grocer.

'You see,' she said, 'here's a man who knows how to take care of himself. Some of you could learn a great deal from – I'm sorry, *kyrie*, your name escapes me.'

'Diaktoros,' said the fat man, directing his reply towards the men. 'Hermes Diaktoros, of Athens.'

'An Athenian amongst us!' said the elderly man. As he spoke, he pulled strands of tobacco from his pouch and pressed them with his forefinger into his pipe-bowl; the action seemed to demand all his attention, so his eyes stayed on his pipe and didn't meet the fat man's. 'And what line are you in, *kyrie*, that brings you here amongst us bumpkins?'

'Bumpkins?' asked the fat man, in surprise. 'Are you bumpkins? Had I known, I would have brought a notebook to take notes; the anthropologist in me can't resist the study of new species. I had taken you for men, pure and simple. If I was wrong, forgive me.'

The elderly man put his pipe to his lips and the flame of a match to the bowl, and sucked on the stem with little popping sounds; as smoke rose from the pipe, he said no more, but a smile touched the corners of his mouth.

'Are you an anthropologist, then?' asked the postmaster.

The fat man seemed to consider.

'In a manner of speaking, yes,' he said, 'in that the knowledge and prediction of the habits and behaviour of men forms an important base to my work. Let us say I am part anthropologist, part investigator.'

Behind the counter, a pan sizzled as Evangelia slipped beaten eggs into hot oil.

'An investigator?' asked the man with thinning hair. 'And what are you investigating amongst us?'

'My business is the blinding of your doctor.'

'You're a policeman, then. If you're a policeman, why not say so?'

The fat man laughed.

'I'm no policeman,' he said. 'There's no police force in this country that'd take me. They find my methods – unorthodox. No, you are quite wrong. My employers are based in Athens, but their interests are wide ranging.'

'Wide ranging indeed, to reach so far as this. Are the police not investigating the assault, then?'

69

'I think you'll find the doctor has not reported it. He doesn't wish to press charges.'

'I see,' said the thin-haired man. 'So he's wanting to sue. There'll be a suit for damages, before summer's out – and I assume you are the man hired to make his case. Is that what you're about – a private investigation, on his behalf?'

The fat man regarded him intently.

'I see you have an inquiring mind yourself,' he said. 'But the true skill in investigation is to answer your own questions by observation. That's an art I have spent many years perfecting. Are you a betting man, *kyrie*? Would you like a small wager with me? Though I warn you, if we're betting, it will have to be worthwhile. Here's what I'll wager.' From the little finger of his right hand, he removed a ring – a plain band set with an unusual coin, stamped with a rising sun on one side and a young man in profile on the other. He laid the ring before him on the table, where it shone with the glow of old gold. 'This antiquity was a gift from my mother. You can see, I hope, that it has considerable value. Do you have anything to wager against it?'

Pulling a half-clean plate from the sink of dirty water and rinsing it under the tap, Evangelia watched with interest.

The thin-haired man laughed, nervously.

'You're cavalier with a gift from your mother,' he said. 'Most men would respect such a gift.'

'Oh, I do respect it,' said the fat man. 'But I respect my own abilities, too. I am 100 per cent confident that I can beat you at this game.'

'You haven't said yet,' put in the pipe-smoker, 'what the game is.'

Evangelia slid the omelette on to the plate and arranged a sliced tomato along its edge.

'Don't get carried away, Dr Dinos,' she called out. 'Don't bet more than you can afford to lose.'

The fat man looked with interest at the pipe-smoker.

'Another doctor,' he said. 'This town seems overflowing with them.'

'I am no longer practising.'

'Perhaps today's misfortune will persuade you from retirement. The wager is, that you can ask me any question about any of the men here, and I can answer it correctly.'

At this, the men all smiled like conspirators. The grocer nudged the doctor, urging him to take the bet, whilst the postmaster felt in his pocket for what cash was there, keen to take such an easy bet himself.

The fat man held up his hand.

'But because I'm a fair man,' he said, 'I want first of all to demonstrate my skill. It would be unfair, after all, to ask you to bet on a horse you've never seen – though remarkably, men do so, every day. So let me show you. Who'll volunteer to be my subject?'

'Well,' said Dr Dinos, picking a strand of tobacco from his tongue, 'it seems your only candidate is Vangelis here.' He pointed his pipe stem at the thin-haired man. 'Evangelia has announced my profession to you. Apostolis I believe you have already met in the post office, and Lambis you know as our grocer. Vangelis is the only stranger to you; so let him be your subject. What can you tell us about him?'

With narrowed eyes, the fat man regarded the man with thinning hair.

'Well, Vangelis,' he said. 'Would you hold out your hands for me, please?'

With reluctance, the man offered his palms to the fat man, as if he were to have his fortune told; his hands were small and pale, with the careful manicure of a woman.

The fat man leaned forward, and, taking Vangelis's

fingertips in his own, turned his hands to see their backs, and then back to the palms.

'Thank you,' said the fat man, sitting back in his chair. 'Your hands tell me a great deal about you. You are no manual labourer, for certain – though it seems to me your work is, to an extent, with your hands. A man of science, perhaps. And you wear no wedding ring, so I know you are unmarried.'

There was silence, until the postmaster gave a bark of laughter.

'There's no detective work there!' he said. 'Any fool could take a lucky guess, and say as much. With hands like those, it's obvious he's no bricklayer. Take the bet, Vangelis!'

But the other three, thinking of the fat man's reference to science, seemed doubtful.

'Shall I give you a little more, then?' asked the fat man, smiling round at them. 'Vangelis is not unmarried, he's widowed, and the sad event of his wife's death was clouded by the circumstances – an accident involving falling masonry, which has left him a victim of suspicion, and has made him bitter.' He held Vangelis's eyes with his own. 'But the authorities know of your innocence, Vangelis; your name is clear, and though you and your wife were not ideally suited, and your escape from the marriage was not entirely unwelcome, you grieve for her in your way.'

Vangelis was about to take a drink, but froze with his beer glass only halfway to his mouth. A flush of deep red spread across his face.

'We were talking, just a moment ago, about doctors,' went on the fat man, 'and it is your lifelong regret not to have followed that profession. Sadly, you didn't make the grade, and so have had to content yourself with being a pharmacist, which you have always seen as second best. But your business does well, and your services are much needed. I think you're more appreciated than you think.' He smiled, and crossed his hands over his stomach. 'Well, gentlemen? What will you bet?'

From behind the counter, Evangelia waddled across to his table and laid his omelette before him, along with a basket of bread. There was cutlery in the basket; the knife blade bore small flecks of a previous diner's food.

She wished the fat man *kali orexi* – good digestion – and turned to the other table.

'He's very good, isn't he?' she said. 'He's summed you up, Vangelis, in a nutshell.'

Frowning, Dr Dinos held up his empty glass.

'Whisky,' he said, shortly.

'You're a government man,' said the grocer, accusingly. 'Only a government man could know these things.'

As the flush receded from Vangelis's face, he drank what remained of his beer, and, handing his glass to Evangelia to be refilled, stood up from the table and disappeared through a door marked *WC*.

The fat man covered his ring with the palm of his hand, and pushed it across the table towards the grocer.

'Come, take the bet,' he said, quietly. With the ring at the edge of the table where the three men remaining could see it clearly, he uncovered it; but no longer lusting after it, they shrank back both from the ring and from the fat man, who now addressed the doctor. 'You, Mr Mayor. How about you? You have cash in your pocket, I'm sure, and money in the bank.'

'Why do you call him mayor?' asked the postmaster, flicking a length of ash from the end of his fresh cigarette. 'You met our mayor this morning: young Petridis.'

The fat man smiled.

73

'The usurper,' he said. 'A mere boy, almost, who displaced Dr Dinos here after – how long in office, *yiatre*? Fifteen years, sixteen? And the boy's moving mountains! How galling to see what's been possible in so short a time.'

Dr Dinos took his pipe from his mouth.

'There wasn't that kind of money about when I took office,' said the doctor. 'These grants are a new invention. He'll blow himself out, before long. The bureaucracy will clip his wings.'

'Perhaps it will and perhaps it won't,' said the fat man. 'Perhaps his commitment to doing real good in the community will keep him airborne. Too many in public office are there for prestige or to line their own pockets.'

'We did many good things for this community,' said the postmaster.

'Did you, Councillor? Forgive me – *ex*-Councillor. Well, no matter, now. You have an excellent man in your new mayor. You'll be there, no doubt, to honour him when the minister visits?'

Evangelia brought full glasses to the table. As she picked up a few more emptied bean pods, the pharmacist slipped back into his chair.

'I wouldn't miss it for the world,' said the postmaster. 'Your health.'

And, as one man, the four of them clinked their glasses in the toast.

Upstairs, the fat man's room was cold. From the head of the bed, the view was of objects kept in permanent storage: dusty boxes tied up with string, a wicker carpet beater with broken struts, an antique typewriter with keys marked in the Roman alphabet. The seat of the bedside armchair had been chewed by mice, which might – from the droppings under the seat – still be in residence. Beside the bed, Evangelia had cleared space to lay a faded *kilim*, whose once-rich patterns were faded and eaten by moths. The weak light from a frilly shaded lamp flickered, and the plug crackled in its socket; the casing of the wires was damaged by the gnawing of rodents.

The bed was narrow, with springs which creaked whenever the fat man moved; the mattress was too thin for any comfort. He turned out the lamp, and stripes of light from the room beneath shone through the floorboards. For a while, he shifted from his side to his back, and to his other side, trying to find a position where he was comfortable; but every movement caused squeaking in the bed-springs, and so the best option seemed to be to lie quite still and wait for sleep to find him.

When he was quiet, others were not. Amongst the dusty boxes, clawed feet ran. And in the *kafenion* below, four men, slightly drunk, talked too loudly.

'The whole town there, the newspapers and television and – what? – no minister.'

They laughed: a head-back, back-slapping, whisky-inflated laugh.

'What will he do?'

'What can he do?'

'You should step in! Prepare a speech!'

Upstairs, the fat man lay quite still, trying to identify each speaker.

'There'll be no speech from me. I shall be enjoying his humiliation from a suitable distance.'

Then, a woman's voice.

'Well, I feel sorry for him,' said Evangelia. 'The time he's given to this town, and all he's done preparing for this visit!'

'He's a gullible fool, then, and an arrogant one! Only a fool would believe the Minister of Public Works would have time for us!'

'He should know men like that have no time for backwaters like this! There aren't enough votes here to make any difference to a minister's career!'

'Why do you call him arrogant?' asked Evangelia. 'He didn't invite the man. You wrote and announced his visit. The letter looked genuine. He was proud to receive it. He showed it to me himself.'

'The stationery is genuine enough. Friends in high places.'

'Then it's not arrogance to believe in the letter, is it?'

'Hush your noise, woman! Gentlemen, another drink before we go?'

But the others demurred. As they rose to leave, their chairs scraped on the marble tiles.

'Well, I think it'll be fine entertainment,' said one of them.

'Nothing to see won't be much entertainment, will it?' persisted Evangelia. 'You've a strange idea of entertainment if you think that'll amuse people. And if you've such influence in high places, why didn't you persuade the minister actually to come? You've no friends in high places, just friends in the minister's stationery cupboard! And if it's votes you're thinking about, playing pranks on the whole town won't win you any!'

'Women know nothing about politics. If there aren't any votes won, at least he'll lose a few! There'll be no more landslides in this town, will there, gentlemen?'

Their talk died away into goodbyes and goodnights, and the door banged shut.

The fat man closed his eyes, and as she locked the locks and barred the shutters, he heard Evangelia muttering to herself. But he didn't hear her pour herself a nightcap of cheap cognac, or pour milk into a saucer for the cat, or check the mousetraps in the cupboards were all set. The day had been a long one, and, despite the creaking bed and hard pillow, the fat man drifted quickly into sleep.

So he didn't hear, either, the murmuring of a man's voice as he asked her to sit by him; and he didn't hear the striking of a match, as the man who hadn't left put a flame to the bowl of his pipe.

Nine

The fat man bought his breakfast at the bakery, where the baker's unsmiling wife slipped his two apple pies into a waxed paper bag. The fat man handed her a small banknote and invited her to keep the change; the woman, scowling, insisted he pay another thirty drachmas.

Following a lane leading off the square, he bit into one of the pastries, finding the filo crisp and buttery and the sweet fruit still warm from the oven. Deciding a pastry of such quality deserved his full attention, he took a seat on a bus-stop bench; and finishing the first pie quickly, started on the second.

As he was eating, around the corner came an old man and a donkey which wore no saddle. The old man walked slowly, with one hand on a painful hip; but the donkey was lively and well ahead of the old man, so it seemed the donkey led the old man by its rope rather than the old man leading the donkey.

The donkey grew close, its feet clipping on the road almost at a trot. The fat man swallowed the last bite of his apple pie, and touching the corners of his mouth to remove stray crumbs, stood up from the bench and called out to the old man.

'*Kali mera sas!*'

In reply, the old man – breathless with the effort of keeping up with the donkey – touched two fingers to the peak of his seaman's cap.

'Can you help me?' the fat man called again. 'I need directions to a certain house.'

The old man stopped walking, and planting his feet firmly, hauled back on the halter with both hands.

'Whoa!' he said. 'Whoa!'

But the donkey, ignoring him, kept up its pace and pulled the old man into a stumble. Quickly, the fat man stepped up to the donkey, and putting a hand on its head-collar, held the animal firm. The donkey jerked its head and tried to shake him loose; but the fat man's grip was immovable, and in a few moments, the donkey conceded and stood still.

'This beast's the very devil,' said the old man. 'She leads me such a dance!' With each breath, he wheezed. 'I can't ride her, because I haven't got it in me to get on her back, but she won't be left behind. Everywhere I go, she has to come; and if I don't take her with me, she uproots her tethering post and follows me like a hound. And if she can't get loose, she brays and brays until the neighbours come to find me to make her stop. She's too feisty for me, *kyrie*, too feisty and too young. Though if she were a woman, I wouldn't complain.'

The old man removed his cap and wiped his sweating forehead on his sleeve. The fat man patted the donkey's neck; her coat was heavy with powdery dirt.

'She's full of spirit,' said the fat man. 'But a donkey that wants to be a dog isn't practical. Why don't you sell her to someone who'll put her to work?'

'I could never sell her,' said the old man. 'I've had her from a foal. I had her mother twenty years. Now the daughter's all that's left to me.'

'Then load her up. Make her carry some weight. That would slow her down, at least.'

'She makes such a fuss. As soon as the saddle's on, she digs in her hooves and won't move an inch. Beating makes her worse.'

The fat man rubbed the donkey between the ears.

'I'm afraid you're not well matched,' said the fat man. 'She needs a firm hand, a stricter master.'

The old man looked the fat man up and down, taking in the good cut of his clothes, his affluent appearance.

'You're quite right, *kyrie*,' said the old man. 'Maybe selling is the only answer. But if I was going to sell her, it would have to be to someone who'd treat her well. I'd ask a fair price, mind, a very fair price. Now, I can tell you're a man who knows a bit about horseflesh. Perhaps you'd like to make me an offer yourself?'

The fat man laughed.

'You're a poor salesman,' he said. 'You've listed all the animal's flaws – and they are many – and now you want me to pay you to take on your burden. I'm sorry, but I have no need of a donkey. Even one as full of character as this one.' He stroked the donkey's muzzle, and its mouth moved to the fat man's pocket, where it snuffled and sniffed for food. 'You'll find nothing there, young lady. I've nothing for you.'

The old man's eyes narrowed to a myopic squint, and he took a step closer to the fat man.

'I know you,' he said. 'Haven't we met before?' He moved closer still, bringing his own face close to the fat man's. He smelled unwashed and of habitual drinking; the whiskers in the crevices of his skin were long and sparse, and his breath was so heavy with garlic that the fat man took a step away. The old man pointed at him with a black-nailed finger. 'I do know you,' he said. 'I'm sure of it.'

'You have the better of me, then,' said the fat man. 'Can you help me find the house I'm looking for? The family name is Kaligi; there was to be a wedding there very recently, but it never took place.'

The old man laughed, disturbing the phlegm settled in his lungs.

'I know the house, friend,' he said, nudging the fat man. 'Are you thinking of going courting? Because I'll tell you what ...' He coughed to bring up the phlegm and hawked a gobbet to the ground. 'My Stella here, my little girl ...' He slapped the donkey on the rump, so hard he made it jump. 'My little girl here is better looking than any woman in that family, any day of the week. Take the donkey, sir – she's a better bargain!' He laughed again, showing gums toothless behind the canines, then gripped the fat man's arm. 'Be careful if you're going in there, friend – there's two of them, remember! Between them, they'd overpower a man! Starved, they've been, for years! Believe me, you're better off with the donkey!'

At these insults to the women, the fat man's face became stern.

'Which house is it?' he asked.

The old man jerked his thumb behind him.

'The one freshly painted,' he said. 'Freshly painted for the wedding. You can't blame the man for getting cold feet, can you? Not with a face like that.'

'The doctor met with an accident,' said the fat man, coldly. He ran his hand down the donkey's ear and let go of the head-collar. Immediately, the donkey set off at a brisk walk that was almost a trot, and the old man, pulled into sudden motion, staggered off behind it.

As he reached the lane's end, he turned back.

'I do know you,' he called. 'I remember where I've seen you.'

But before he could say more, the donkey had hauled him round the corner, out of sight.

As the old man had said, fresh paint made the house easy to find; the ochre-yellow walls and cerulean-blue shutters emphasised the neglect of its neighbours. Split in traditional fashion into two, downstairs seemed to be the family home, whilst an outside staircase led up to a dowry apartment. Downstairs, the door opened directly on to the street. The fat man stepped up to it, and knocked.

The door was opened by a woman who had always, undoubtedly, been plain; but she had lost, too, the advantages youth gave any figure and skin to the creasing and slippage of middle age. And yet she had not conceded defeat; any grey hair had been coloured chestnut brown and her cheeks were flushed with carefully applied rouge.

'May I help you?'

'I'm looking for Chrissa Kaligi,' said the fat man. 'Is this the house?'

'I am Chrissa Kaligi.'

'May I speak with you?'

'Regarding what?'

The fat man surveyed the neighbouring houses, where all was silent, and knew that silence signalled his being the focus of all attention: that the women within had halted their chores – had turned off their taps and stopped rattling basins and buckets – the better to hear his business.

'It is a matter,' he said, 'far better discussed in private.' More quietly, he added, 'My business relates to your fiancé.'

She glanced up and down the street, then held the door wide, allowing him to pass into a room where attempts to lift its drabness only emphasised its poverty. An offcut of red linoleum was too small to cover the floor, so the old floorboards showed at its edges; a glass-fronted cabinet held cheap china bought from gypsy traders; the doors of a lopsided wardrobe were held closed with a bootlace; the lace curtains at the windows were strung on lengths of dowelling.

'I'll leave the door open,' she said, and did so. 'What they can see, they don't talk about. Gossip needs no carriage in this town.'

'I have no wish to compromise you,' said the fat man. 'If you would prefer, I can return when you have a chaperone.'

'I am already the favourite object in the ladies' tittle-tattle. Entertaining a strange man can scarcely make a difference to that. Has Louis sent you?'

'The doctor?' he asked. 'No.' Her face became sad. 'No, I'm afraid not. Let me introduce myself. I am Hermes Diaktoros, of Athens, and I am investigating your fiancé's accident. I'm hoping you can help me by answering some questions.'

She offered him a chair; as he sat, it wobbled on the uneven floor. Beneath the icon of St Martha on the wall, the lamp was unlit; on the windowsill was a stack of paperback romances, the books' spines creased with reading.

'Will you take coffee?' she asked. 'Or there's sage tea?'

But the fat man declined. From the rustic air of the place and from her demeanour, he knew coffee would mean long rituals of hospitality: spoon sweets and ceremony. He had neither time nor inclination for any of it.

So now she took a seat across from him, her knees tight together, her body closed and rigid in showy modesty.

'I should ask you, first of all, if you have yourself had news of your fiancé's condition,' said the fat man.

Tears came to her eyes, and her face tensed in her effort not to cry. In the fat man's view, distress often made women more attractive. In Chrissa Kaligi, it brought to mind the features of a bulldog.

83

She lowered her head.

'I haven't seen him,' she said. 'He won't see me, or anyone. Noula spoke to the doctor at the hospital; he says Louis wants me spared the shock. That's what he's like, always putting others before himself. It's what makes him such a good doctor. But I'm tougher than he thinks. I cared for Mother practically alone. I'm not afraid of nursing.'

'By coincidence,' said the fat man, 'I was present when the doctor was brought back to town. I think he's being wise in keeping you away, for now. Healing takes time.'

'Is it so bad, then?'

'Chemical burns are always unpleasant, at first. In time, with grafts, much can be repaired. Did they say anything to your sister about his sight?'

'What do you mean?'

'Whether his blindness can be healed.'

Her hand went to her mouth.

'I didn't ask,' she said. 'Noula would have told me, wouldn't she, if they'd said anything about that? I can't believe she wouldn't have told me. I'll tell her to ask them when she phones again. Are the police going to do anything about it?'

'The police? I have no idea.'

'But you said you were an investigator!'

The fat man smiled.

'I work on behalf of the authorities, not the police,' he said.

She frowned, and opened her mouth to question him, but he went on.

'There's no doubt a vicious crime has been committed, and I shall bring the perpetrator to justice. I know you'll want to help me do so, and the best way for you to do that is to answer my questions about your fiancé and your relationship with him. We might start by your telling me how long you have known Dr Louis, and how you met.'

He expected her face to soften with romantic reminiscences, but instead, she seemed thoughtful, and fixed her eyes on the cabinet of china; whether one object or several held her interest, was impossible to say.

'We haven't known each other very long,' she said. 'About a year ago he came to town. Bad health forced our old doctor – Dr Dinos – into retirement. Dr Dinos was doctor here for decades.'

'I have met Dr Dinos,' said the fat man.

'Well, the new mayor put the word about that the town was needing a doctor. We have a lot of old people who can't travel far; we need a doctor prepared to live here in Morfi, but we weren't hopeful. Professional men and women don't want to bury themselves in a backwater like this. They find the work more interesting in the cities. So Louis was the answer to our prayers. He found his way here by chance, and liked the town and wanted to stay.'

'And stay he did. Fortuitously for you.'

'Not just for me.'

'But for you especially. Tell me, how did your romance blossom?'

She turned to him, as if suspecting herself the butt of a jibe; but the fat man's face was impassive.

'We're too old for romance,' she said. 'There was no wine and roses. He liked me, I liked him.' She shrugged, as if that fact answered all questions.

'Louis,' said the fat man, 'is not a Greek name. And I noticed when I met him, his Greek is very good, but not that of a native. Where is he from?'

'He's French, from some village in the south, I don't remember where. A small place, quiet like this. He said Morfi reminded him of home.'

'Does he still have family there?'

'His mother. A brother, I think.'

'Have they been contacted?'

'I couldn't say. Not by me, or Noula. I don't know where to find them. He wasn't close to them. There'd been some unpleasantness, a falling out.'

'About what?'

Again, she shrugged.

'I don't know. I didn't like to ask.'

'And what brought him to Greece?'

'Love of this country. He'd travelled here as a young man. And he saw opportunity here, the chance to grow a practice, learn new techniques. He wanted to be a pioneer.'

The fat man raised his eyebrows.

'And yet he chose, as you say, a small, quiet place like this.'

She frowned.

'What are you suggesting?'

He smiled.

'Nothing,' he said. 'I am suggesting nothing, merely gathering facts. But if I were to suggest anything, it would be that something – or someone – must have been a big incentive to keep him here. A compliment to you was all I meant.'

At the house opposite, a woman carrying a wicker basket stepped into the street, and set off in the direction of the square, peering in as she reached the open doorway of the room where Chrissa and the fat man sat. The fat man believed himself unseen, but Chrissa called out to her neighbour.

'Anna, *kali mera*!'

The woman took the greeting as permission to stop, and stared in with curiosity.

'*Kali mera sas*,' she said.

'The gentleman's a visitor from Athens,' said Chrissa, 'on family business.'

The neighbour looked from Chrissa to the fat man.

'Oh,' she said. For a moment, she waited, in case Chrissa would say more, but Chrissa remained silent, a polite smile on her face. 'I have to go,' said the woman, when the silence grew too long. 'For bread. *Yassas*.'

'She's been to the baker's already today,' said Chrissa, as the neighbour walked on. 'Her reason for going again is to let them know you're here. Still, she was a godsend whilst Mother was ill.'

'In what way, a godsend?' asked the fat man.

'I couldn't always leave Mother to run errands. Anna fetched prescriptions from the pharmacy, a loaf of bread sometimes ...'

'Did she not offer to sit with your mother so you could go yourself? In my experience, those nursing the sick benefit greatly from time away.'

'I couldn't have asked her to do that. And Mother would not have tolerated it. Noula sat with her, when she was here. And when we knew each other better, Louis – Dr Louis – sat with her sometimes for half an hour. He thought the same as you, that I needed a break. It was the care he showed for me, and Mother, which drew me to him.'

'Your mother didn't object to having a man sit with her?'

'This was towards the end of her illness, and she couldn't speak to say one way or the other. But she wouldn't have objected, I know. I felt she liked Louis, in her way.'

'She approved of the match, then?'

'She was not able to approve or disapprove, in words. But I know she was proud. I could sense it.'

'So it was your mother, in fact, who brought the two of you together?'

'Yes. He came to attend to her. She was bedridden for some time before she died, and infirm before that. I cared for her almost single-handedly. Whatever she says, my sister had little part in her care. Caring for Mother was down to me. Washing, feeding, changing, dressing. It was like taking care of a giant baby. But I didn't mind. I didn't complain. It was my duty.'

'So why did your sister have no part in her care?'

'My sister is committed to her career. All possible hours God sends, you'll find her at her workplace. She calls herself our breadwinner.'

'Ah. And what work does she do?'

'She works at the public library, in Platania. She was a librarian. Then they gave her something else: she said it was a promotion. I don't know exactly what she does now.'

'So when Dr Louis was attending your mother, how often did he come to the house?'

'Once a week at first. More often, later.'

'You mean as your mother deteriorated?'

'In part, yes.'

The fat man smiled.

'I see,' he said. 'You must miss your mother.'

Chrissa made a triple cross over her heart, and raised her eyes to the icon of St Martha on the wall, as if the sweet-faced, haloed head was that of her own parent.

'Mother was highly respected,' she said. 'Until she became ill, in over twenty years she never missed a mass. She was greatly admired for her devotion.'

'I'm sure she was,' said the fat man. He hesitated. 'I suppose it is too early for you to have considered your future?'

'What do you mean?'

'I am asking whether you intend to set a new date for the wedding.'

Her expression showed displeasure.

'Without doubt,' she said. 'Why shouldn't we? Of course I know there'll be a delay ...'

'With respect, Miss Kaligi, your fiancé is unlikely ... That is, he may not make a full recovery from his injuries. What then?'

'My cousin is an orderly at the hospital, and she tells me they can perform miracles these days. Eye transplants, if necessary. They'll make him as good as new.'

The fat man shook his head.

'They can do much,' he said, 'but in the world of medicine, miracles are still in short supply. Of course they will do their best, but my advice is to be realistic in your expectations. In the meantime, you must be strong for him. If it is your intention to stand by him, regardless of the outcome.'

In silence, she looked at him.

The fat man stood.

'I must leave you, for now,' he said. Outside, a courtyard door opened, and someone unseen emptied a bucket of water into the road. He smiled down at her. 'I almost forgot. My memory is not all that it was. I must ask you if you've any idea who'd attack your fiancé in this brutal way.' Like a child holding in a secret, she pressed her lips together. 'Because it will be impossible for me to bring anyone to justice without your help. You understand that, I'm sure.'

She turned her face from him, her eyes again on St Martha's lovely face.

'You shouldn't protect anyone,' he went on. 'This is a particularly nasty crime which may have ruined your prospects. What you know, you must tell me.'

'I'll tell you nothing,' she said, bitterly. 'But I'll show you something, and you may draw your own conclusions.'

Abruptly, she stood, and brushing past him, went out through the open door. The fat man followed; she led him up the staircase at the side of the house, and stopped at the doorway to the apartment there.

'Take a look inside,' she said.

As best he could, he looked through the wrought-iron grille covering the glass pane in the door. Where downstairs was ageing and rustic, dour and make-do, the apartment was a remarkable contrast: modern and comfortable, furnished in the urban style of Athens.

'Most attractive,' said the fat man.

'Mine,' said Chrissa, at his shoulder. '*My* dowry, now. And she's trying to take it back! My own sister's locked me out of the home that's rightfully mine!'

In surprise, the fat man faced her.

'Do you accuse your own sister of the attack on your fiancé?' he asked. 'That's a serious charge, Chrissa. Take care what you say, because some things, once said, have repercussions which cannot be helped. Sometimes, there can be no retraction – so be sure of what you are saying before you speak again.'

'Who else?' Rage she had so far suppressed filled her face. 'Who else is bitter enough to want to ruin my happiness? Who else is there who'd want to make a fool of me this way?'

Indeed, thought the fat man. *Who else, indeed?*

Down in the lane, the households again fell silent as he went by. At the lane's end was an old orchard, where the trees still bore their winter-hardened fruit: figs too high to reach and pomegranates too numerous to pick. In places, the orchard wall had fallen, giving a view of long grass scattered with poppies and yellow daisies.

Passing one of these gaps in the wall, the fat man heard the fall of stones, as if a foot had slipped, but giving no hint of awareness, he walked on to the corner, where he stopped, took out his cigarettes and slowly lit one. As he drew in the first of the smoke, unobtrusively he turned his head. A man was crossing the orchard, making for a wooden door in the wall on its far side. It was no one the fat man recognised: a mountain man, long-haired and heavy-bearded, who loped away, wrapped against the winds of his terrain in the shaggy skin of one of his own sheep.

Ten

The smell of hospitals, thought the fat man, was universal: rubbing alcohol and carbolic, starched laundry and soiled sheets, flowers and boiled vegetables. On the ward to which he had been directed, the doors of many rooms stood open, and curious patients and their relatives inside craned their necks to watch him as he passed.

But the door of room 112 was shut. In 111, the volume on a small radio was turned up high, broadcasting an interview with a farmer about the rising costs of cotton production. An elderly man lay pale and dozing on a metal-framed bed; in a chair beside him, his black-clothed wife was knitting a baby's bonnet, her needles working an intricate pattern from a ball of pale-blue wool.

At the closed door, the fat man hesitated. The old woman looked up from her knitting, and seeing him, bustled across to the doorway.

'Can I help you?' she asked. Her tone was proprietorial, as if the hospital employed her as receptionist.

The fat man hesitated, considering whether to indulge her. She was the type who would miss nothing in the comings and goings on the ward, and that type was often useful; and so he turned to her and smiled.

'I'm looking for Louis Chabrol,' he said. 'They told me 112, but I don't want to disturb him.'

'Oh, don't you worry about that.' She placed a hand on the small of his back to usher him forward. 'Go in, *kalé*, go in. He doesn't mind. He's used to me being in and out.'

'But if he's sleeping ...'

'Sleeping, waking, it's all the same in here,' she said. 'All they have to do is sleep. He'll be glad to be woken up. He's had no visitors; you're his first. He wouldn't want to miss you.'

On the fat man's behalf, she opened the door. Room 112 seemed identical to the room next door, although there was no radio, and the man lying on this bed was somewhat younger, with his eyes heavily bound in white bandages. The room was pleasantly warm, the heat rising off the aged radiator comforting.

Aware that the doctor might be sleeping, the fat man was about to speak gently, but the old woman pushed past him to the window.

'Pouf! So hot in here!' she said. 'I keep telling them, fresh air is what they need. Heat slows the blood, and the sickness takes root. If you keep the blood moving, they get better much faster.'

Lifting the latch on the window, she threw it open, letting the warmth out and much colder air in. On the bed, in silence, the doctor moved his arms beneath the blankets.

'See?' she said, turning to the doctor as she did so. 'He's livening up already.'

She leaned over him as if professionally assessing his condition, and as she leaned, she raised her voice to speak, as if the doctor was suffering from deafness.

'There's a gentleman to see you, *kalé*,' she said, so close to his ear and so loud, the doctor flinched. 'When he's gone, I'll come back and help you with your lunch.'

93

Touching the fat man's arm, she drew him away from the bed.

'Are you a relative, *kalé*?' she asked, in a low tone. 'Because there's been no one, no one at all. I've done what I can; it's my duty, as a Christian, to help him. He needs a lot of help, as you can see, and the hospital food's not much. We've been glad to share what we have, my husband and I. We're a little out of pocket – you're bound to be, aren't you, when you give charitably? – but I ask for nothing. I ask for no repayment of the debt, *kalé*. We've given what we can out of charity.'

She stood before him, waiting, as he knew, for reimbursement.

The fat man smiled.

'Your good deeds do you great credit,' he said, 'but I am not a relative.'

Muttering, she left them. The fat man crossed silently to the door and quietly closed it; but instinct told the doctor he was not alone, and he moved his head from side to side, as if to give his ears their maximum range.

'Is someone there?' He spoke uncertainly, as if he mistrusted all his senses.

'Yes,' said the fat man. 'Shall I close the window?'

'Please do,' said the doctor. 'Every time the room gets warm, she makes it her business to come and open it. If my care's left to her, I'll die of pneumonia. Who are you?'

'You don't know me,' said the fat man, 'though we met very briefly when you were brought down from the chapel.' He closed the window firmly, slotting the latch back into place. 'I am Hermes Diaktoros, of Athens, and I'm investigating the attack which has been made on you. Would you mind – if you feel up to it – answering a few questions?'

'They should have told you,' said the doctor. 'I won't be

94

pressing charges. I asked for no police involvement. There was no need for you to come.' His voice was rough from lack of use, his words somewhat unclear, both because of his reluctance to move his painful jaw, and because his accent – perhaps under the influence of painkillers – seemed more pronounced.

'May I sit?' asked the fat man.

Without waiting for a reply, he picked up a tubular-framed chair from the corner of the room, and placing it at the doctor's bedside, tucked his holdall between his feet and sat down. Bending close, he scrutinised the visible injuries on the doctor's face. The skin where he could see it was stained yellow-brown with iodine, and coated in parts with thick, white cream of zinc. Beyond doubt, the damage was serious. There were places where the skin was lifting as dead tissue peeled away; elsewhere, where the chemical had eaten deeper, dark scabs had formed.

'You're looking at my face, and I'm sure it isn't pretty,' said the doctor bitterly. 'Do they not say we should count our blessings? Perhaps I should count as one of mine the fact that I shall never see the damage.'

'No, it isn't pretty, at the moment,' agreed the fat man. 'But never despair. A few more days are needed yet before the likely long-term outcome can be even guessed at. As you, as a medical man, will know.'

'I know what the outcome will be; I need no sugar-coating. I won't see again. I'm blind for life.'

'Prognoses may be affected by attitude.'

'Mind over matter? Be reasonable. I'm a practical man by nature, and as you say, medically trained. I'll leave here with a white stick, no doubt of it.'

'If you believe that, then my first question must be, why do you want no investigation? If some malicious person has robbed you – as you believe – of your precious sight, why do you not want that person caught, tried and punished for their crime?'

'I have my reasons. And since I do, I ask you to respect them, and leave me.'

But the fat man folded his arms, and made himself more comfortable in his uncomfortable chair.

'I have given this some thought,' he said, 'and I think your wish to avoid any investigation has three possible sources. Firstly, you may yourself be known to the police, and be avoiding contact with them. That strikes me as unlikely in your case. Secondly, you may already know who attacked you and have decided to mete out your own justice, in your own time – a more vicious justice than you could ever hope to win going through the courts. Many people in your position want an eye for an eye, and believe there must be a physical element to any true justice – in short, you wish to inflict pain in return for what you have suffered. I must counsel you very strongly against this course. It would, beyond any doubt, catch up with you in the end. Or thirdly, you may wish – for reasons of your own – to protect the perpetrator from the scandal of prosecution. You may wish to protect that person's family. But whatever your reasons, you have no need to hide them from me. I am not a member of any police force. I act on behalf of a higher authority, and you have my word that, whatever I discover in the course of my investigation, I will report nothing to the police without your permission. I can be very discreet if I choose to be, and I am always pleased to keep secrets if the situation warrants it. So you may confide in me in absolute confidence.'

In the hall outside, china rattled on a trolley, and a coarse female voice called out for coffee orders.

'I want no investigation,' said the doctor, 'and it is painful for me to talk. Please leave me.'

'I'm sure you're missed in Morfi,' said the fat man, as if he hadn't heard the doctor's request. 'The people will be anxious for you to come back and take care of them.'

'Not all of them.'

'Oh?' queried the fat man. 'Who wouldn't be?'

'That old fool of a doctor they had before me, for one,' said Dr Louis. 'He'll be glad to step back into his old shoes, with me out of the way. Poor beggars! He'll see them all buried before he's done.'

'Is he not competent, then?'

'It's only recently he nearly killed a girl. He diagnosed a pelvic inflammation instead of appendicitis. If I hadn't stepped in, she'd have died. He dislikes me because I showed up his incompetence. When this attack took place, where was he? Of course I was in pain and couldn't see, but I don't remember him being there to help.'

'No,' said the fat man, thoughtfully. 'No, I don't think he was there.'

He stood, and from the window looked down on the everyday world of the street below – businessmen and shoppers, hawkers and loiterers. He glanced back at the doctor, who would, in all likelihood, never see any of it again, and considered the drastic and life-limiting consequences of that probability.

'I spoke to your fiancée,' he said. 'She's desperate to see you.'

The doctor's face turned a little in the fat man's direction.

'I want to see no one,' he said, 'including you, whoever you are. Please ring the bell for me as you leave, or there'll be no coffee again for me this morning. They leave me for hours with no attendance at all.'

'Can I do anything for you?'

'Unless you wish to feed me coffee or fetch a urine bottle, no.'

'Your fiancée would leap at the chance to nurse you,' said the fat man gently. 'She does not strike me as such a shallow woman that she would desert you – though obviously your condition will be a shock to her at first. Shall I ask her to come and take care of you?'

'The sooner she sees me, the sooner she'll leave me, and then what? She'll be praising the skies for her lucky escape, and I'll be shipped home to rot in some institution. No. Tell her she must wait. The more time that goes by, the better a prospect I'll look. She might yet be persuaded to marry me, if the approach is right.'

'You'll forgive me for saying that you show more concern for your own welfare than you do for the woman you should love.'

'If you've met her, you'll know Chrissa is not young. She and I are both well into middle age. We were rescuing each other from a lonely retirement, not stepping out on a path strewn with rose petals. I am no romantic, and I don't think she is, either. Our arrangement was a practical one.'

The fat man raised his eyebrows.

'Are you sure that is her view?'

'How should I know? Probably not. Sometimes I think the older women get, the more starry-eyed they grow. It's hormonal.'

'You don't love her.'

'Our marriage would be convenient to us both. Ask her if she loves me, and look into her eyes when she gives her answer.'

'And now it would be highly convenient for you if she became both eyes and nursemaid.'

98

The doctor gave no answer. His hand patted the bedclothes to find the call button, which, unseen by him, hung on its wire over the side of the bed. The fat man picked it up.

'I'll leave you then, for now,' he said, placing the call button silently on the bedside table.

'Tell them, please, to bring me more painkillers.'

'Are you in much pain?'

'Look at me, and tell me what you think!'

'Creatures in pain are often angry at the world. The pain will pass. That, at least, will get easier. I'll see you again before I leave, Louis.'

But by the door, he hesitated.

'Of course there will be no investigation if none is required,' he said. 'But oblige me by answering one further question. What took you to the chapel? Why did you go there in the first place?'

'I went because of the boy.'

'Boy? What boy?'

'He gave me a note.'

'Saying what?'

'He came to my room. The note asked me to go to the chapel immediately, that there was an emergency.'

'Where is your room?'

'Behind the butcher's shop. People come to me there, sometimes. They knock on the window; it overlooks an alley.'

'Who was the boy?'

'I have no idea. There are so many.'

'Age?'

'How should I know?'

'More child than youth, or well grown?'

'It's impossible to tell their age these days. Boys of ten outgrow their fathers.'

'And at the chapel, you saw no one?'

'I opened the courtyard door and – pouf! – my life was over.'

'No one spoke to you? No words were said?'

'Nothing. Straight away I felt the pain and begged for help. I dared not open my eyes. But he just stood there; I could sense him watching. And then he left; I heard him go.'

'How did he leave? On foot? Did you hear an engine, or a motor?'

'Nothing but my own voice.'

The fat man looked at him.

'I'll fetch the nurse,' he said.

As he passed the door of room 111, the old woman jumped up from her chair.

'Are you leaving so soon?' she asked. 'Do you know the relatives? I've done my best, you know, but it isn't easy, caring for two. My husband's in a bad way.' The old man had not moved. On the table beside him, the radio announced the weather for farmers.

'I'm sorry,' said the fat man, 'but I don't know the family. You must excuse me.'

She watched him down the full length of the corridor, as far as an office where he found two nurses considering the entries on a batch of three-part forms.

'Ladies, *kali mera sas*,' he said. 'One of your patients is asking for more pain relief. Dr Louis Chabrol, in 112.'

Together, the nurses turned to a board on the wall, where a badly drawn grid held the names of patients on the ward. The crossings-out and pencilling-ins were many; they made the grid impossible to read.

'I know who you mean,' said one, at last. 'The Frenchman. Is he a doctor? I didn't know that. Did you know that, *kalé*? The Frenchman's a doctor.'

The other shook her head.

'They tell us nothing,' she said. 'They keep us in the dark.'

'But you ladies strike me as having considerable experience, professionally,' said the fat man.

'Twenty years, I've done this job,' said one.

'Twenty-two,' said the other, 'and I've paid for it with my back. They all want lifting and hauling, in and out of bed. We shouldn't be doing this, at our age.'

'But with all your experience, surely you know all the medical men in this area?' asked the fat man.

'Oh yes, we know them all,' said one.

'All their foibles, their little ways,' said the other.

'But you don't know Dr Chabrol? He's been practising in Morfi.'

'Has he?'

'What happened to Dr Dinos?'

'So you've had no contact with Dr Chabrol at all? No referrals, no phone calls?'

'Not that I recall. Do you remember any referrals from him, *kalé*?'

The other nurse shook her head.

'It rings no bells with me,' she said. 'Chabrol, Chabrol. No, *kyrie*, it rings no bells at all.'

Eleven

Leaving the hospital by the main entrance, the fat man made his way through the town's busy streets. From time to time, he paused at shop-window displays where items caught his eye: a shirt by a French designer in a particular shade of mauve, a collection of baseball caps in the colours of American football teams, a well-chosen selection of imported wines at a delicatessen.

On a corner by the park stood a lottery-ticket vendor, whose cap showed the logo of the Chicago Bears. His vast beer-gut swelled over trousers his belly had long outgrown; a tight belt held their waistband in a slant from the top of his buttocks to the underside of his gut. Pinned to a long pole held over his head, the pink and white lottery tickets fluttered in the wind.

The fat man stepped closer to the vendor, and noticing his interest, the vendor bellowed his repetitive cry.

'Lottery! Get your lottery tickets!'

'*Kali mera*,' said the fat man. 'I'll take two from you.'

'Here you are, *kyrie*, here you are.' Lowering the pole, the vendor stood it on the ground to allow the fat man his choice. 'Take your time, you know, take your time. I've a feeling you're going to be lucky. I can always tell winners, you know, I can always tell. So choose two lucky ones, *kyrie*. You've a lucky face, you have. Take your time, and choose two lucky ones.'

But the fat man made his choices quickly, taking one ticket from the top of the pole and one from the middle before handing over his payment.

'Both lucky ones, they are,' said the vendor, 'both lucky ones.'

'Do you think so?' said the fat man, smiling. 'Time will tell, my friend. Time will tell.'

The public library was imposing: scroll-topped Ionic pillars beneath a triangular portico, a graceful run of broad steps, two stone lions watchful on high plinths. From the far side of the avenue, the fat man stood for a moment to admire the building's pleasing lines; then, spotting a gap in the passing traffic, he made his way across the road and up the library steps.

He passed through the revolving doors, and found the entrance lobby some degrees colder than outside, with the never-warmed chill of a cavern. A splendid chandelier hung unlit from the ceiling; on the shadowed walls, gold-framed portraits of the library's long-dead founders faced a selection of scenes from the myths, whose colours were muted by the grime of decades.

Through swing doors, the library itself was no warmer. Bookshelves ran round the perimeter of the circular room; more shelves branched into the centre, where several tables were pushed together to form a workspace. Here, students in down jackets scribbled notes from open volumes; a man in scarf and overcoat read a newspaper. More students stood by the bookshelves, reading or searching through indexes; in the travel section, a woman flicked through an outdated guide to Tibet.

At the counter, a librarian was sticking new labels in old books. The librarian had dressed for the cold: a tank-top over a grey sweater; beneath the grey sweater, a floral-patterned shirt.

For a minute or two, the fat man waited patiently for the librarian's attention. The librarian smoothed a label on the first page of a book, pressing down the corners with his thumb. Satisfied at last that the label was properly stuck, he closed the book, and – not, apparently, having noticed the fat man – reached out for another book from his stack.

The fat man was too quick for him; the book was in his hand before the librarian touched it.

The fat man read the title aloud.

'*Economics of the Market.*'

As the librarian glared, the fat man opened the book at the inside cover and ran his eyes over its record of loans. Its readers had been few; the last loan was over two years previously.

'Not your most popular volume,' said the fat man. 'Perhaps you should requisition a more recent edition. Markets, as I'm sure you're aware, evolve. Current data is essential in the study of economics.'

'There are no funds available for new editions of books we already have in stock,' said the librarian, shortly. He held out his hand for the book. 'May I help you?'

The fat man smiled.

'Indeed you may. I'm looking for a colleague of yours – Noula Kaligi.'

'Through the double doors, upstairs, first on the right.'

The fat man placed the book on the counter and his own hand on top of the book.

'Before I see Miss Kaligi,' he said, 'there's a book I've been looking for. Perhaps you could check the catalogue to see if you have a copy.'

For a long moment, the librarian regarded him.

'Title?' he asked, at last.

'*A Short Guide to Etiquette and Modern Manners*. It was published some years ago. I'm afraid the author's name escapes me.'

The librarian sighed. Leaving the counter, he crossed to the bank of wooden drawers which housed the catalogue. Opening a long, narrow drawer packed with yellowing index cards, his fingers riffled deftly through them, until, close to the back of the drawer, he found the title the fat man had requested. Turning the card behind it vertical to mark its place, he removed the card and read the fading ink script.

'It seems we do have a copy,' he said. 'You'll find it ...'

'Excellent,' interrupted the fat man, smiling. 'Perhaps you'd be good enough to retrieve it for me. My time here is limited, and I need to speak with Miss Kaligi. I'll come back to you on my way out.'

Upstairs, the first door on the right bore a nameplate: Director's Office. The fat man knocked, and a woman's voice invited him to enter.

He stepped into a small room no warmer than the library downstairs. A well-organised desk was positioned to bar easy access to an inner office, whose door was closed. At the desk, a woman sat with her hands over a typewriter's keyboard, a letter half finished between its rollers. The woman's likeness to Chrissa Kaligi was clear, but her looks were more unfortunate; and as if accepting the fact of her unattractiveness, she'd made no effort at all with herself: no make-up to bring out the eyes or enhance the skin, no bleaching of the dark-haired upper lip, no dyeing or styling of the greying hair, no pretty jewellery or clothes which flattered.

The fat man smiled.

'*Kali mera sas*,' he said.

She did not return his smile, but instead looked down at a black-bound diary, open at today's date.

'Do you have an appointment?' she asked.

'Appointment?'

'The director sees no one without an appointment. He's a busy man, as you would expect. But he has an opening on Monday afternoon.'

'You mistake the purpose of my visit,' said the fat man, politely. 'My business is not with the director. If you are Noula Kaligi, my business is with you.'

'Me?'

'Allow me to introduce myself. I am Hermes Diaktoros, of Athens, and I have been asked by the authorities to look into the circumstances surrounding your sister's wedding.'

'There was no wedding. My sister remains a spinster.' She bent to the floor; he heard the snap of a handbag clasp, and she reappeared behind the desk, wiping her nose on a handkerchief trimmed with lace. 'Excuse me,' she said, 'but from October to March, I'm a martyr to colds. They've made cutbacks on the heating.'

'What a pretty handkerchief,' said the fat man. 'Such fine lace. Is it your own work?'

'The only work I have time for is here. It's my sister who's time for hobbies and needlecraft.' She tucked the handkerchief up the sleeve of her cardigan, out of sight. 'I have work to do now, and I don't know anything about Chrissa's wedding she can't tell you herself.'

She positioned her fingers over the typewriter's keys, and looked down at the shorthand notes she was working from.

'The wedding was prevented by an attack on your sister's

fiancé,' said the fat man, ignoring her show of disinterest. 'A vicious and malicious attack.'

With reluctance, Noula again gave him her attention.

'We are aware of that, now. At the time it appeared that he had – well, it seemed she had been stood up.'

'That must have been very hard for her. Such embarrassment and such disappointment! How did you cope?'

'How did I cope? I sent the guests packing and paid for food we never ate. It was all down to me, as usual.'

The fat man gave a small shake of his head.

'You misunderstand me,' he said. 'What I meant was, how did the two of you together cope? How did you comfort your sister?'

'Comfort her? How should I comfort her when she will barely speak to me? Chrissa blames me for everything, and acts like a character from one of her silly books. She makes herself ridiculous, moping and sulking.'

She pulled out the handkerchief from her cardigan sleeve, wiped her nose once more and bent to return the handkerchief to her handbag.

'She has suffered a great shock, surely?' said the fat man. 'Any woman who has looked forward to her wedding day would feel the same. Wouldn't she?'

'I have not, myself, had the pleasure of looking forward to my wedding day. So how could I possibly say?'

The phone on her desk rang, and she answered it with a formal greeting; continuing to speak, she flicked through the days ahead in the director's diary. As she made the caller's appointment, the fat man cast his eyes around the office, noting the lack of personal touches – no photographs, no favourite china cups, no plants, no personal effects at all, except for a black woollen jacket hanging on a hat-stand behind the door. The single radiator was rusting around its pipework. The fat man touched it with the back of his hand, and found it cold.

Noula replaced the phone's receiver, and with a newly sharpened pencil, made an entry in the diary. The fat man waited until she had finished writing before putting his next question.

'Your sister tells me you have phoned the hospital on her behalf, for news of her fiancé. Did you pass on to her all that was said?'

She placed the pencil in a beaker containing several more, all well sharpened and of identical length.

'My sister's not good on the telephone, whereas I – as you may have noticed – spend half my life on it. I thought I would get more sense out of them than she would. She would run up the bill, and be no wiser at the end of it.'

The fat man smiled.

'With respect, I didn't ask why you made the call. I was wondering if you told your sister all that was said.'

She hesitated.

'Not all, no.'

'So what did you leave out?'

'The long-term outlook.'

'Ah. You didn't tell her he is likely to remain blind.'

'No.'

'Why not?'

She looked directly into his eyes.

'I thought it would be unnecessarily cruel. Just at the moment.'

'So you were waiting for the right moment to break the news?'

'I suppose so.'

'When I asked your sister if another date had been set for the wedding, she told me Dr Chabrol won't even see her. Is that correct?'

'He's no fool, is he? He's not a pretty prospect at the moment, I'm sure; in my opinion, he wasn't such a pretty prospect before, either.'

The fat man raised his eyebrows.

'What do you think, that my sister landed herself some handsome, wealthy surgeon? Louis – Dr Chabrol – may have been a medical man, but he wasn't – in my opinion – such a great catch. If he was, how come he hadn't been snapped up before? He finished off our mother, if you ask me. Dr Dinos was always firm with her, made her get up in the mornings and keep moving, however tired she felt. When he came on the scene, Louis was the opposite. *Rest, Maria, rest*: that's what he used to say. She took it as licence to put herself to bed. Bedridden in three months, she was, and dead in nine. What kind of doctoring is that?'

The fat man fixed Noula's eyes with his own.

'Did you really dislike him so much, Noula – or only because he preferred your sister to you? Be honest with me: if he had courted you instead of her, would you have found him more attractive or more likeable?'

She blushed, and her face grew angry.

'You insult me, the same way she does! My sister, of course, has been very pleased with herself – unbearably so. She wants to believe in that hearts-and-flowers romance she reads about all the time. She'll tell you I was jealous, that I couldn't bear her happiness. I couldn't bear her gloating, that is true, but I didn't envy her that man. Something about him isn't right. I told her so, many, many times. But she wouldn't listen. My words were wasted, white lines drawn on white stone. She knew best.'

'What if I tell you, Noula, that your sister takes the view that you were so bitter, it was you who blinded her fiancé.'

She gave a short laugh.

'I? She's losing her mind! But if she says I am bitter, it is not over wanting that man! Did she tell you about the sacrifices I was to make for her marriage? I was persuaded by my family – by my aunt, mainly – to give up rights to my possessions – to things I bought myself, with money I earned, and to things which were bought for me by my mother, as my dowry – and my sister has not even thanked me! A "thank you" would have at least softened the blow! I shall remove the items I paid for, of course. Or I may perhaps move upstairs myself. She has no claim on upstairs, now she's not married.'

'Is that why you have locked the place up?'

'My aunt and I agreed – the apartment must be kept as a dowry, for either her or me.'

'She states she will still marry him.'

'Then she's a bigger fool than I thought. A man who's sightless and can't work? He'd be nothing but a millstone round her neck. And Chrissa's not capable of work, not even as a cleaner. She's never worked. She'd take all day to clean one window. She cannot, surely, be thinking I will work for all three of us? Please, tell me she was not suggesting that.'

'She didn't talk about practicalities.'

'No. Chrissa does not think in practicalities.'

'What if she loves him?'

She eyed him shrewdly.

'Have you spoken to her face to face?'

'I have.'

'Then your impression is probably the same as mine. What she loved – if anything – was the idea of love and the prospect of status: not just as a married woman, but as a doctor's wife. To my sister, she and I, as spinsters, were two of life's failures. She saw our spinsterhood as our disgrace, and the doctor as a chance – at last – to end it.'

'You don't feel that?'

'I have eyes in my head,' she said. 'I used to watch my mother, scrubbing floors and laundering my father's underwear. She seemed nothing but a servant to me. What status is there in being someone's servant? I work for my own living and my sister's, and my mother's too, until she died. There are better jobs, but there are worse. Like laundering other people's underwear.'

'Do you see yourself as a feminist, then?'

'If being a feminist is being independent, yes.'

The fat man smiled.

'Bravo,' he said. 'I applaud you. But you're quite right that your sister sees it differently. She thinks you blinded him to keep her tied to you.'

'She's mad. Mad to think I'd be that mad.'

'Greater crimes have been committed with less reason.'

'I resent your suggestion! When this person's caught, they'll go to prison, for certain. Why on earth would I risk getting locked up to keep myself tied to her? To live upstairs instead of down? You must ask the doctor. He must have seen his attacker.'

'He saw no one at all.'

'Well, that's unfortunate. But he must have an enemy somewhere, wouldn't you say? I am not his enemy; I wish them good luck, whatever they make of it, though I think Chrissa is a fool if she goes through with it now. And I shall tell her that I will not support them. There'll be no help from me.'

'You're right. The doctor has an enemy somewhere – a dangerous one – and it is my intention to track him down. Him, or her. Can you remember what you were doing on the morning of the wedding?'

'Easily. I was running errands for my sister, as dogsbody – flowers, whisky, table linen. You name it, I was responsible.'

'How did you run these errands – on foot?'

'In my car. I bought it for myself. I work long hours, sometimes. The buses between here and home are not always convenient. Why are you asking me these questions? Are you really thinking I might be guilty? Do I look like someone who'd throw acid in a man's face? I didn't hate him, and what was done to him was a crime of hate. Maybe there's a jilted woman somewhere; had you thought of that?'

'As a matter of fact, I had,' said the fat man. 'Do you think it's possible?'

She hesitated.

'Is this discussion confidential?' she asked.

'If you wish it to be so.'

'Nothing I say will be repeated to Chrissa, or to him?'

'Nothing you tell me will be repeated and attributed to you.'

She hesitated again, seeming to decide whether or not to speak.

'I took some papers from amongst his things,' she said at last. 'I shouldn't have done, but I was curious. I thought I might make sense of them, learn something about this man who's marrying my sister. But they're in French. I borrowed a dictionary from downstairs, but I don't know the alphabet. It was hopeless; it took me an hour to translate one line. So if you think you can do something with them, I'll pass them on to you. But they must go back, in due course, into his suitcase.'

'You took them from his suitcase? That was very – enterprising of you.'

'It was theft; I realise that. I'm not proud I did it, but I was thinking of Chrissa.'

Again, the fat man raised his eyebrows.

'Are you sure, Noula, that was your motivation?'

She looked at him, and, with a sad smile, shrugged.

'Shall I relieve your conscience, then,' he said, 'and take the papers from you?'

She slid open the top drawer of her desk and withdrew the manila envelope taken from the doctor's suitcase. As she laid it on the desk, the door she guarded opened and a tall, balding man stood there. Seeing the fat man, he raised his chin to make himself seem commanding; but the cloth of his suit was shiny with over-wear, and his shirt cuffs sat too high above his wrists. Between finger and thumb, he held up a letter. Regarding the fat man with suspicion, he spoke to Noula.

'I need the file on next year's budget,' said the director. 'That idiot Velomoutsos has got his numbers wrong again.'

Head bowed in obedience, Noula rose from her seat and crossed to a filing cabinet by the window, the colour in her cheeks a little high. Waiting, the director watched the fat man.

The fat man gave him his broadest smile.

'I'm so sorry,' he said, 'I haven't introduced myself. You must be the Director of Libraries. I am Hermes Diaktoros, of Athens. I was asking Miss Kaligi a few questions about her sister.'

'Between the hours of 8.30 a.m. and 2 p.m.,' said the director, slowly, 'Miss Kaligi is paid by this district to do this district's work. Perhaps you could arrange to speak to her at a time when she is not working.'

At the filing cabinet, Noula withdrew a heavy cardboard file.

'Shall I bring it through?' she asked the director.

'Yes,' said the director, turning back to his office. 'Bring it through.'

Noula followed him, closing the door behind her; she offered the fat man no goodbye.

113

Picking up the manila envelope, he glanced inside it, and smiling to himself, tucked it away inside his raincoat.

Downstairs in the library, the librarian was sticking more new labels in old books. By his left hand lay the book the fat man had requested.

'Ah,' said the fat man, smiling, 'I see you found it. Excellent.'

'Do you have a borrower's ticket?' asked the librarian.

'A borrower's ticket? I'm afraid not.'

'Well, you can't borrow the book, then.'

'I think you have mistaken my intention,' said the fat man. 'I have a copy of my own – though it's a little dog-eared now, after loans to the many people I felt might benefit from a little teaching in good manners. I didn't mean the book for me; I meant it for you. I strongly suggest you read it; it will make a better man of you, by far.'

He didn't wait for the librarian's reply. Outside, the clouds had dispersed. The fat man turned his face to the weak warmth of the sun, and judging the temperature acceptable for the drinking of coffee alfresco, set off from the library steps in search of a café.

Twelve

Leaving Platania, the fat man felt in no hurry to return to Morfi. A kilometre or two along the new dual carriageway was a junction with the old road, and here he carefully signalled a right turn and took the quieter route along the coast.

The day held all the freshness of spring; the cobalt sea was lively with crests of foam, the rocky flatland between road and sea was bright with flowers – the purest white of rock roses, the purple of wild mallow, the blue of campanula. On the empty beach, a fisherman wore his down jacket zipped to the neck and the flaps of his Russian army hat pulled over his ears; as he cast a line from a long pole into the shallows, waves touched the toes of his leather boots. Where a sign boasted a new hotel opening soon, the builder's gang had already left for lunch; a perplexed architect stood, shoes muddy, at the site entrance, holding the blueprints up to the wind, failing to match the drawings on the flapping sheets to the brick lines of foundations on the ground.

Along the road, the sign to an ancient monument had lost one of its post screws, and pointed at an angle, down and right. Here, the fat man slowed the Mercedes and turned on to an unmade track, which led across the flatlands towards a promontory jutting out into the sea. At the track's end, he parked the car and surveyed the land around him.

The site was exposed, the wind blowing sharp and salty across rock and sand. Ruins lay all about him, the sad remains of ancient walls: stones laid in lines, the deteriorating foundations of shops and houses, schools, temples and stadiums. What had been here, was impossible to say: the city's time had passed. For a while, he wandered amongst the stones, crouching now and then to examine the remnants of inscriptions or carved details on the stumps of fallen pillars. Grass grew amongst the stones; weeds flourished on the barely discernible pathways. At the water's edge, the lines of the walls ran into the sea, disappearing into the deeper water. Here, by the toe of his tennis shoe, he found a pottery shard, a fragment of some plate or bowl broken centuries before. He picked it up, and rubbing it clean with the pad of his thumb, examined the faded marks of the potter's tools, and – on the rim and very faint – the traces of an ancient fingerprint. The fat man smiled, and placed the fragment back on the dirt.

He walked by the water's edge towards the promontory, where at high seasonal tides the land would be under water. Here, at a distance from the ancient city, were a number of gravestones marking the limits of a cemetery whose greater part now lay beneath the sea. Each stone was engraved in the simplest fashion, though clearly by different hands: they bore a name and a single word: *Xhairé – Be happy*. At one grave, he bent and ran his fingers over the name, then patted the stone as if in affection, or gentle reproach.

As he made his way through the graves, an object almost buried in the dirt caught his attention. From his raincoat pocket, he took an empty matchbox and a penknife, and with great care, dug out his find with the knife tip and placed it in the matchbox, adding a scraping of grave dirt for good measure. Closing the penknife, he slipped it with the matchbox back into his pocket. Then, offering a small bow to the grave where he had made his find, he turned his back on the cemetery and walked thoughtfully back to his car.

Around the next bend on the coast road stood a small taverna. Its shutters were closed, there were no summer signs offering cold beer and *souvlakia*, and its tables and chairs were stacked up and roped down under plastic tablecloths on the terrace; but two men sat outside the open kitchen doorway, tossing coins to the centre of their table as bets on hands of cards.

The fat man parked his car. As he approached the men, they paused in their game to watch him, both holding their cards against their chests in mistrust of the other, each with one eye on his opponent.

The fat man smiled.

'*Yassas*,' he said, and the two men returned his greeting. From their appearances, they were related: cousins, maybe even brothers. Their oiled hair was receding to the same degree, their noses were equally noble and equally wasted: sprouting excess nasal hair, and on unshaven faces spotted with blackheads. In build, however, the men contrasted like a pair of stage comedians: one had run to fat, the other was too thin. The plump one of the pair wore a chef's apron, its strings wrapped twice round his hefty waist and knotted at the front; the thin man had the red eyes of a drinker, and kept a tumbler of Metaxa at his elbow.

'I was wondering,' said the fat man, 'if I might get something to eat.'

The cook glanced at his cards.

'The hell with this,' he said. Throwing his cards on the table, he swept half of the stake money towards himself and nodded towards his companion. 'He may not be much to look at, but he's the luck of the devil at cards, this one.'

Looking at his own cards, the thin man scowled and silently gathered up his stake money, placing it with the coins and small notes by his glass before taking a drink.

The cook stood up from his chair, revealing the stains on his apron.

'Sit,' he said to the fat man, indicating the empty table beside theirs. 'There's rabbit *stifado*. I shot the rabbits myself yesterday.'

The fat man waited for the rest of the cook's menu, but the cook only looked at the fat man for his agreement.

'I can do you an omelette,' he said at last.

The fat man smiled.

'Rabbit sounds excellent,' he said. 'I'll have a little salad, from whatever you have fresh.'

'And to drink? I have a very good red, from the barrel.'

'Thank you.'

'*Amessos*.'

The cook disappeared into the kitchen as the fat man took his seat. He watched the card player count his winnings, stacking coins and notes in 1,000-drachma piles.

The view from the table was through the trunks of the pine trees which overhung the terrace, giving vital shade in summer; at this time of year, they gave some shelter from the onshore breeze, which nonetheless blew strongly enough to force the card player to weight his banknotes with a salt pot. Between the trees and at a little distance were the contrasting blues of sky and sea; between there and the terrace were straight lines of stone: more of the ruined city.

'You have a view of the archaeology,' remarked the fat man, pointing through the trees to the decaying walls.

The card player looked up from his counting, and squinting, followed the fat man's finger with his red eyes.

'Rubble,' said the gambler. He waved a dismissive hand before his face. 'They call it archaeology. But it looks like rubble to me.'

The cook brought out a ceramic jug fired with a pattern of black olives. Slamming down a tumbler before the fat man, he filled the glass with wine from the jug. The wine was richly coloured, dark as bull's blood. Still holding the jug, the cook urged the fat man to drink.

'Try that,' he said. 'Tell me what you think.'

The fat man sipped from the tumbler. The wine was complex, with the sweetness of figs on the tongue and the light perfume of plums; but as he swallowed, a pleasing dryness came through to balance it, hinting at the tartness of blackcurrants and the smooth wood of the barrel.

The fat man looked at the cook in pleased surprise.

'Truly excellent!' he said. 'One of the most characterful wines I've tasted in some years.'

Delighted, the cook filled up the glass.

'I make it myself,' he said, 'from my own vines. I combine two grapes – *krassato*, and *xinomavro* so it will mature well – but the secret's in the picking. When you think the grapes are ready, when you're sure they're so ripe they'll fall from the vine, wait a week longer. Then the wine is already being made inside the grapes before you even pick them.' He kissed his thumb and forefinger in the Italian manner. 'Superb.'

'Ask him how he knows,' said the card player, taking another drink of cognac. 'No, don't ask him, I'll tell you. Because every year, he's too idle to get out there and pick grapes when he should be picking grapes. Every year, he's weeks behind everyone else. Lazy. That's what he is – lazy.'

'Then there's something to be said for laziness,' said the fat man, 'in this instance, at least. Sometimes, rushing about is the wrong thing to do.'

The cook spoke to the card player.

'See,' he said. 'Here's a gentleman who knows the value of good timing.'

He placed the jug on the table, and returned to the kitchen. As the fat man savoured his wine, the card player tallied his stacks of money, and pile by pile, slipped them into the pockets of his trousers; and when the table was cleared of money, he drank down the last of his Metaxa.

The cook brought the fat man a salad of crisp lettuce leaves and green onions and a dish of pickled vegetables – young carrots, hot peppers, stalks of cauliflower and black olives; returning to the kitchen, he fetched a saucer of brine-soaked caper leaves and a basket of fresh bread topped with toasted sesame seeds.

'*Oriste*,' he said. '*Kali orexi.*'

'This looks excellent,' said the fat man.

'All my own produce,' said the cook. 'You'll not find better. All grown within a kilometre of this place and all natural; no chemicals and no fertiliser, except for my own special ingredient: goat's shit.'

He disappeared back into the kitchen. A gust of wind moved the tops of the pine trees, causing a fall of loose needles. Unconcerned, the fat man picked a needle from the salad, and with a fingertip hooked a second from his wine before flicking it to the ground.

'I expect,' said the fat man to the card player, 'this place is busy in summer?'

The card player sighed, and shook his head.

'We work all the hours God sends,' he said, 'and we try. There's only four of us. Dmitri's wife helps in the kitchen, and my eldest and I wait tables. In the old days, summer brought work for a dozen, but since they built the new road, folk pass us by. A few adventurous souls find us, as you have today. And the odd one or two who come to see the rubble. Why they want to see it, I couldn't say.' He leaned across to the kitchen door. 'Dmitri! Bring another Metaxa!'

From the kitchen came no answer but the rattling of pans; but moments later the cook appeared, a plate of *stifado* in one hand, a tumbler half-filled with brandy in the other.

'*Oriste*,' he said, laying the stew before the fat man. He placed the brandy beside the card player, and sat down beside him at their table.

The savoury smell from his plate was quite delicious: tiny onions, cloves and cinnamon, the meat of young rabbits and above all, garlic. The fat man broke off a piece of bread, and dipping it into the thick sauce, began to eat. Swallowing the first mouthful, he smiled at the cook.

'First class,' he said. 'My compliments.' He tasted a piece of tender white meat. 'Your food does you great credit. But your colleague was just saying, this place doesn't draw people as it used to.'

The cook shook his head, as if in despair.

'We work like mules,' he said. 'Right through the hottest months, we never stop. It's a hard life. And these days, there's no money in it.'

Taking a forkful of the salad, the fat man raised an eyebrow.

'Six months of work and six months of rest seems a reasonable bargain to me. You'll forgive me for saying that, to a stranger's eyes, your life seems blessed. Your own business, land and the skill to produce your own wine, meat and vegetables, and talent as a cook – surely the gods have smiled on you? A beautiful view, and your health – more gifts! Who could possibly ask for more? You're a happy

121

man, I'm sure. And here's to your continued health.' He held up his glass, then drank more of the excellent wine.

But the cook and his relative looked dour, staring out through the trees, across the ruined city to the sea.

The fat man finished his meal, lit a cigarette, smoked half and stubbed it out. Putting his cigarettes away, his hand touched the matchbox in the pocket of his raincoat.

'Let me show you something, gentlemen,' he said. 'Here's a curiosity which may interest you.'

He slid open the matchbox and picked out the dull-grey object he had found by the ancient graves. The cook and his relative looked dubious; at their doubting faces, the fat man laughed.

'Appearances deceive,' he said. 'Look more closely.'

He handed his find to the cook, who held it up to study it. It was a piece of flattened lead, formed into a roll; piercing the roll was an iron nail.

The cook handed it back to the fat man.

'I'm none the wiser,' he said. 'What is it?'

'To begin with,' said the fat man, 'it's an antiquity. This piece of metal was buried by someone when this rubble, as you call it, was a flourishing town. It carries, I think we'll find, something intriguing. Chef, can you find me a pair of pliers? If you have none, scissors might do.'

The cook rose from his seat; from the kitchen came the sound of drawers opening and the scattering of cutlery.

'If that – whatever it is – has been there all that time, how come no one's found it before you?' asked the card player.

'Sometimes an object waits for the right person to find it.'

'Better keep it hidden, if it's archaeology. Those museum folks'll throw the book at you.'

'I have a safe home in mind for this, if it's what I think it is.'

The cook returned holding up a pair of fine-tipped electrician's pliers. The fat man took them, and with great care pulled the iron nail from the lead, laying it on the table by his glass.

'Now,' said the fat man, 'our museum friends make heavy weather of these. It takes them weeks to open one and decipher it. But if you have the knack, it isn't difficult. Watch.'

Working it gently with the pliers, he teased the rolled lead into a resemblance of its original form – a square of beaten metal. When the lead was as flat as he could make it, the fat man laid it on his palm, and held it out for the two men to see the writing on the metal – tiny letters scratched with some kind of pin.

'I'll be damned,' said the cook. 'It's a scroll.'

'Of a kind, yes,' said the fat man.

'What does it say?'

'Let's find out.'

Bending to his holdall, he took a jeweller's loupe from a front pocket. Removing his glasses, he dipped a thumb into his wine and rubbed it across the lead scroll, darkening the metal to provide a deeper contrast with the dusty lettering, so the words were somewhat clearer. Fitting the loupe to his eye socket, he squinted at the writing on the scroll. For a minute he was silent, studying the script.

'What does it say?' asked the cook, impatiently.

'It's ancient Greek, of course ...'

'Can you make it out?' asked the card player.

'Oh, quite easily. It says, *Great Hermes, bind him who stole my good name and so ruined me, and let him suffer punishments eternally*. And there's a name, but that I can't read. It's a curse tablet, obviously. Quite a nice one, actually. It makes you wonder, doesn't it, if its target is still suffering the eternal punishments he was wished.' The two men looked at each other, grimacing. 'Of course this part of Greece – the hard north – was famous for its witchcraft, magic, that kind of thing. Thessaly – Thrace – was the capital of spiteful magic. Binding, as they called it. An important part of your ancestors' rich history.'

'History be damned,' said the cook. 'They're at it still, in some of the smaller places – cursing, evil-eyeing, whatever you call it. Don't cross anyone whilst you're here, friend, or there'll be old women binding you too.'

A breath of cold wind passed over the terrace. The thin man shivered.

'Superstition,' said the fat man, 'nothing more.'

'What will you do with it?' asked the cook. 'If it were me, I wouldn't walk about with such an object on me. To carry a man's ill wishing can't do you any good. If I were you, I'd take it back and bury it where you found it.'

The fat man held the scroll in the flat of his hand.

'The ill wishing died with the writer,' he said. 'This is a piece of metal, nothing more – and yet in the right hands, it might bring benefit instead of trouble. And I think I know where to give it a suitable home; and if I find the right place, you two might be amongst those who reap the benefits.'

By the time the fat man arrived back in Morfi, it was late afternoon. He found a phone booth on the far side of the high school, on a street that was quiet when the school was closed.

Taking a handful of coins from his pocket, he pressed several into the slot and stacked the remainder on top of the phone. He knew the long-distance number by heart; he knew, too, the uncertainties of OTE, the Greek phone operator, and so dialled slowly and with care. The phone was answered quickly, but the line was not good; the cable connecting the receiver to the phone was loosely wired.

'*Yassou*, cousin!' said the fat man. 'Do I find you well?'

He listened to exclamations of delight; he was chastised for being so long absent; he was questioned on his whereabouts and activities, and asked whether he was staying out of trouble. As soon as there was opportunity, he spoke again.

'Listen,' he said, 'I'm arranging a little surprise. If you're free, you're the ideal one to help.'

He explained what was required; the cousin laughed, and readily agreed. The fat man named the time and place, and they wished each other goodbye, until their meeting.

Thirteen

Early evening brought the townspeople outside. Youths gathered by the new fountain, shouting like louts, shoving and cuffing each other, impressing the passing girls with stunts performed on old bicycles. Slippered housewives made their way to the grocer's for small necessities – a tin of milk for coffee, a little sliced salami for supper – and stayed there half an hour, gossiping.

The streets and alleys grew dark, and the green cross over the pharmacy door was lit. Behind iron grilles, the window displays were visible in the shop's fluorescent light, and for some minutes, the fat man studied an arrangement of relics from an earlier age of medicine: cornflower-blue syrup jars – *Syr Marrubii, Syr Rhei, Syr Simplex, Syr Rhamni* – and a run of hexagonal poison bottles arranged from large to small, all stamped 'Not to be taken'. The right-hand window carried advertising: a photograph of a woman with glowing, unlined skin, and before the photograph, a pyramid of jars of face cream linked by fine strands of cobwebs, the jars' sun-faded labels painted with long-stemmed roses.

Pushing open the pharmacy door, the fat man found himself at the back of a gathering of black-clothed women, all shortened and bent in some degree by age – bandy legged, or hump-backed, or stooping a little at the neck – as if bowing under the weight of their years. Behind a counter carrying a till and a small stand of wintergreen lozenges, the pharmacist's face had grown red, and his thin hair stood on end where he'd run his hands through it. Now, he leaned forward with both hands pressed on the counter, as though set in defence against attack.

At the front of the gathering, the most elderly of the women held up a box of blood pressure tablets, along with her health-service-issued booklet of entitlement, validated and stamped.

'Eight years, I've been taking these,' she was saying. 'You know it, and I know it. And now for lack of a piece of paper, you deny me this medicine which keeps me alive.'

'The law,' said the pharmacist, 'is very simple: no prescription, no free medicine. You're welcome to pay. I can't break the rules; it's more than my job's worth.'

'You'll kill us all,' came a querulous voice from the back of the gathering. 'You sentence us to death!'

'You could catch the bus to town and see a doctor there,' said the pharmacist. 'Come back with a prescription, and the medicine's yours.'

'All that way!' objected the woman at the group's head. 'Look!' She opened up the booklet, flicking through the pages of ink-stamps and signatures in the pharmacist's own hand, the records of the prescriptions he had dispensed. 'All these, you gave me. All I ask is another box of what I always have.'

Without warning, the pharmacist reached out, and grabbing the box from her, opened it and pulled out two blister packs of tablets, one part used and one untouched.

'How many of these do you have to take a day, *kyria mou*?' he asked.

'Three. I have to take three.'

127

'Then you have …' He made a quick count '… a full week's worth of medication remaining. You have at least a week of life left. Your situation is not of life and death, this evening. You must wait until they send us a substitute.'

Amongst the women, there was a murmur of disgruntlement.

'And how long will that be? The vacancy was unfilled for many months, last time. There'll be no doctor here within a week!'

'You'll kill us all,' came the querulous voice again.

'For God's sake!' The pharmacist raised his hands. 'Listen,' he said, 'listen, all of you. Is there anyone here who does not have medication for at least two days?'

'Mine runs out on Friday.'

'*At least* two days?'

There was silence, and a shuffling of feet.

'Then go away, now. I will phone to town, and tell them we need to borrow a doctor for our surgery. You can all see him when he comes, and get your prescriptions renewed.'

'But how will we know when he's coming?'

'I'll put a notice in the window.'

With reluctance, the women began to leave. The fat man promptly stepped forward and held open the door, smiling and offering a small bow to the back of the group, and wishing them *kali spera*. The women filed out, not thanking him, as though respect and good manners were rewards due to age and infirmity, whatever they had been in their younger years – grasping or selfless, good-humoured or bitter, faithful or faithless.

As they left, a small child watched from the doorway where the pharmacy became the pharmacist's home. Anxious for the pharmacist in his difficulties, she sucked hard on her thumb, and followed the old women with wide and lovely eyes as they reassembled on the square outside to continue their complaining.

The fat man closed the door behind them. As the pharmacist saw him, his expression changed; frustration and forced patience became displeasure.

But the fat man's smile remained, and, as he laid down his holdall, he turned to the child in the inner doorway.

'Who have we here?' he asked, as he approached her. 'Who is this gorgeous little creature, quiet as a mouse and pretty as a picture?' The child dipped her head in shyness, but her eyes brightened at his compliments. Grasping the hem of her skirt, in delighted modesty she twisted it in her fists. 'What do they call you?'

'Kokkona,' she whispered, not daring to look at him.

'Kokkona.' He repeated the name as if he'd known it all along and she had merely confirmed it. 'My very favourite name: Kokkona.' He crouched beside her, reducing himself to her height; the pharmacist busied himself with the lozenges. 'A pretty name for such a pretty girl! And I know when you grow, Kokkonitsa, you'll be a real beauty, and that beauty will lay all the world before you. So use your gift wisely, *koritsi mou*; use it to draw to you the handsomest and wealthiest of princes.'

The pharmacist gave a cough of disapproval, but the fat man ignored him and went on.

'Do you like magic, little one?' he asked. Hesitantly, she gave a nod, and at this signal, he pulled a silk handkerchief from his pocket, and wafted it before her to display its colours – purples, blues and greens. 'Watch,' he said. 'Watch very carefully.' He held out his palm to show its emptiness; the gold of the ring on his little finger shone. Draping it with the handkerchief, he covered his outstretched hand. 'Now, very quietly, we say the spell.' Eyes fixed on the child, he touched his finger to his lips and whispered words the pharmacist couldn't hear; then, with a flourish, he whipped away the handkerchief. Between his forefinger and thumb he held a sugar mouse with a short tail of pink thread and dots of gaudy colouring giving a bright blush to its cheeks.

Smiling with delight, she stepped forward to take the mouse, and he, laughing, tousling her black hair, gave it to her. He stood and put the handkerchief away in his pocket, whilst she called to her mother and ran away into the house behind the shop.

The pharmacist still seemed busy with the lozenges.

'Quite the magician, aren't you?' he said. 'Any more tricks up your sleeve?'

'Mere sleight of hand – a little conjuring I've practised that's quite impressive when it's mastered. But, since you ask, I never run out of tricks.'

Outside, on the square, the old women were still complaining to one another. The fat man crossed to the window and looked out at them, over the photograph of the woman with perfect skin and the jars of face cream. 'They feel the loss of their doctor. They believe, no doubt, he is the only thing standing between them and death. They put a lot of faith in him, and in the products you supply. Do you have faith in them yourself, Vangelis?'

The pharmacist shrugged.

'It doesn't matter whether I have faith or not,' he said. 'When your time's here, it's here. Taking your tablets every day won't stop you falling off a cliff.'

'Quite right,' said the fat man. 'I was admiring the display you have in your window, the common cures of days gone by. Syrup rhei, you have there, I noticed – rhubarb syrup, not used, strangely enough, as a laxative, but as a cure for loose stools. Whereas the syrup marrubii – syrup of horehound – is a laxative, and also, I believe, is very good for colds. And the rhamni – buckthorn – is a purgative. In other words, a poison.'

'Are you a medical man, then?' asked the pharmacist.

'I'm afraid not. Perhaps you were thinking I might step into the vacancy and get the angry mob off your back? No. I have a cousin who takes a great interest in such things, and he's taught me some of what he knows. Little Kokkona there, by the way, is quite charming and so lovely. Is she your daughter?'

'My granddaughter. I had only sons.'

'The way we live, sons are much easier. The Kaligi sisters are a case in point. Have you, by the way, any tincture of merbromin? It's hard to find, these days, but I'm lucky sometimes in these smaller places.'

Frowning, the pharmacist turned to the bank of drawers behind him, all labelled with a range of letters from the alphabet. Opening a drawer marked 'M–O' he rummaged through the medicaments – pills, salves, ointments, linctuses – until he put his hand on a small brown bottle, which he extracted and placed on the counter.

'What do you mean about the sisters?' he asked.

'Well, we very often judge women by their looks, don't we?' said the fat man. 'Their looks are a large part of their value.' Picking up the bottle, he unscrewed the cap, sniffing the bottle before he replaced it. 'Excuse my checking this; as it gets older, it loses its potency. As do we all, I suppose. So, on the face of it, the Kaligi sisters had little value to begin with; and as spinsters past their prime, well … Not like little Kokkona. She'll be a real prize. There'll be plenty of offers there. You'll get a good match, for her.'

'Her value is not only in her looks.'

'Is that so? What, then, left the Kaligi women on the shelf? Some vice of character? Were there debts in the family or genetic flaws? Or were they perfectly nice girls no man would be seen dead with?'

There was a short silence.

'Three hundred drachmas.'

'You know, I'm very partial to wintergreen. I'll take some of those lozenges. It must have been a great relief to Chrissa to find someone to take her on, so late in life. Wouldn't you say?'

'I don't know.' The pharmacist placed a box of lozenges beside the tincture bottle. 'I barely know the woman. That'll be four-fifty.'

'When did you first meet the doctor?'

'He came into the shop, just wandered in to talk. He was here as a visitor and found he liked the place. I told him there was a vacancy and he said he'd put in an application. Couple of weeks later, here he was. At first he practised privately; he took a room off the square, close to where he rented a room to sleep in. He had a sliding scale of charges, charged folks by how much he thought they could pay.'

'How altruistic.'

The pharmacist looked at him, sharply.

'People thought so. Was there a reason they shouldn't?'

'In my experience, a willingness to work for less than the going rate is not common amongst doctors in private practice. Was that how things remained?'

'He borrowed the key to the public surgery from time to time; there was equipment there he needed, and it seemed absurd for the community to go without a decent diagnosis when the paraphernalia of the profession was there, gathering dust. Before long, the move was permanent and he saw all his patients there; I assume when his public appointment was confirmed.'

'So at that point he no longer charged for his time?'

'I have no idea. My family and I did not require his services.'

'Why did he not take the public appointment from the first? Much easier for everyone, surely?'

'I asked him that myself.'

'And?'

'Taxes, was what he said to me. I wondered, between us, if he lacked the papers to work, with his being a foreigner.'

'But you assumed that, in the end, he had squared it all away?'

'It seemed a reasonable assumption to me, yes. Your tone suggests there may have been a problem.'

'You liked the man?'

'I didn't know him well. It's not relevant whether I liked him or not. I found him easy enough to deal with, professionally. He didn't prescribe obscure medicines I had to send away for. And our ladies there –' he pointed to the gathering in the square '– well, with them he was charming. That's why they want him back, if you ask me.'

'So you don't know for certain, then, that his appointment was official? There was no notification to you from the Medical Board, nothing like that?'

'The Medical Board has no obligation to inform me of its appointments.'

'You took his word for the fact he had been given the job?'

'He never told me he had the job. I just assumed it.'

The fat man turned away and seemed for a moment drawn into the changing scene outside, where a battered truck piled high with freshly picked oranges had pulled up outside the grocer's, and the truck's driver – swarthy, dirty and with the Arab-dark eyes of a gypsy – had begun to call his wares. The grocer had abandoned his customers inside the shop to remonstrate with the hawker, pointing to his half-filled box of oranges. But ignoring him, the gypsy called out to the women; smiling his amusement at the grocer's annoyance, he picked up three of his fruits and began expertly to juggle them, tossing one higher than the others from time to time, or passing one beneath his leg. From nowhere, small children appeared to watch. When the first of the old women crossed the square to the gypsy, purse in hand, the grocer threw up his hands and retreated inside his shop.

The fat man laughed.

'Your friend is beaten in the fruit market, at least for today. The entrepreneur wins out over the traditionalist, the innovator over him who stands still too long. As I think you found, at the last election. Let me pay you what I owe.' He took coins from his pocket and laid them on the counter. 'By the way, when the doctor was brought down from the chapel, it caused quite a stir. It pulled a crowd in the end almost as big as our juggling friend here. And yet, you weren't there. A man with a little medical knowledge – and a pharmacy – might have been invaluable. But you weren't there.'

The pharmacist slipped the coins, rattling, into the till.

'I have commitments,' he said. 'I can't be there for every dog-hanging and drama.'

'Maybe not.' The fat man smiled. 'Well, I'll say goodbye for now, and go and see what this young fruit seller has to offer. We'll speak again, perhaps.'

Picking up the small bottle of tincture, he put it in his pocket; and as he made his way to where the crowd was gathering, he opened up the box of wintergreen lozenges, and removing the paper from one of the sweets, popped it in his mouth.

Fourteen

With reluctance, the fat man accepted Evangelia's offer of dinner. He knew the state of the kitchen; he had seen the liberties the cat took with the food and how she let it lick the unwashed dishes; the evidence of rodents found in his bedroom was even more compelling here downstairs. He had noticed, too, how the cockatoo (when allowed its daily half-hour of freedom) flew around the *kafenion* to stretch its wings, letting feathers and debris from its cage fall everywhere; and wherever its droppings landed, Evangelia, complaining, cleaned up with some dry rag or sheet of newspaper and did not go back to wipe the table tops with soap and water. But the evening was dull and uninviting, and so the fat man decided he would dine in.

Examining his cutlery for cleanliness, he stirred meat sauce into his pasta, and winding strings of spaghetti around his fork, took a mouthful. The spaghetti was soft and tasteless, left to stand too long in the water it had boiled in; the sauce had an undertaste of burning, as if scraped off the bottom of a pan. He tried the salad (a roughly cut, under-ripe tomato, a few slices of red onion going soft and the tired end of a Kos lettuce, all doused in vegetable oil and sharp vinegar) but pushed the plate away and drank down half his beer to take the taste away.

He was considering a second mouthful of pasta when the *kafenion* door opened, letting in a draught which caused the cockatoo – miserable in its cage – to huddle into itself on its perch and hide its face amongst its feathers. A man entered slowly, tapping ahead of himself with a bamboo cane, which carried the weight his right leg should have taken. He closed the door, and not noticing the fat man, was making his way slowly to the empty table where the four men had sat the previous evening.

But the fat man, recognising him, spoke up.

'*Kali spera, yiatre,*' he said.

Somewhat startled, Dr Dinos looked across the room. Realising who had spoken, he smiled and made his slow way towards the fat man. His clothes, though still immaculate in appearance, were those he had worn last night, and as he reached the table, the fat man noticed the strong, sweet scent of violets, as if the doctor had overused cologne to mask the consequences of irregular hygiene.

'Our visitor from the capital,' said the doctor. 'We meet again.'

'Please, join me,' said the fat man. 'I dislike eating alone.'

The doctor looked down at the fat man's plates, and his smile grew wider.

'I believe that's my dinner you're eating,' he said. 'Eva is always fickle with her favours. Where is the lovely lady, by the way?'

'She's gone to the grocer's,' said the fat man, 'so I think we may assume she'll be back soon.' He laid down his fork. 'Forgive me. It was not my intention to deprive you of your meal.'

The doctor laughed, and as he took a seat at the table, patted the fat man's shoulder.

'Eat, friend, eat!' he said. 'You're doing me a favour, giving me a night off from dyspepsia and heartburn. Eva's no cook, as you'll have found; unfortunately, food is her favourite weapon, these days, in her fight to bag a man. I'm her usual target, but for now it seems she's turned her sights on you. So eat, friend, and I'll enjoy the spectacle of you taking the punishment. Just be sure you've plenty of Milk of Magnesia on hand for when you've finished. I can drop you off a bottle, if you're stuck.'

The fat man took another forkful from his plate. The food had not improved.

'You think I'm ungallant, of course, criticising the lady's good intentions,' said the doctor. 'But believe me, the good intentions are all on my side. It's not every man who'd sit night after night and eat food not fit for a dog.' He took out his briarwood pipe and his pouch of tobacco, and taking a pinch of soft-looking strands, began to pack them into the pipe's bowl, watching the fat man with eyes bright with mischief. 'So, tell me, how's the detective work coming along?'

'Well enough,' said the fat man. 'But you'll understand it's not appropriate for me to discuss my findings.'

'He'll not see again, of course. And just as well, if you ask me.'

The fat man looked at him in surprise.

'That's an extraordinary remark,' he said, 'especially as a medical man, who must understand both the pain and the psychological trauma of such a terrible injury.'

'We must look on the bright side. It'll stop him ever practising medicine again.'

Again, the fat man showed his surprise.

'Is this the view of a man who wants his job back?' he asked. 'Now the situation's vacant again, will you be putting in an application, *yiatre*?'

The doctor shook his head.

'Indeed I shall not. Almost forty years I doctored these people, and shall I tell you something? Doctored or not, they die. Some die quickly, and some die slowly, but we're all on the same road. You can't keep any alive indefinitely, and many you wouldn't want to. With some of them, you have to restrain yourself not to help them along. And those that are worth saving, you can't save either. Modern medicine just masks the symptoms and buys some a little time. You might just as well stick to the old cures – honey and bed-rest and a couple of aspirin. They work just as well, in the end. If you've finished eating, I'll light my pipe.'

The fat man laid down his fork, and the doctor put a match to his pipe-bowl, puffing on the stem until the tobacco glowed red and rich smoke filled the air.

'May I suggest, *yiatre*,' said the fat man, 'that with your fatalistic view of modern medicine, the people here perhaps were better off with Dr Chabrol.'

Slyly, the doctor looked at him.

'Do you think so? I think in Dr Chabrol – Dr Louis, as he was fondly known – the people thought they had a general practitioner. But I found him to be something of a specialist.'

'What sort of specialist?'

'Perhaps specialist is the wrong word. Shall we say, his range of expertise seemed very narrow. If you ask Vangelis, you'll find the range of his prescriptions was limited to match. Almost as if, in fact, he knew of very few medicines to prescribe. Perhaps at heart he was, like me, a believer in the simple cures of healthy diet and fresh air.'

'You didn't like him.'

'I didn't like him, no. Is that a crime?'

'Not unless you took your dislike to a malevolent degree.'

'On the contrary. My dealings with him were professional and polite. Let me tell you something. When I studied for my degree, we learned all there was to know about modern medicine, as it was then. I came here to practise what I'd learned, and what did I find? Superstition and fear. So I gave most of them aspirin or prescribed the old cures. But when this new man came along, I was keen to hear what was new and exciting, how the world had moved on since my days at the university. But our French friend wasn't one for professional discussion. He didn't respond to my interest. I found him stand-offish.'

'Really? Yet according to the pharmacist, his patients loved him.'

'Especially the ladies, yes?' He touched the stem of his pipe to his nose. 'There's nothing like a Frenchman to charm the ladies, is there?'

'Would I be wrong in thinking,' asked the fat man, with a wink that Dr Dinos almost missed, 'that you have been, in the past, a bit of a ladies' man yourself?'

The doctor sucked on his pipe, but the pipe had gone out. He reached for his matches, and took his time in striking one and putting its flame to the tobacco.

'You're not asking me to be indiscreet?' he said, at last.

'Absolutely not.'

'Then we'll leave it at that.'

'Would it be fair to say, then,' said the fat man, 'that Dr Chabrol's practice of medicine was perhaps a little more modern than your own? Is that where your differences lay?'

'I didn't say we had differences,' said Dr Dinos. 'You're putting words into my mouth. And it wasn't his "modern ways" that I had problems with. It was his incompetence.'

'Incompetence?'

'Misdiagnosis would be a kinder word.'

'Please, tell me,' said the fat man, drinking the last of his beer. 'I'm sorry our hostess isn't yet here, or I'd gladly buy you a drink.'

'You may not be a policeman,' said Dr Dinos, 'but you operate like one. Buy me a whisky, and loosen my tongue – is that how it works? No matter. In fairness, all doctors – including myself, on thankfully rare occasion – are prone to error. Symptoms may mask each other; one disease looks very much like another. Experience is the great teacher and there's no substitute for it. I bailed him out, that's all. There was a young woman with stomach pains; he diagnosed a pelvic inflammation. When she grew worse, the family turned to me, and I recognised the case for what it was – appendicitis. If she had been left much longer, she might have died. I was glad to have been able to help. I said nothing to him, of course.'

'But surely, as a professional, you should have taken him to one side and pointed out his error.'

'Do you think so? Unfortunately, I could think of no way of approaching the subject discreetly; I didn't want him to think that I was crowing. Besides ...'

The door opened, and Evangelia entered, carrying a bag of potatoes in the crook of one arm, in the other hand a bag full of groceries.

'Here she is,' said Dr Dinos, 'our lovely hostess. Lay down your burdens, *koritsi mou*, and be good enough to bring us both a drink.'

Evangelia kicked the door closed behind her, and making her way puffing to the counter, put down her bags.

'A whisky for me, if you please, and for our Athenian friend, another beer.' Dr Dinos turned to the fat man. 'No bribery needed here, you see, my friend,' he said. 'I'm happy to give you all the help I can, and for nothing.'

'I'll get the gentleman a beer in a moment,' said Evangelia, taking dried chickpeas and canned mackerel from her bag. 'But there's no time for you to be drinking, *yiatre*. Orfeas the sheep-man has come off his motorbike, and they're waiting for you to patch him up. A lot of blood, they say – a lot of blood. If you go quickly, you might be in time to save him.'

Paternally, Dr Dinos shook his head. Evangelia began putting away groceries in near-empty cupboards.

'They never learn, *kyrie*; take it from me, they never learn. This generation is obsessed with speed and their own convenience. And old Orfeas is a hypocrite, to boot; it's not five minutes since he told me he'd never own one of those things. But I'll go, of course I'll go.' The doctor knocked the ash from his pipe and held out his hand to the fat man. 'You see how it is? As soon as the Frenchman is gone, they call for me, night and day.' His smile was cheerful. 'It seems I must step into the breach, once again, so I'll wish you *kali spera*. Eva, put this gentleman's next drink on my bill.' Leaning on his cane, he stood. 'There's no rest for the wicked, friend; that never changes. There's no rest for the wicked, in this town.'

Fifteen

The morning sky was still heavy with the rain that had fallen all night. Around the new fountain, the leaves on the plants were vibrant green, their flower buds swollen and ready to bloom. Adonis Anapodos rode his moped carefully between the puddles on the square, the hood of a quilted anorak pulled over his head, his bald tyres hissing through the wet. With a boat hook, the grocer knocked pooled water from the summer-striped canopy outside his shop, not moving fast enough to dodge the deluge which soaked his shoes. The men who should have been working on the sewerage pipes had left their shovels in the truck and taken coffee at the *kafenion*; now they'd finished coffee, they called to Evangelia for a round of beers. A youth in a shirt so wet it clung to his skin rattled by on a bicycle without brakes; a blond-haired youth called out to him, and waved.

The fat man had waited patiently for the rain to stop, and as it did so, he stepped from the *kafenion* doorway into the square, and crossed the wet cobbles to the side street where he had parked his car. From the overhanging trees, water fell in cold and weighty drops on to his head and shoulders, and as he slid into the driver's seat, he brushed them from his coat. Putting the car in gear, he drove up to the junction.

The rain began to fall again in earnest, blurring his view through the windscreen. The fat man threw the switch for the windscreen wipers, but the wipers did not move.

With care, he reversed back into the parking spot he had just left; and, rain pattering on the roof, he folded his arms over his chest, and settled down to doze until the weather cleared.

At the garage, the fat man pulled up alongside the pumps. Reaching down to his holdall, he unwrapped his galoshes from their newspaper and folded the newspaper for reuse. Slipping the galoshes over his tennis shoes, he stepped out of the car.

There was, today, no hammering or banging from the workshop; instead, the air was noxious with the fumes of paint, and the ghost of its scarlet colour hung in the finest of mists across the forecourt. The workshop door was closed; inside, a radio played loud enough to be heard over a paint sprayer's pneumatic hiss.

Leaning back into the car, the fat man pressed the Mercedes's horn, twice. For a minute, there was no response; then the workshop door opened and the mechanic appeared, a woollen hat pulled down to his eyebrows, his face covered by a gas mask of the type issued to civilians in the last world war. Peeling heavy-duty rubber gloves from his hands, he handed them to someone unseen inside the workshop; he handed over his hat and mask, too, and whoever took them closed the workshop door behind him. The mechanic rubbed his face to restore the circulation inhibited by the mask's tight seals, and ran a hand over his blond hair to ensure that it lay flat. Then he turned towards the pumps.

'We meet again, mechanic.' The fat man strode towards him, hand outstretched.

The mechanic seemed wary, but held out his own hand, with black oil behind the fingernails and grime in the creases of the palm.

'How can I help you?' he asked.

'My car still has a small defect,' said the fat man. 'You did your work too well; the windscreen wipers have gone from working constantly to not working at all. Do you have a few minutes, perhaps, to look at the problem?' He looked up at the sky. Towards the sea, grey clouds threatened. 'It's a disadvantage at this time of year to have a car that can't be driven when it rains.'

The mechanic crossed his arms over his chest.

'I fixed it,' he said. 'It worked fine; you saw it did.'

'I agree; but the old girl is temperamental, and what's fixed one day fails the next. If you could oblige me, I'd be grateful. Of course your rate will be the same, and I'll pay cash, as before.'

The mechanic hesitated.

'My lad's helping me on this re-spray,' he said at last, 'so I'll have a quick look. But if it's a big job, it'll have to wait till tomorrow.'

'I'm sure it will be straightforward – a loose wire or something of that kind. But may I wait inside the workshop? I'm afraid I'm prone to feel the cold.'

'Five minutes in there without a mask'll set your lungs like concrete,' said the mechanic. 'You can go up to the house. My wife is up there.'

The fat man remembered the cake and good coffee; he remembered too the mechanic's hard-eyed suspicion, and his remarks about the doctor's too-regular visits. But the cake had been excellent.

'Thank you,' he said. 'I will.'

Close to the house, the air lost the choking stink of paint. Instead, the fat man breathed the scent of wet grass, the rain-battered blossom of a crab-apple tree and the slightly acrid scent of the lemon-yellow margaritas which flourished amongst the long grass, out of the goat's reach. The kitchen door was closed against the breeze blowing off the sea, and when he knocked, there was no answer. Cautiously, he turned the handle, and opening the door a little way, called out. A woman's voice invited him to enter, and so he stepped inside, wiping his feet on the mat.

The kitchen held the damp warmth of boiling pans and the savoury smell of lunch – melted cheese, baking pastry. A girl's fur-trimmed jacket was draped round the back of a chair; a bag of school books was thrown down in a corner. From the dresser, the faces in the silver-framed photographs were still smiling.

He crossed the kitchen, looking back to check he had left no footprints on the clean floor tiles. The far door opened on a hall from which other rooms led off; at its end was a bedroom, where an elderly woman was propped up on several pillows in a bed. In a chair beside her sat the mechanic's wife.

'Forgive me,' said the fat man. 'I didn't mean to intrude.'

He turned away, but the mechanic's wife beckoned him forward.

'No, no,' she said. 'Come in, come in.'

She didn't smile as he approached. The lines of worry in her face seemed deeper than they had only a day or two before.

'Do excuse me,' said the fat man. 'I don't want to disturb you. Your husband said I might wait in the house. I'll sit in the kitchen, if I may.'

The old woman did not move; there was, from her, no turn of the head, no blink of the eyes, just the stillness of catatonia, as if she were already a corpse. But the mechanic's wife again beckoned to the fat man, inviting him into the bedroom.

145

'Come,' she said, 'come and meet my mother. She'll enjoy the company. Won't you, Mama?'

The fat man gave a small bow of his head and entered the bedroom. It was a small room, with a single window looking out towards the hen house and beyond that to the mountains, where the clouds were clearing and sunlight touched the highest slopes. On the head-board of the bed, five icons hung on nails hammered into the wood: St Nektarios and St Ilias, St Marina and the Virgin, the largest and most splendid of Christ himself. On a pre-war dressing table whose deteriorating mirror reflected the mountain view, a plaster statue of the Virgin was draped in amber worry beads; a lamp burned before the statue, giving off the smell of hot oil and smoke. At the end of the bed stood a dowry chest of greater age than the dying woman, ornately carved and carefully polished.

But the walls made the room extraordinary. Everywhere, there were photographs – in black-and-white and sepia, a few in poor-quality, early colour, all mounted in rough, home-made frames of pine and panel pins. Simple, almost naive in composition, they illustrated a rural life now extinct: men scything fields of grain; women stirring pans of goats' milk on a fire; a donkey being whipped to turn the grinding stones of an olive press; a chandler outside his shop; a fisherman holding up a pair of octopuses; men struggling in mud to haul a cart out of a stream. But the pictures' simplicity was also their genius, and the fat man moved in fascination from photograph to photograph, studying faces alive with character and settings which captured perfectly the landscape's soul.

Then his eyes fell on a portrait on the dressing table, the only photograph professionally framed. The head and shoulders of a woman of singular beauty were caught against an uncertain background; turning from the camera, she was beginning to laugh, as if distracted from her pose by some irresistible joke. The shot was natural and relaxed, emphasising her lovely profile and capturing the fall of sunlight on her shining hair.

The fat man's eyes lingered on the portrait; the mechanic's wife noticed.

'She was lovely, wasn't she?' she asked. She turned to the old woman in the bed. 'You were a real beauty, weren't you, Mama?'

The old woman made no movement, nor gave any sign of having heard; she lay as still as the dead, except for the working of her jaw and a faint clicking as her false teeth slipped over her receding gums, and as the fat man looked at her, a muscle spasm at its corner made her eye twitch in a parody of a wink. The hair that had been luscious in the portrait was sparse and white; fluffed with recent washing, it lay thin on the shoulders of the moss-green cardigan she wore over a nightdress buttoned tight at the neck. The bed sheets were recently changed, with the creases of ironing still in them, and the blankets which covered them were clean; but the once lovely woman carried the smell of age: behind the talcum and soap was something insanitary. As if suddenly aware of it, the mechanic's wife stood up and opened the window behind her, just a crack.

'Please, sit,' she said, indicating the chair she had vacated. 'Sit a while. Mother will enjoy the company. Will you take coffee? Mother's no doubt ready for her tea.'

'Thank you,' he said, taking her seat. 'As I recall, you make excellent coffee.'

Giving no smile, or word, or sign of pleasure, she let his compliment pass unacknowledged. She pulled open one of the deep drawers of the dressing table, where there were no clothes but stacks of photograph albums, varied in size and colour and giving off the equine smell of leather. Choosing one from near the bottom of the drawer, she handed it to the fat man.

'Whilst I'm making coffee,' she said, 'perhaps you would turn the pages for Mother.'

As she walked away down the hall, he opened the heavy album to its waxed cover sheet, through which he read its handwritten title page: '1959'. A little awkwardly, the fat man slanted the album towards the old woman, positioning it where he thought she might best see it, and turned to the first of the photographs. The page's fabric was spotted with pale grey growths of mould and smelled of must and damp, as if he had opened some long-sealed vault; but the photographs were brilliant with light, and sparkled with memories of that summer. He turned the pages, and each turn seemed to lead him down a forgotten road, each page a day in that long-past year; and it seemed too that the silent woman beside him called to him from the place where he was heading, as if she had taken the road ahead of him, and was pleased to guide him to the place she was quite content to be.

When the mechanic's wife called him to the kitchen for his coffee, the fat man carefully closed the album and laid it on the chair he was vacating. For a long moment, he looked down on the frail figure in the bed. At the corner of her mouth, a bubble of spittle rose and shrank as she breathed. He touched her forearm, and finding the skin cold, closed the window and secured the latch. Glancing again at the portrait of her in her prime, he lifted her hand up to his lips and lightly kissed its veinous, bony back.

On the kitchen table, a plate held a slice of sponge cake topped with cinnamon-spiced apples.

'I used the apples you brought,' said the mechanic's wife, 'so Mother can eat them, softened.'

The fat man took a seat with a view of the forecourt, where the mechanic was half-hidden beneath the Mercedes's bonnet. The mechanic's wife placed his coffee on the table. Putting water to boil for the old lady's tea, she added a twig of wild sage to the *kafebriko* and a teaspoonful of honey to a spouted invalid cup.

He cut his first mouthful of cake, and ate it with a fork.

'Has your mother been ill long, Litsa?' he asked.

She didn't look at him as she replied; she seemed busy watching for the water's boil.

'It's over a year now, since her stroke. It seems so cruel to us. She was always the busiest of women, always doing; always active. If she has to go, why doesn't God just take her?'

The fat man had no answer, and a silence grew between them. At the stove, the gas burner whispered; as the water grew hot, the sage's scent displaced the stronger smell of coffee.

Cutting once again into his cake, he asked, 'Who took the photographs?'

'My father,' she said. 'It was his life's work – though not his real work. His real work was a smallholding. But photography was his passion. Every spare drachma went on photographic essentials: film, chemicals for his darkroom, wood for framing. He made the frames himself. Mother used to say if he'd applied himself to that trade, he'd have made a useful living as a carpenter.'

'He was quite an artist.'

Turning to him, she gave a short laugh.

'Do you think so? I certainly never did; nor did Mama. She saw it as an expensive hobby that made life difficult.

He came home one day with a camera he'd bought off some traveller, and that was it. To him, it was a marvel of the age; it's just a piece of worthless junk, now.'

'You still have the camera?'

'Somewhere.'

'But the photographs themselves – they might be worth something.'

'They're just snaps. But he spent hours, days on them. We never saw him. He had a shed he used as a darkroom; that's where he preferred to spend his time. When he died, and Mother came to us, she wouldn't leave anything behind; everything from that shed came too. It's all there in the workshop now, getting in Tassos's way and gathering dust. If I told Mother there was money in the photographs, she'd still not agree to part with them. And anyway, what use is money to her now?'

Steam was rising from the *kafebriko*; turning off the gas flame, she poured the sage tea into the invalid cup.

'With respect,' he said, quietly, 'the day will come when she's not here to object.'

'You think I'm ridiculous, of course, with her in that condition.' With an emotion he read as anger, she banged the *kafebriko* down on the stove, spilling the tea remaining in the pot on to the stove top. 'I'm sure you're thinking it could make no difference to her, the state she's in. But I know she's still here with us. She hears and she understands. And she feels things, too; I know she does. Excuse me. I must take her her tea.'

She touched the cup and burned her fingers. In frustration, she looked round the kitchen for a cloth. The fat man leaned forward, and taking a folded tea towel from the back of his chair, held it out to her.

'Here you are,' he said, 'but the tea's too hot for her, just yet. I shall say no more; your husband will be finished soon

150

and I shall leave you in peace. And you must believe, Litsa, that people respect you for respecting your mother. You are treating her as she deserves and I approve wholeheartedly of that.'

'You think she deserves any of this?' To hide gathering tears, she faced the window. 'Life was hard for her and the ending's harder still. Day after day bedridden like that, with me wiping her backside and feeding her like a baby, with nothing to look forward to but the end.'

'You may think she sees it like that, Litsa, but perhaps she sees it as a blessing, to be cared for in her last days by someone who loves her enough to do it.'

'I know how embarrassed she must be. She was always such a modest woman.'

'I think she is beyond embarrassment,' said the fat man. 'She has, I think, one foot in this world and one in the next. She sees where she is going, I'm sure. She seems comfortable to me, and content.'

She seemed about to answer him, but instead shook her head. Picking up the cup with the cloth, she blew on the tea to cool it.

'She'll be thirsty,' she said, 'if you'll excuse me.'

'Gladly,' he said. Through the window, he watched the mechanic lower the Mercedes's bonnet. Drinking down his coffee, he swallowed the last of his cake and rose from the table. 'It appears it is anyway time for me to leave you. My thanks to you for the refreshment, especially the cake. Your light hand is appreciated.'

'You're welcome.' Unsmiling, she watched him to the door. As his hand touched the handle, she stopped him. '*Kyrie*. About the photographs – don't say anything to my husband. If he thinks they're worth anything, he won't care what Mama or I think about it.'

'You need have no worries about that,' said the fat man. 'You'll find I'm very good at keeping secrets, when the secret deserves to be kept.'

As the fat man approached, the mechanic's eyes were watchful. He wiped his hands on an oily rag and tucked it into the belt of his trousers.

'She kept you entertained, did she?' he asked.

'Your wife, as I'm sure you appreciate, is a woman of worth, a hard worker and of a very sober nature. I trust you value her as you should.'

The mechanic scowled, as if about to take issue with the fat man's remarks; but before he had formed his words, the fat man smiled and reached for his wallet.

'All fixed?' he said. 'I think we agreed the same as last time, didn't we?'

He counted out several notes, and taking them, the mechanic stuffed them into his trouser pocket.

'I know where to find you if I've any more problems,' went on the fat man. 'But hopefully she'll cope now, rain or shine.' Inside the workshop, the paint sprayer hissed, and he nodded in that direction. 'Your son's a great help to you, I'm sure; and what a benefit for him to start life with a good trade.'

'He's always been keen to join me in the business. Twice the labour, twice the income, I say.'

The fat man opened the Mercedes's door. On the driver's seat, a smudge of oil had dirtied the leather, and thinking of his raincoat, he hesitated to get into the car. But the rain was falling again, heavy drops creating ripples in the puddles; so he got in anyway, and waving cheerily to the mechanic, drove away.

Sixteen

The fat man took the road towards the foothills, driving across the plain between smallholdings where the leaves of spring crops were already showing, and empty fields were ploughed and ready for planting cotton. Where the road began to rise and its bends became sharper, he slowed the Mercedes to look for the track Evangelia had told him was there; and where a fast-flowing stream was crossed by a timber bridge, he left his car.

The path was clear at first, leading him through woodland of beeches and wild chestnuts; but beyond the trees, the path grew rockier and less marked, until at the edge of an upland meadow it disappeared, hidden by mountain grasses and flowers. The breeze had moved the morning's rain inland, and a blue sky carried only the remnants of clouds, so, out of the shaded woods, the sun was pleasantly warm. Walking at a fast pace uphill, the fat man inhaled deeply and deliberately, taking in air sweetened by pollen and the scent of spring. At the brow of the hill, he stopped and looked around to take his bearings. The place where he was heading was above him and to the north, and so he made his way in that direction. A few paces on, the grass was rutted; here and there, the ruts were deep and churned to mud. Placing his holdall beside him, the fat man crouched to examine the ground. Beyond doubt, a motorbike had been ridden this way.

Shadowed by a mountain outcrop at the far side of the meadow was a stone-built cabin, its corrugated-iron roof held on by rocks and rope. As the fat man grew close, a dog began to bark; as he grew closer, a rangy mongrel – grey-muzzled, with tumorous swellings on its inner thighs and belly – strained at its chain, snarling in frustrated rage at the fat man, who stopped just out of its reach. Bending to the dog, the fat man held out his hand for it to sniff; but the dog was mistrustful, and cowering, tucked its tail between its legs and slunk into the rusty oil barrel which made its kennel. There, it stood on its bed of dirty straw and faced the fat man to protect the bone it had been gnawing on: the lower leg of a sheep, with a few bloody scraps of meat and the sheep's hoof still attached.

For a few moments, the fat man waited, expecting the dog's barking to have roused anyone inside, but the door remained closed. Moving without noise, he made his way to the back of the cabin, which fell in the shadow of the mountain. A crop of spearmint filled an old tin bath, and the fat man plucked a sprig in passing, holding the herb to his nose to sniff its fragrance. Behind the bath, a large tarpaulin – ripped in places into holes, in others patched and stitched, weighted at its corners and its edges by heavy rocks – covered some large object. Tossing several of the rocks behind him with obvious ease, the fat man released one corner of the cloth and lifted it to see what was hidden underneath; and the dog, which watched at the end of its chain, began to bark again.

Orfeas the shepherd judged the hour by the light and length of the day, and when he came in from the lambs, it seemed to be an hour or two after noon: too early for a drink, but a good time to eat. There were tins left on the shelf, and hard bread and crackers in the tin, so he chose luncheon meat and a tin of pears in juice, and took a handful of the crackers. With his forearm, he swept the breakfast crumbs from the table top to the floor, and laid his lunch out on the table.

The room was dark (the room was always dark, regardless of the hour, midday or midnight; only the depth of darkness varied, because the shutters were never opened to let in daylight or the faint light from the stars). The ashes in the grate were cold, and lifted in puffs of grey powder each time the wind breached the hopeless chimney or drove through the unfilled holes in the stone walls.

As he wound the steel key on the tin of meat, the dog whined, and having whined, began to bark in earnest, its chain rattling on the ground as it ran backwards and forwards before the door. He called out to it for silence – the damn dog barked at everything, from a sheep knocking the pen rails to a crow cawing overhead – and, briefly, it was quiet; but then its racket began again, and so he left the meat on the table and threw open the door.

No one was there. The dog had stretched its chain to its limit, and with sorry eyes looked back at him from the corner of the cabin.

'Hush your noise,' said Orfeas, and the dog wagged its tail uncertainly.

Orfeas went back inside the cabin.

He finished opening the luncheon meat, and with the can opener, opened the tin of pears, then found his knife and spoon and wiped the knife blade on his trousers. He set the two tins – both with their lids still hanging – in his accustomed place at the table. Sitting, he dug out a wedge of meat, and stuffed it in his mouth with a damp-softened cracker, which tasted of nothing but flour as he chewed it into pap. There was nothing else, and so he took another. Finishing the meat, he ate the pears, snapping off the lid and drinking the juice from the tin. He lit the primus stove, poured water from a bottle into a saucepan, and added coffee and sugar from their packets. As the coffee heated on the flame, he stood in silence, looking at the bottle of rough spirit on the table; he looked at it until he thought he might as well, and then folded his arms and turned his back on it. The coffee boiled. Orfeas unscrewed the cap off a tartan thermos flask, decanted the coffee into it and fastened the flask into his shoulder pouch.

Outside, the dog lay, head on paws, beside the oil barrel. Orfeas unfastened the chain from its collar and took a few steps mountainwards, expecting the dog to follow him, but the dog bounded away and disappeared from sight. Orfeas cursed, and putting finger and thumb under his tongue, gave a sharp whistle to call it back. But the dog did not respond, and so Orfeas followed it.

Behind and beyond the cabin, under the branches of a solitary fig tree, was a table where the shepherd ate in summer, and seated there, on Orfeas's chair, was the man he had recently seen talking to Chrissa – a man tall as himself, though somewhat fatter, seeming comfortable in the mountain terrain despite his inappropriate dress. The fat man was eating off Orfeas's table, with Orfeas's dog sitting by his knee, and as Orfeas watched, the fat man broke off a piece of whatever he was eating and fed it to the grateful dog.

As Orfeas approached, the fat man seemed not to notice him; but as he drew closer, the fat man smiled and raised a hand in greeting.

'*Kali mera sas*,' he called, and fed another morsel to the dog. 'Forgive my intrusion. I was enjoying your view with my lunch.'

As Orfeas reached the fig tree, the dog left the fat man's side, and pressing its hard body against the shepherd's thigh, licked at his fingers in apology for its defection. Orfeas looked down at the fat man's meal: a wax-paper packet of mortadella sausage, spotted with rondels of pork fat and pale green pistachios; two varieties of white-marbled salami, both crusted with coarsely crushed peppercorns; fine-cut slices of mature yellow Gruyère, more holes than cheese. There was a paper bag of fresh bread rolls, which the fat man was using to make sandwiches, and to drink, Italian mineral water, in an elegant, sapphire-blue bottle.

'Please,' said the fat man, offering the food with spread hands, 'join me. There's plenty, as you can see.' Splitting a bread roll with his thumb, with relish he folded inside it a slice each of mortadella, salami and cheese, and bit into it.

'What do you want here?' asked Orfeas.

The fat man looked up at him. The shepherd's skin was dark from windburn and sunburn; his hair was receding, but long on his neck. Above the garlic from the sausage and the pungent cheese, his odour was strong, of sheep and sour milk, of the summery sweetness of hay; there was, too, the musk of the human male and, faintly, the smell of alcohol. The shepherd was not handsome; the features of his face seemed mismatched, though his eyes were distinctive, silver-grey and – at this moment – suspicious.

And beside one eye, his cheek was cut; a graze ran from his chin to his eyebrow.

'You've been in the wars, my friend,' said the fat man. 'You've made a mess of your face. The back of your hand, too; that looks nasty. And I couldn't help but notice that you're walking with a limp. Have you had some kind of accident?'

'I'm prone to accidents,' said Orfeas. 'The ground up here is rough.'

The fat man took a bite out of his roll.

'Please,' he said, gesturing again at the food, 'help yourself.' He peeled a slice of mortadella from the packet, and held it out for the dog, but the dog, back under its master's jurisdiction, was afraid to take it, and hid behind the shepherd's legs. 'I know this terrain is treacherous, especially on a motorbike, and especially when the rider is an amateur. I should tell you I was with Dr Dinos when he got the message to come to you. The usual exaggeration in its passing from mouth to mouth had you at death's door.'

'It's just a few cuts. I'll mend.'

'Do you know,' said the fat man, 'I have something that will help. An old cure that's not very often used, these days.' He reached into his pocket and took out the bottle of merbromin tincture he had bought at the pharmacy. 'Use this,' he said. 'It'll do a better job of healing than time alone. But be careful not to get it on your clothes; it stains red and is very tricky to get out. I am impressed that you managed to get the motorbike back home again in your injured state, if this is, indeed, your home. It's a charming spot, though the facilities seem somewhat basic for permanent occupation. Forgive me!' He laid down his sandwich, and stood up from the table. 'I have you at a disadvantage; I have not introduced myself. Hermes Diaktoros, of Athens. I am here investigating the recent attack on Dr Chabrol.'

He held out his hand, and the shepherd reluctantly took it with his own. The fat man's height matched the shepherd's; like a close friend, the fat man draped an arm around Orfeas's shoulder.

'Walk with me a moment,' he said. 'There's something I want to ask you which might help me with my investigation.'

He led the shepherd back towards the cabin; the dog fell back and followed them, nose down. 'You know Dr Chabrol, of course. It was he who recently failed to attend his own wedding.' Beneath the fat man's arm, the shepherd tensed. 'Were you a guest at that wedding?'

'No.' Needlessly, the shepherd turned and called to the dog, which still followed close behind them.

'You surprise me,' said the fat man. 'In a small town like Morfi, I thought the community was close.' They had reached the back of the cabin; the fat man pointed to the tin bath filled with herbs. 'You have a wonderful crop of spearmint there,' he said. 'I am particularly partial to mint in courgette fritters. I have a housekeeper who makes the best you'll ever taste, and she is always generous with the mint. But what I wanted to show you, was this.'

Stepping away from the shepherd, he lifted the freed corner of the tarpaulin, revealing the handlebars and front wheel of a silver motorbike.

'This is a very fine bike,' he said. 'Yamaha, 500cc. A powerful machine, and dangerous in the wrong hands, as I think you discovered last night. It seems unusual, to me, to keep such a bike so far from any road. It must be difficult, I would think, to get it up here at all. One might be forgiven, in fact, for suspecting that this bike has been brought up here only to hide it.' The fat man laid a hand on the bike's front lamp. 'There's something else, my friend,' he said. 'I pride myself on reading people; it is a little vanity of mine. And I would never put you with this bike, if only because – forgive me – to buy a bike like this, a man would have to spend a good sum of money.' He glanced down at the shepherd's well-worn boots, at the muddied hems of his trousers, at the rough jerkin and holed sweater beneath it. 'And it would be unusual for a man to spend that kind of money on such a machine, just to hide it away. And you know, Orfeas, I'd put money on your being a man who prefers to walk. So I don't think this is your bike at all.'

'It's none of your business, anyway,' said Orfeas. 'The bike belongs to a friend.'

'Ah,' said the fat man, 'that would explain a great deal. Your friend isn't a doctor, by any chance?'

The shepherd strode forward, and, snatching the corner of the tarpaulin from the fat man's hand, re-covered the motorbike.

'I've work to do,' he said, 'so I'll wish you *kali mera*.'

He whistled to the dog, which stayed close by his heels as he set off towards the mountains.

The fat man watched him go, noticing the route of the path he followed. Glancing at his watch, he found that it wasn't as late as he had thought; so, returning to the table under the fig tree, he took his seat and settled down to enjoy a leisurely lunch, and the view.

Seventeen

Noula walked, head bowed, along the street, uncomfortable with notoriety. As the women in the houses saw her pass, they turned their attention from their chores, and made the sisters the subject of their prattling. A neighbour's husband was loading a mattock, hoe and fork into his van, preparing to head up to his smallholding; as she reached him, he bent inside the cab, sparing both of them the embarrassment of speaking. Only old Pandelis seemed as normal. He sat in his usual place inside his doorway, fiddling with the worry beads in his fingers, and raised a hand to say hello; half deaf, half blind, half simple, he was still grateful for anyone who'd speak.

She had hurried to reach the house, but at the door, Noula hesitated. Behind the garden wall, one neighbour called out to another, and afraid of being seen, Noula quickly went inside.

The house seemed deserted; the stillness of their mother's absence lay as tangible as settling dust. She passed through the cramped *salone* to the kitchen, where the old TV Mama had loved so much was silent in its place. They had put it on the dresser so Mama could see it from the bed – the bed she and Chrissa had carried in together from the bedroom; the bed Mama had refused, one day, to leave; the bed she had died in. The chair placed at the bedside for her visitors – relatives and neighbours, the priest and the doctor – stood vacant with its back against the wall.

It had been a grave error, to fall in with Mama's planned idleness; as her body grew fat and her muscles softened, her brain had seemed to lose its sharpness, too. The bed had taken Mama prisoner, and Mama had made Noula and Chrissa slaves to new routines, of bedpans and TV shows and her medicines.

The lamp before the icon of St Martha was out; yet, with oil in the glass, and the lamp standing in no draught, it seemed that Chrissa must have blown it out on purpose.

On Chrissa's wedding day, these rooms had smelled of polish, and baking, and flowers. And on workdays, Noula came home to the smells of cooking – fried fish or a soup of pulses, a stew or baking pasta – but today, there was nothing. Her breakfast dishes were on the drainer where she had left them, the crusts of her bread and honey still on the plate. Noula's stomach growled with hunger. It was annoying that Chrissa hadn't bothered to cook; if Noula had known, she could have bought something in Platania.

'Chrissa!'

She listened for the noises Chrissa would make – the clatter of a mop and bucket, the calling to the chickens in the yard, a brush's bristles scrubbing the steps.

There was silence.

'Chrissa!'

There was no response; but now she noticed the back door to the garden was ajar.

She crossed to the window, and Chrissa was there, kneeling in the worn grass beneath the lemon trees, in the place where they put the chairs in summer. She knelt with her head low, and spread around her knees was a cloud of white, something soft like drifts of snow.

What the devil was Chrissa playing at, whilst there was no lunch? Marching to the door, Noula flung it open, and called again.

'Chrissa!'

With a start, her sister turned, showing Noula a face creased with pain and wet with tears. In her hand she held an object: small, bright yellow.

Noula didn't shout again, but hissed at her sister. She didn't know what Chrissa was doing, but whatever it was, instinct suggested it was something that the neighbours shouldn't see.

Noula hurried out to Chrissa, and looked down. The billowing clouds of white were Chrissa's wedding dress, the yellow object in her hand a lighter. Noula kept her voice low; behind the wall, the neighbours might be listening.

'What on earth are you doing?'

'I'm burning it. I'm burning my dress.'

She flicked the lighter, and a tall flame appeared. Noula blew it out.

'Why? Why would you do that?'

'He doesn't want me. No one wants me.'

Noula felt a stab of pain, a portion of the hurt felt by her sister; and yet the words she said were platitudes, wholly inadequate.

'Don't be ridiculous. Of course he wants you. He asked you, didn't he?'

'He won't even see me. I was supposed to be his wife, and he won't even see me.'

'Give me the lighter.' Like a child caught in misdemeanour, Chrissa gave it to her. 'Now come inside, for pity's sake. He's sick, Chrissa. When he gets better, he'll send for you.'

'That isn't true. You don't believe that, do you?'

She was calling on Noula to give her reassurance, and Noula's hesitation could only undermine any confidence which, hour by hour, was seeping away. Yet Noula couldn't bring herself to say the right words: her dislike of the man, the dread of her own loneliness, the stigma of being the one left titled 'spinster', all prevented her.

The dress would be spoiled; already there was dirt around the hem, from Chrissa's melodramatic flouncing down to the beach. But the sequins on the bodice still sparkled, the flowers in the lace were still fresh, and the urge came over Noula to help her sister do the job, to snatch the lighter from Chrissa's hand and be the one to set the frippery on fire; *in fact*, she almost said, *let's fetch that can of paraffin from the outhouse, and make sure the damn dress really burns*: burn it, and be finished with this business once and for all, and let them go on together, as they were, sharing their shame into old age.

'Look, Chrissa,' she said. She kept her voice low, always anxious they were being overheard, and reached out to touch her sister with a gesture that was uncertain; but Chrissa knocked her hand away. 'I don't know what he's thinking. You know him better than I do. But if it comes to it that things don't turn out the way you planned – it's all up in the air now, isn't it? I can't help that, and I'm not sure you can either – it wouldn't be so bad, would it? We've got each other, haven't we? We've always had each other.'

She knew the words were wrong, inviting Chrissa back into that place where they would be together, but alone, dividing between them the stigma of their spinsterhood. Chrissa's face was angry, as much as if Noula had just slapped her.

'I don't want you!' she said. 'I want him!'

The words were hard, and stung.

Noula went inside.

Minutes went by, before her sister followed her. She carried the dress before her, bundled up over her belly like a pregnancy. Her knees were deeply indented from dirt and stones, so Noula knew she must have been in physical pain, like a penitent. Noula was peeling potatoes; a pan of oil was heating on the stove.

'I'm sorry,' said Chrissa.

'I'm glad you've brought that dress in; it cost too much to spoil.' Noula didn't look at her, afraid Chrissa would notice the tears in her eyes. 'You'll have to get it cleaned. Is there any bread? I don't suppose you've been to the bakery. How long have you been out there?'

'A while.'

'For heaven's sake, Chrissa! What will people say? Here, peel these. Give me the dress.'

She gathered up her sister's gown – the nets and lace, the sequined flowers – and hugged it to her; it held Chrissa's perfume, the special scent she'd bought just for her wedding. The dress was soft and magical, fit for a princess, a dress of transformation. But the nets had picked up debris from the garden, dead leaves of geraniums and small twigs. As best she could, Noula brushed it clean, and took the dress away. When she came back, Chrissa was sitting at the kitchen table, finishing the potatoes. The hair colour which had suited her on her wedding day seemed too bright now, and there was no make-up in her bag of tricks which could put life in her complexion. Noula could see clearly what she was: a miserable, middle-aged woman, suffering life's defeat.

On impulse, Noula placed her hands on her sister's shoulders and kissed the top of her head.

'Do you know what I think?' she asked. 'I think he's protecting you. He doesn't want to burden you with hospitals and caring. You had all that with Mother; he knows that. And

165

he's in shock, Chrissa; the man has lost his sight, perhaps – I'm sorry – for good. Maybe he wants to be alone to come to terms with that. Or he's giving you the chance to walk away. That would be noble of him, wouldn't it?' The words were plausible, the ideas behind them possible. Beneath her hands, she felt Chrissa's shoulders lose some of their tension. 'You know what Mama would have said. Patience. Courage and patience. If you like, I'll go and see him, find out what I can. I could go over to the hospital before work.'

Chrissa lifted her head, and smiled up at Noula.

'Would you?' she said. 'Will you go tomorrow?'

'Maybe not tomorrow,' said Noula carefully. 'I've a lot to do, tomorrow. But I'll go as soon as I can.'

'Promise?'

'Promise. As soon as I have time, I'll go.'

Eighteen

Behind the woman mailing the parcel to Australia, a queue was forming. As she searched through every compartment of her purse for cash to pay the postmaster, a man covered in plaster dust tapped the toe of a paint-spattered work boot, and scowled with impatience; an elderly man laid down his shopping – a few fresh young squid tied tight in a carrier bag, half a dozen lemons, a bottle of hair oil from the pharmacy – to mark his place in the queue, and shuffled to the chair beneath the window.

The fat man stood behind the old man's shopping. The workman turned and looked him up and down, then turned away, still scowling. The postmaster lit a fresh cigarette from the one alight in his mouth, and grinding out its short stub in his ashtray, inhaled on the fresh cigarette with obvious pleasure, like a man taking a cold drink of water after days lost in the desert. The air was blue with smoke; seated on his chair, the old man coughed.

'It wasn't that much last time,' complained the woman. 'Has it gone up?'

The postmaster sighed.

'The rate's the same, but your parcel's weight's gone up,' he said. 'The more it weighs, the more you pay.'

'It'll be those newspapers I slipped in at the last minute, to stop the biscuits breaking,' she said. 'My sister likes to read the local news.'

'It'll be the biscuits,' said the postmaster. 'You're sending half the bakery's stock, I'll bet. Don't they have biscuits in Australia?'

'Not like these. She says they don't taste the same, over there. I told her last time, it'd be cheaper for her to come and eat them here. It's no good. I haven't got enough.' She zipped her purse, and pushed her parcel a little way along the counter. 'I'll leave this here until I've been to the bank.'

The fat man waited patiently for his turn. The builder concluded his business quickly; the old man bought a few stamps and chewed the fat with the postmaster. But as the fat man at last stepped up to the counter, the woman returned, holding up a 5,000-drachma note. Standing beside the fat man at the counter, she leaned across him to reach her parcel, and pulling it towards her, addressed the postmaster as if the fat man wasn't there.

'Here you are, Apostolis,' she said, offering the banknote to the postmaster. 'This will cover it.'

The fat man turned to face her.

'Excuse me, *kyria*,' he said, 'but I think you'll find it's my turn to be served.'

As if he had appeared out of thin air, she looked at him.

'I was here before,' she said. She turned away from him, back to the postmaster. 'Can you change this, Apostolis?'

The postmaster put out his hand to take the note, but the fat man spoke again.

'My business will take only a moment,' he said, 'so you won't have long to wait. Postmaster, would you please check if there is any mail for me?'

A half-burned cigarette hung from the corner of the postmaster's mouth. He gave the fat man a slow, malicious smile.

'I'll be with you very shortly,' he said, 'when I'm finished with this lady.'

For a few moments, the fat man's expression was impassive; but it changed then to one of curiosity, and he leaned forward, peering at a corner of the woman's parcel, where the paper wrapping was changing from buff to coffee-brown as liquid spread across the parcel's base. As the postmaster took the woman's money, the fat man bent closer to the parcel and sniffed.

'Forgive me, *kyria*,' he said, 'but can you smell vinegar?'

As he spoke, the sharp smell reached her nose, and she, too, sniffed.

'Vinegar.' She said the word as confirmation; but then she noticed the condition of her parcel, where the stain was increasing in size.

'My parcel!' She span the parcel round; on its far side, the damage was worse. A wet patch was developing on the counter, and the smell of vinegar overwhelmed even the smoke of cigarettes. 'It's the capers! Everything will be ruined! And I took such care, packing it!'

The postmaster handed back her banknote.

'Perhaps the jar lid came loose,' said the fat man, helpfully. 'Or maybe the jar is cracked. You'll find out, no doubt, when you re-pack it. So, if your business is concluded for the time being … Postmaster, perhaps you have time now to deal with me. I'm expecting some correspondence, addressed to me here, *poste restante*. I think you'll find it there.'

The postmaster turned to the pigeonholes, where, amongst the old and dusty letters that would never now find their addressees, a large white envelope had appeared. With deliberate slowness, the postmaster checked the address.

'Hermes Diaktoros, *poste restante*,' he said. 'Postmark Athens.' This last he said without reference to the envelope, and the fat man knew he'd studied it already.

Holding the dripping parcel away from her clothes, the woman reached the door and stood waiting for assistance in opening it. The fat man took no notice; turning his envelope over, he inspected the seal closely, testing the strength of the glue on the flap to see if it had been opened.

'Must be important, if they've sent it on here,' said the postmaster, eyes alight with curiosity.

'It relates to Dr Chabrol,' said the fat man. He tucked the envelope beneath his arm; the postmaster stubbed out his cigarette.

'So are you getting to the bottom of our mystery?' he asked.

'Oh yes,' said the fat man. 'I reached that point some time ago.'

'So aren't you going to tell us? Surely you're not going to keep us in the dark?'

'It would be easy to shed light on the mystery for yourself,' said the fat man, 'if you knew which stones to look under. *Kali mera sas.*'

At the door he seemed to relent and held it open for the woman, whose face was now as sour as her vinegared parcel. But on the threshold, he paused to watch the preparations for the minister's visit: men up ladders were hanging bunting, more were tipping barrows of tarmac on to filled-in holes, others were collecting rubbish in plastic sacks.

The fat man turned back to the postmaster.

'The town looks at its best, doesn't it?' he said. 'You must all be very proud, and looking forward, no doubt, to the minister's visit tomorrow.'

The postmaster chose a cigarette from an open packet.

'Oh, I'm looking forward to it, very much indeed,' he said. 'You have no idea how much I'm looking forward to it.'

The fat man crossed the square, and took a seat at Evangelia's *kafenion*. Opening the white envelope, he withdrew from it several photocopied sheets – copies of the documents Noula had taken from the doctor's suitcase. To each sheet, a second sheet, typed in Greek, was stapled, and securing all together was a paper clip.

There was, too, a postcard of a dark-haired girl dressed in a bikini, with waves breaking on a beach behind her.

He turned the postcard over. The few words on the back were in a curling, feminine hand.

'Translations enclosed. Good luck,' they said.

There was a signature, impossible to read; but the kiss which followed it was very clear indeed.

Nineteen

With no easy alternative available, the fat man ate another of Evangelia's meals. She boiled him an octopus (the steam from the saucepan filled the *kafenion* all afternoon, clouding the windows like fog) and served it cut in pieces, dressed in cheap oil, sour vinegar and a sprinkling of shop-bought oregano. There was a plate of pale chips, undercooked and cold; the bread brought in a basket was stale, from yesterday.

At his own request, he ate early.

'I'm a bit of a naturalist,' he said, dipping bread in the octopus's juices to soften it, 'and sometimes I like to be out very early in the morning, birdwatching and such; so if you could let me have a key, I'll let myself out and in, and have no need to disturb your beauty sleep.'

She showed him the workings of the latches and the key, then sat down at his table with her chin resting on her fist, and watched him eat.

'Why aren't you married, *kalé*?' she asked. 'An attractive man like you, well dressed, nice manners ...'

'I might ask you the same question,' he said. 'A woman like you, your own business – they should be forming a queue.'

She gave a sigh which lifted her huge breasts, and folded her arms beneath them.

'I never found the right man,' she said. 'There were plenty who spent time with me, but when the time came, they all married someone else. They toyed with my affections, *kyrie*; they used me as a plaything. I was used, and tossed aside, and now I'm all washed up.'

'Really?' said the fat man. He took a chip from those left on his plate; its taste was of raw potato and burnt oil. 'A little bird told me you have a suitor: a certain doctor, maybe?'

'Oh yes,' she said, 'there's him. But he's old, and old men are short on vigour. I always thought I'd like a younger man.' She leaned towards him, studying his face for lines which would give clues to his age. 'How old are you, *kyrie*? I'd put you no older than fifty.'

'I'm older than I look,' said the fat man quickly. 'Besides, you should be very sure, before you go rushing in, that you want a man at all. From where I sit, you're well off as you are. You've the company of men throughout the day, and at night you send them packing to their wives. Men aren't such a desirable species, when you look at it. They might start out so, but marriage has a strange effect on them. It makes them fat, and bald, and short-tempered. They belch and snore and eye up pretty girls. You're better off without, believe me. Too many women trade their freedom for bad bargains. So if the doctor asks you to make it legal, take my advice, and turn him down.'

'Turn down a medical man! Chance would be a fine thing!'

'The choice is yours, of course,' said the fat man, suppressing a grimace as he swallowed the last of his chips. 'But a medical man is no better than any other. You can take my word for that.'

At the very first lightening of the sky, the fat man rose from his hard bed. The muscles in his back and shoulders were tight, as if bruised by the unyielding bed-springs. Barefoot, he stood on the faded *kilim*, and, arms bent, pulled his shoulders back to stretch his chest; then, placing his hands on his hips, he twisted at the waist to right and left, and bent forwards and backwards, until he felt the tension in his muscles ease and his body felt loosened and limber. Bending forward, he touched his toes quite easily, and pleased with himself, he smiled.

He took off the pyjamas he had slept in to reveal a body that was admirable for his age. His skin was tanned to golden, as if he had recently spent time lying in the sun; but in the hair which spread generously over his chest, grey was more prominent than black.

From his holdall, he took out a T-shirt and athletic socks in white, and a navy blue tracksuit whose sleeves and legs were piped silver on the outside seams; as he zipped up the jacket, he smoothed out the logo of a half-risen sun on the left breast. Over the socks, he pulled on his pristine tennis shoes and laced them tightly; and making his way silently down the uncarpeted stairs, stepping over the treads that creaked, he crossed the *kafenion* to the doorway and opened it as Evangelia had shown him.

He took the road at a fast pace. The sky was heavily overcast, and there was scant light, as yet, in the dawn. As he ran through the streets, his feet made little noise, his breathing was unlaboured. No lights shone in the houses and there was no traffic on the road; only the startled cats foraging in the public dumpsters saw him pass.

He followed the road beyond the sign which marked the town's limit, to the loop in the carriageway where the garage stood. As he drew level with the mechanic's house, he stopped. For several minutes, he watched and listened, but there was no sign of movement from within. Across the forecourt was the workshop, all in darkness.

Silently, he ran across the grass verge to the petrol pumps. Remembering the filthy ground between the hard standing and the workshop, he glanced down at his shoes and grimaced; but every minute, the sky was growing lighter and his time shorter.

Moving swiftly, he crossed to the workshop door, pressing himself close against the building to hide himself from the house. The door was padlocked. In the weak light, he bent down to search for a tool around his feet, and found amongst the scattered rubbish a length of rusting hacksaw blade. With finger and thumb, he plucked it from the oily dirt and inserted its end into the padlock's keyhole; and with a practised twist and a little manoeuvring, he snapped the padlock open.

He gave a small smile of satisfaction and turned the hacksaw blade in his hand, admiring its efficiency for the job; then he laid it back on the ground, making sure to fit it into the depression from which he'd taken it.

Hanging the padlock through the hasp, he lifted the latch and opened the workshop door just wide enough to slip through.

He pulled the door closed behind him. Inside, the workshop was dark, and for a full minute the fat man peered into the gloom, waiting for his eyes to reach their optimum usefulness. As they did so, he began to see the layout of the place. The long, barn-like building stretched before him, lit faintly by cobweb-covered skylights. Above him, something moved, and startled, he prepared to hide himself; but the movement was the fluttering of sparrows, nesting in the joints of the roof supports.

A length of cable ran by his feet. Following it to its end, he found it attached to the mechanic's lamp – a high-wattage light bulb, encased in a metal cage to prevent breakage. Picking up the lamp, the fat man considered: using the lamp would speed up his task, but any early riser would notice it shining through the skylights.

He decided to take the risk. Lamp in hand, he tracked the cable back to the wall and a set of electrical sockets over a workbench. He flipped the switch and the lamp was lit.

The workbench where he stood was covered with tools, paints and spares in disarray. A radio with one knob missing was playing very low; a plate with uneaten food might have been there several days. On the floor were rags, newspapers and tyres; at the bench-end, a drum was overflowing with viscous, tar-black oil.

Overhead, the sparrows fluttered from beam to beam. The fat man made his way to the back of the workshop, where the chaotic spread of rubbish grew thinner and it was easier to find clean places to put his feet. Against the back wall was a sideboard with the generous proportions of the 1930s; a utility piece rather than a craftsman's, it had doors on either side and three drawers at the centre. Its top was in use as storage, for cans of house paint, paintbrushes left to fester in preserve jars of white spirit, and roughly folded blankets used as dust sheets.

The fat man opened the top drawer first, tugging it hard because the wood had swollen from damp. But that tightness had sealed the contents and protected them. The drawer was filled with photographs, both black and white and colour, loose and mounted in cardboard frames. Taking out a handful, he sifted through them, finding them to be more extraordinary recordings of that life now gone. The second drawer held cutlery and kitchen implements, the third table linen, all hand-embroidered and pressed.

Opening the right-hand sideboard door, he found supplies for framing – lengths of wood and dowelling, sheets of glass in various sizes, backing card and glue. In the left-hand cupboard were two boxes, one on the upper shelf, one on the lower. Both boxes held chemicals for developing film, in antique-looking bottles of brown and clear glass. Pulling a box towards himself, he lifted out a bottle and read the label, then chose another, and another. He tried the lid of one, but the contents had crystallised around the neck, forming a seal which had not been broken in years.

But it was the largest bottle which most interested him. Taking it from the box, he read its label and, frowning and with great care, twisted the black lid off the brown glass. The lid moved easily, as if opened only yesterday. He glanced inside, at the powdery white crystals; the bottle was two-thirds empty. Returning it to the box, he pushed the box back into its place and closed the sideboard cupboard.

The skylights overhead showed growing daylight. Moving quickly back to the wall switches, he turned off the lamp and put it back carefully where he had found it. He slipped out through the workshop door and snapped the padlock back in place.

At the house, there was still no sign of life, but the fat man took no further risks. Screened by the workshop, he climbed the fence into the field on its lower side, and crossed it at a jog. At the field's far side, he rejoined the road and ran at a leisurely pace back to the square.

Twenty

The fat man returned to his room, hoping for another hour of sleep, but it was the day of the minister's expected visit, and soon after the fat man climbed back into bed, the mayor's task force arrived in the square.

Their first job was to rig the sound system through which the dignitaries' speeches would be broadcast. Two of the men were designated to haul the noisy diesel generator into its position behind the post office; the others rolled out great lengths of wiring off enormous wooden reels. The workman tying the loudspeakers in the plane trees blew on his hands to warm them, and damned his own lack of competence as his cold fingers struggled to knot the string. Four surly, sleepy youths were made to put out chairs; they cursed the electrician, who, when he finally arrived to install the microphones beside the fountain, pointed out that the youths had laid out all two hundred chairs facing the wrong way.

As the morning went on, young children ran excitedly amongst the rows of seats and knocked them out of line. When the sound system was fully operational, a member of the council – in consultation with the youths, the electrician and the street-sweeper – set up a broadcast of martial music. The music was tinny and distorted (and, in one corner of the square where the speaker had slipped off its branch, inaudible) but its mood was appropriate: upbeat and celebratory, it invoked civic and national pride, so the women laughed and chattered on their way to the bakery, and the men took seats at the *kafenion* and watched, critical and relaxed, as others worked.

Hot-faced and flustered, Evangelia brought coffee after coffee from the kitchen, whilst Adonis Anapodos did his best to clear the empty cups and glasses, dodging the flats of hands and spiteful, pinching fingers of men who judged him, being not quite normal, as fair game. A *souvlaki* vendor parked his van outside the pharmacy; whilst his grill and deep-fat fryer were heating up, he strung bags of candyfloss around the serving hatch, so the children all ran home, clamouring for money. An outside broadcast unit arrived from the area's TV station, with technicians who erected an aerial so high it knocked the branches of the plane trees; the people passing craned their necks to spot any famous faces, and rumours flew that the reader of the evening news was here, in Morfi.

The square was filling with expectant, smiling people, and many of the chairs in front of the microphone were already taken. At the *kafenion*, however, the fat man noticed that four faces were missing from the crowd: of Dr Dinos, the pharmacist, the postmaster and the grocer, there was no sign.

Adonis brought him Greek coffee and an ashtray, but the fat man had no cigarettes.

'Adonis,' he said, 'would you like to earn yourself a tip?'

Adonis smiled and nodded, but looked nervously behind him, in case Evangelia should accuse him of slacking.

'Take this empty box to the *periptero*, and ask if they have any of my brand,' said the fat man. 'Tell them to look carefully. They're bound to have a box or two in stock.'

Adonis looked doubtfully at the cigarette box's lid, admiring the picture of the starlet.

'She's pretty,' he said, 'but I don't think they'll have these, *kyrie*. I've never seen a box like this before, and I fetch a lot of cigarettes for a lot of men.'

'Try,' said the fat man. 'Try, and if you persuade them that they have them, you'll have a special tip, from me.'

Adonis ambled away; the fat man tasted his coffee. In the rush to serve so many, Evangelia had been generous with her spooning, and made an excellent cup.

A little breathless, Adonis returned, and placed two boxes of cigarettes by the ashtray, along with change.

'They said they didn't have them,' he said proudly, 'but I made them look again, and then they did.'

'*Bravo sou*,' said the fat man. 'Now, here's your tip. Have you ever played the lottery, Adonis?'

Adonis shook his head.

'I've wanted to,' he said, 'but my mother says the lottery's for fools.'

'Fools or not, it's a game for optimists,' said the fat man. He pulled out of his pocket the two tickets he had bought in town. 'Either of these might be a winner, or neither might be. Take your pick.'

Adonis chose the ticket on the left.

'Do you feel that's a winner?' asked the fat man, and Adonis nodded. 'Then the trick is, be optimistic. If you know that it's a winner, then it is.'

The fat man took one of the side streets from the square, and when he reached the promenade, followed it in the direction of the port. The promenade was decorated with blue and white bunting strung between the lamp-posts, but the task force had brought insufficient cable to wire speakers along the road, and as his distance from the square grew, the music of marching bands faded away. By the steps down to the beach, a police car waited, its blue roof lights pulsing; two policemen leaned on the car's side, smoking and watching the fat man with suspicion as he passed.

At the port were more police cars, their officers inside, out of the wind. Close to the dock was the minibus the mayor had borrowed for the occasion. Its windows gleamed with polishing, its paintwork was washed and waxed; the flaking rust around its wheel arches was hidden by daubs of gloss paint so recently applied, its smell was in the air. Beside his minibus, the driver stood in his borrowed suit, his hair slicked down with oil and his face pink and nicked from the hasty shaving of several days' stubble.

And with the driver stood four men, who, amongst all the cheerful townsfolk, smiled wider, spoke louder and laughed more heartily than any other; they peered together in apparent anticipation towards the sea's horizon, from where the Athens ferry carrying the minister would appear.

At the heart of a group of his supporters – his mother, wife and children, the street-sweeper, a troop of high-school pupils smart in uniforms they never normally wore – the mayor waited with his council at the dockside. The councillors (the women, especially) were overdressed and nervous; the mayor himself betrayed some signs of agitation but looked handsome and comfortable in his suit. A reporter from the local newspaper touched his arm and drew him to one side to interview him; the mayor answered the questions put to him with confidence, becoming passionate about his plans for the town, whilst the uninterested reporter wrote down everything he said in a laborious shorthand. Behind the police cars, the band held their instruments in their laps, the cases stored beneath their summer chairs; the leader of the band (a middle-aged man, renowned for his bad temper) glanced at his watch repeatedly, stealing frequent nips from the brandy flask inside his jacket.

Then across the water came the blast of a foghorn, and the bulk of the ferry came into sight.

The fat man made his way towards Dr Dinos and his friends, who were sharing another joke with the minibus driver. As he approached them, a gull flew low overhead, startling the men with its sudden cry. A skinny dog sniffed at the fat man's heels, and slunk away to cock its leg on a police car's tyre.

The fat man glanced up at the overcast sky, where dark, rain-laden clouds were moving in. As he joined them, the men offered no welcome or greeting. The postmaster took the end of a cigarette from his mouth, and spat on the ground.

The fat man's expression showed concern.

'Gentlemen, *kali mera*,' he said. 'You'll no doubt be sharing my anxiety that all the mayor's hard work and preparations for today will be marred by bad weather.'

The muscles in the men's faces grew tight as they repressed smiles; the postmaster's moustache twitched. The grocer was standing close to the pharmacist; with a subtle movement of his elbow, he gave the pharmacist the lightest touch of a nudge.

It seemed none of them was inclined to reply; but then Dr Dinos straightened his shoulders, and said, 'I don't think, *kyrie*, that anything could spoil the satisfaction this day will bring us, not even if it rained from now till doomsday.'

'I have just come from the square,' said the fat man, 'and the air of pride and celebration is quite extraordinary. It would be a huge disappointment to so many if anything were to spoil it. No, not a disappointment, but a crime. Do you not agree, it would be a crime?'

The minibus driver was a lanky youth, whose borrowed trousers were too short to cover his white-socked feet. He stuck his forefinger into his mouth to wet it and held it up to the breeze.

'South-westerly,' he said. 'We'll be all right. The sea'll take the rain and we'll stay dry.'

Dr Dinos smiled, and laid a hand on the young man's back. 'Well said, Socratis,' he said, turning to the fat man. 'This lad is better than any forecaster you'll see on television. He's never wrong, are you, Socratis? But my own forecast is, that we shall have a very interesting day, regardless of the weather.'

The ferry was drawing closer. On the quayside, men stepped forward to be ready with the mooring ropes; the port police officers – splendid in full-dress, white uniforms – stood officious and unhelpful beside them, whilst the senior officer removed his cap and smoothed his perfect, close-cut hair one last time. The mayor shook hands with the reporter and moved with his party closer to the dock, where the council formed an official line of welcome.

'He's a splendid young man, isn't he?' said the fat man, looking across at the mayor. 'I have a feeling he'll go far in political life. He's a man of vision, a man who gets things done. It's quite a coup he's pulled off here, to get such a senior man from Athens to this small place. One wonders how he managed to persuade the minister.'

'The gift of oratory, no doubt,' said Dr Dinos, turning his face away. 'He talks a good story.'

The grocer allowed a smile to cross his face; the postmaster ground out his cigarette under his shoe, and reached into his pocket for another. At the quayside, the newsmen were moving in close to get good pictures.

'Often too little is done to nurture talent, don't you agree?' went on the fat man. 'And often, people put obstacles in talent's way. It is one of humanity's most common failings, that men cannot bear to see other men succeed. In my work, I see examples of it almost daily.'

But Dr Dinos and his friends did not hear him; their attention was on the huge ferry which, gracefully and improbably, was executing a mid-harbour turn to approach the quayside stern-on.

The mayor's party and the port police pulled down their jackets and set their feet apart like the military; the newsmen had their cameras at the ready. With the minister's arrival now so imminent, even the policemen climbed from their cars and looked expectantly towards the dock.

'This minister, Mr Semertzakis,' said the fat man. 'I'm not certain I shall recognise him when I see him. He's not one of those who's often in the media, is he? Perhaps he will appreciate this opportunity to get his face known. Do you know, postmaster, what he looks like? Fat, thin, short, tall, what?'

The postmaster's expression was of innocence.

'I've really no idea,' he said. 'As you say, a man who works away in the background. We shall no doubt find out, in a few moments.'

'Indeed,' said the fat man. 'Well, if you gentlemen will excuse me, I shall move a little closer. I want to be sure I have the best possible view, when the show begins.'

Dr Dinos smiled.

'Do you know, I think we'll join you,' he said.

On board the ferry, the crewmen secured the ropes and hauled the boat's stern up to the quay. The ramp descended, and in curiosity the small crowd on the harbourside strained forward. At the moment it touched the ground, the port police officers jumped on to the ramp, and took up the 'at ease' position down each side, as their senior officer had instructed them.

The ferry's interior was smoky, dark and dirty, sulphurous with exhaust fumes from disembarking vehicles, and echoing with the throbbing of their engines. Behind the shouting crewmen, nothing could be seen. The foot passengers waiting to board stepped up to the ramp, but were held back by the outstretched arms of the port police, who ordered them imperiously to wait.

No disembarking passengers were visible. The first of the arriving vehicles – a truck laden with German beer – edged forward.

The mayor looked anxiously at his fellow councillors. The newsmen turned whispering to each other.

The beer truck moved cautiously towards the ramp; a crewman stepped in front of it and waved the driver on; and Dr Dinos, the pharmacist, the postmaster and the grocer all smiled.

Then, from the rear of the deck, a shout went up. A second crewman ran in front of the beer lorry, and raised both hands.

'Wait a minute, *vre*!' he shouted. 'Wait a minute!'

The truck driver pulled up short, banging his fists on the steering wheel and tapping on the face of his watch; the bottles in their wooden crates rattled like a shiver of fury.

From amongst the smoking vehicles, a man stepped out of the shadows. Slender and elegantly suited, grey-haired and distinguished, with an air of lifelong privilege, he was as handsome as the maturer stars of Hollywood. Walking into the deck space between truck and ramp with the assurance of an actor used to an audience, he ran his eyes with interest and a little amusement over the people gathered on the quayside, then raised his well-defined chin and ran the knot of his silk tie more perfectly into the collar of his shirt.

For a moment, no one moved. Behind him, a young girl in a navy-blue suit appeared, hair pulled back in a pleat and glasses concealing real beauty, high heels on tiny feet, and beneath one arm, a very full leather briefcase; she was followed by a short man, whose suit fitted him so well it hid a well-fed belly, and whose nervous eyes seemed to look everywhere for trouble.

The girl stood at the handsome man's right shoulder, the short man at his left. The handsome man's eyes came to rest on the mayor, who hesitantly took a step forward, and the man strode towards him, hand outstretched and smiling to reveal enviable teeth.

Cameras flashed. They met at the foot of the ramp, and joined hands in a handshake.

'Mayor Petridis?' asked the man. His accent was beautifully clear, his words carefully enunciated in the perfect Greek of TV newscasters.

'Minister,' said the mayor. His colour was high, but he was broadly smiling. 'Thank you so much for coming.'

The newsmen were calling for pictures, and with practised ease, the minister turned the mayor to face them, holding his hand in a faux-handshake until the newsmen were done. Then the mayor, pink with delight, led him to the blushing councillors, where he introduced them at some length, one by one.

And the fat man, himself smiling, turned to Dr Dinos and his friends. They stood apart and silent, watching the mayor escort his minister and his party to the waiting minibus.

The minibus sped away, towards the speechmaking in the square. The fat man took his time on his way there, diverting by way of the beach, walking at the water's edge, stopping from time to time to pick up an object of interest – a pebble with unusual markings, a piece of driftwood, a foreign bottle cap.

By the time he reached the square, the speeches were coming to an end. He bought a *souvlaki* from the vendor, and found himself a seat on a low wall with a view of a merry-go-round, where little children sat, bewildered or delighted, in spinning cars and motorbikes. The *souvlaki* was first class: the pork was tasty from the smoking charcoal, crisp outside but succulent; the onions were sweet but with a pleasing heat; the *tzatziki* was boldly flavoured with garlic; the pitta bread was warm and satisfyingly doughy to chew. He finished the *souvlaki* and sipped the tumbler of cold retsina the vendor had given him as a gift; then he was hungry for something sweet, and bought a plate of *loukoumades* – doughnut balls hot from the frying oil, sticky with honey syrup and generously sprinkled with cinnamon.

The mayoral party finished their speeches, and turning off the microphone, made their way towards the town hall, followed by a small group of invited citizens, whilst those uninvited made their way to the amusements. For a while, the fat man browsed the offerings of the gypsy hawkers, who spread blankets on the ground to display their tat: transistor radios with no reception; sharp-edged, wind-up toys the children begged for; tools – pliers, mallets, wrenches – picked up in job lots; cheap paintings of views these people would never see – the Alps, the rivers of China, the boulevards of Paris.

The band took up their instruments and began a familiar song, whose notes of yearning and longing spoke to all their souls, and immediately the women – matrons, young wives, grandmothers – got to their feet to join the dance, whilst the men passed the bottles round. The TV crew and newspaper men had their equipment packed away and were ready to leave; but the music called to them, too, and, talking amongst themselves, they decided they might stay just a while – what was the point in rushing back? – and helped themselves to wine.

At Evangelia's *kafenion*, all the tables were taken by men out-buying each other whisky, and the only seat available was with two fishermen still bloodstained, fresh from the sea; but as the fat man was about to ask if he might join them, someone touched his elbow.

The fat man turned, and found the short man who had arrived with the minister at his side. The short man looked suspiciously about them, as if his whole life was troubled by eavesdroppers and spies.

'A word, *kyrie*, if I may,' he said. He drew the fat man away from the crowd, so no one would overhear. 'A message from the minister. He asks me to pass on his regrets that he is not able to invite you to lunch, but the room, he says, is small, and the dignitaries many. But I am to tell you that the food looks excellent: in his words – which he asks me to repeat to you ...' a smile came to his lips '... a veritable country banquet.'

The fat man laughed, and clapped the short man on the back.

'Thank you, Arsenios, for playing messenger,' he said. 'I suspected there'd be a good meal in it. And tell my cousin he's filled the minister's shoes extremely well. Perhaps he should consider a career in politics, some day. But then, perhaps not: he's bored too easily, and would never sit through all those dull debates. Tell him to enjoy his banquet and his moment of celebrity; I've eaten well already. And tell him his precious car's been temperamental, but I've managed to get it fixed. The repair bills are on me, since he's doing me this favour. Now go, and enjoy your lunch.'

Giving a small bow of the head, Arsenios left him. At the *kafenion*, the odiferous fishermen had ordered brandy, and made the fat man welcome. The fat man asked for coffee and an ouzo, and waiting for his drinks, looked out across the crowd filling the square. For some time, he searched amongst the faces; but of the four men who had conspired against the mayor, there was no sign.

Twenty-one

The hour was late, far past the acceptable hours for visitors. At the hospital's upper windows, the lights were dimmed, and blended with the warm glow of night lights lit as comfort for the sleepless through their worry or their pain. In the lobby, the reception desk was deserted. Along the corridor, the TV in the nurses' room was turned up loud (on a game show, an unlucky contestant was being bid goodnight), and from there came the rustle of food wrapping – biscuits, or chocolate – and a female voice pressing treats on another – *Take two, kalé – here, have another.* The woman who answered had her mouth full – *She was unlucky, there,* she said, in a voice which held a sad shake of the head, as if she identified closely with the game show contestant's lack of fortune.

The fat man knew where he was going, and moving silently in his newly whitened shoes, crossed the lobby's polished lino and went up the stairs. At the ward entrance, he pushed the swing door open just wide enough to slip through, but the door squeaked on its hinges. He guided the door shut carefully, so it made no further noise.

The ward was quiet. At the far end, at the nurse's station, an anglepoise lamp burned, lighting folders of patient records, some thick with papers from long treatment, some holding just a sheet or two of notes. Inside the doorway was a tall cabinet, and the fat man slipped around its side, hiding himself. The doors to all the patients' rooms were closed, though not all their occupants slept: in one, a radio played Beethoven, in another, someone was running water into a glass.

The hands of the clock on the wall moved on, two minutes, then three, until the fat man was certain all was safe; only then did he move silently down the corridor, to the door marked 112, where he quietly turned the handle and let himself in without knocking, closing the door behind him with a click.

He stood with his back to the door, and placed his holdall between his feet. Soft light revealed the doctor in his bed, but he did not have the relaxed limbs of a sleeper; he lay on his back, his arms at his sides, his eyes still covered in bandages. The room smelled antiseptic, of sterile lint and iodine; the jug of water and the glass on his bedside table were empty. Through the open slats of the window blinds, a full moon shone silver in a black sky; below the window, amongst the dumpsters, fighting cats yowled.

'Who's there?'

The doctor's voice was anxious. The fat man didn't answer him immediately, but stood quite still before the door.

The doctor asked again, 'Is someone there?'

Still the fat man didn't answer, and slowly the doctor relaxed. The fat man crossed silently to the window, where he separated two slats of the Venetian blind with his fingers, and looked down on the fighting cats below.

At the sound of the slats bending, the doctor started.

'Who's there?' he demanded; the anxiety in his voice was pronounced. 'Answer me, for God's sake – I know someone's there!'

The fat man turned from the window and moved close to the bed. Smiling as he bent down to the doctor's ear, he whispered, 'It's me.'

The doctor gave a small scream.

'What do you want?' he asked, in real fear.

Straightening up, the fat man laughed.

'You remember me, Louis,' he said. 'We met before. We had a chat about investigations, or lack of them.'

'For God's sake,' said the doctor, angrily. 'What the hell are you playing at? You frightened me half to death. I'm a sick man. And what are you doing here, at this time, so late? It's the middle of the night.'

'Is it?' asked the fat man, teasingly. 'How do you know? On what do you base your assumption? Is it the middle of the night, or is dawn breaking – how can you tell? Am I late, or am I early? Or am I, in fact, just about on time? Do you mind if I sit?' Without waiting for a reply, he picked up a chair and placed it by the head of the bed, and leaning back in it, examined his nails as he spoke. 'I do hate to be late, but from time to time it's unavoidable. In your case, I managed to be slightly early. But, late or early, I'm here, and that's what counts.'

Below the bandages, the doctor's mouth was set in a frown.

'What the hell are you talking about?' he asked bad-temperedly. 'Are you demented? Be good enough to leave me in peace – and as you go, you might call the nurse for me. These sleeping tablets aren't working, and the pain is getting worse. Go now, or I'll call the nurse myself.'

'You may call the nurse if you wish to,' said the fat man, 'and I'm sure you're capable of shouting the place down, if you put your mind to it. But I must say, I find your attitude to me a little bewildering. I remember telling you I was making it my business to find out who assaulted you, so your having no wish to speak to me is somewhat baffling. I expected to find you all eager curiosity.'

'I was sleeping,' said the doctor, 'and you frightened me out of my wits. I suppose that tempers a welcome, somewhat.'

'Then I expect your welcome will grow warmer when you find out I have news.'

'News? What news?'

'I have brought something with me,' he said, 'which I think goes a long, long way towards solving this mystery. Just excuse me, one moment.'

He rose, and went to his holdall at the door. Unzipping it, he withdrew the white envelope he had collected from the post office. Re-taking his seat, he opened the envelope and took out the stapled sheets it contained.

'You can't see these, of course,' he said, 'but I know you've seen them before. I had them translated from your native language.' The papers rustled as the fat man scanned the sheets; at the sound, the doctor tensed. 'The heading is – the coat of arms is very smart indeed, by the way, most distinguished and attractive – the heading is "The National Medical Council of France", and it's addressed, I believe – yes, here it is – to your good self.'

'You've been through my personal belongings!' objected the doctor. 'It's an outrage! How dare you, without a warrant!'

'I, go through your things?' laughed the fat man. 'Indeed I have not. I came by your papers almost honestly, without having to resort to anything as sordid as riffling through your belongings. And warrants are a tool used by the constabulary, never by me. What I have in my hands are not your originals anyway, but Greek translations. Has your fiancée seen these papers, by the way? With them in the original French, I suppose you were quite safe. But it would certainly be unfortunate, would it not, if she set her eyes on these translations?'

193

The doctor was silent, so the fat man went on.

'When I first interested myself in this crime, I thought it rather crude. It seemed most likely, on the face of it, to be a crime of passion. I was thinking of jealousy, in fact. But this was not a crime of jealousy; in fact I am not persuaded that it is, in any sense of justice, a crime at all. What we are looking at here – metaphorically, of course, in your case – is revenge. And I think you knew that all along, didn't you – you suspected it, or at least you knew of the possibility. As I suspected it when you so vehemently objected to any police involvement. Someone came after you for what you had done. And the punishment they chose for you is, to me, a perfect fit, a punishment that truly fits *your* crime.' He held up the papers and wafted them to make a noise the doctor could hear. 'It's all here, isn't it? The court papers, the medical council's decision. Here's the reason you didn't take the doctor's job officially, didn't draw the salary – because you were struck off. You were never to practise medicine again. And I'm sure your face was known in your home country. Better to come here, and re-establish yourself in a practice where no one knew your name. Get yourself married and establish your legal right to be here. And then, of course, you did what you had done again.'

'I have no idea what you mean.'

'I know that you do. But you won't be doing it again now, will you? Striking you blind was an act of pure genius. I might even have thought of it myself. Even so, I accept this kind of judicial anarchy is not ideal. I shall speak to your attacker, of course, but I shall offer my protection from official prosecution.'

'You know who did this.'

'Yes, I do. And I think you do, too. When you told me you didn't know who brought you the note that morning,

I think you lied, because I think you understand, now, the connection between them and this attack. But I shan't be spelling it out for you or anyone else, because I think the attacker's motive – their desire for revenge on you – was entirely justified. And you have years ahead of you to decide whether or not you agree.'

Outside in the corridor, the nurse's station was still unoccupied. Leafing quickly through the patient files, the fat man found the one labelled 'Chabrol, Louis', and slipped the documents he had brought with him inside, taking care they were on top of the other paperwork and would be seen immediately the file was opened.

There was a spring in his step as he descended the stairs and made his way past the reception desk and into the street. The night was filled with moonlight and still young enough for the town's entertainments to be explored; and as he set off to find a restaurant where the cook knew how to cook, the fat man was cheerfully humming.

Twenty-two

Noula set off in good time the next morning, and reaching Platania, parked her car in its usual place on a quiet street at the back of the library. Then, breaking the habit of many years, she passed the *kafenion* where she bought the director's morning coffee, and passed the library's front entrance without climbing the grand steps. Instead, she made her way through a district she rarely visited, heading in the direction of the general hospital.

The businesses in this part of town were late opening. At the cobbler's on Ptolemon Street, a woman still in housecoat and slippers unbolted the shop door, and called with a saucer of tinned pilchards to an absent cat. There was a stationer's Noula knew on Angelaki, where the window hadn't been changed in several years and dead bluebottles lay on the displayed merchandise. At the florist's at the bottom of Angelaki, flowers were being prepared for a wedding, and the florist's girls chattered away excitedly as they tied ribbons around frothy blossoms of baby's breath and white roses.

Opposite the hospital was a French-style café well known for excellent coffee and first-class croissants. Noula walked past the café, and crossed the street to the hospital entrance;

and at his café table, from behind his newspaper the fat man watched her go.

The nurse at the hospital's reception was occupied, thumbing through a cabinet of files whilst a young couple waited impatiently in front of the desk. Glad to be unnoticed, Noula followed the 'All wards' sign up the stairs and then along the corridor to the door she wanted.

The ward was quiet. She made her way down the central aisle, noticing the numbers of the rooms she passed, until she reached the open door of 111. The old man in the bed there was sleeping, his face to the wall; a woman sat at the bedside, knitting a baby's jacket in soft blue wool. The moment she saw Noula, she laid the knitting on her husband's bed and came to the open door.

'Are you lost, *kalé*?' The woman's voice was loud, almost a shout; her husband, suddenly woken, raised his head from the pillow, then, muttering, lowered it back. 'Who are you looking for?'

'I'm just a visitor,' said Noula shortly. 'Please, don't disturb yourself.'

As if Noula hadn't spoken, the woman went on.

'Who are you visiting? This place is like a maze, and they don't put up enough signs. But I know the place like my own home.' She gripped Noula's upper arm and pulled her close. 'I know them all in here, *kalé*, I know them all by name and they know me. They know I'll look after them. Any little thing they need, they know they can ask me. Is it a relative you're visiting?'

Noula was unsure how to answer.

'More of a friend,' she said. Her vagueness sounded like subterfuge.

'I understand, *kalé*, I understand.' The woman touched a finger to her nose to confirm compliance in Noula's

197

conspiracy. 'Tell me his name and I'll point you in the right direction.'

'Chabrol. Dr Louis Chabrol.'

In her delight, the woman's face lit up.

'You're the fiancée!' she said, looking Noula up and down; a slight reduction in the width of her smile told Noula she was not what was expected. 'I told him every day that he should call you. He needs careful nursing, *kori mou*. In the absence of family, I've done what I can, of course, and I don't ask for any repayment, even though I'm out of pocket. I told my husband, it's our Christian duty to do what we can for a man whose family aren't caring for him, regardless of cost. We'll get our reward in heaven, I said. The money from my own purse isn't important. This way, *kalé*, this way. Right next door to us.'

'I'm not his fiancée,' said Noula, but the woman wasn't listening.

'It's time he had a visitor or two. He's had almost no one, except for me. I've done my best by him. In here, here you are; in here. And I'll be here, if you need me. I've made him as comfortable as I can.'

With a hand on Noula's back, she threw open the door of the doctor's room.

'You've a visitor, *yiatre*,' she announced, 'a friend of yours. I've been telling her you needed brightening up. You've been a bit down these past days, haven't you?'

The doctor's room was cold; the open window let in the morning's chill and the noise of passing traffic from the street. The doctor sat in a wheelchair by his bed, his knees covered with a hospital blanket; beneath the blanket, he was dressed as Noula had often seen him, in shirt, sweater and trousers.

But it was only by his clothes she knew him. His eyes were bound in bandages; the skin of his lower face was the raw red of newborns, and greased with ointment. On his chin, the

198

peeling skin formed curls; around his mouth, deep burns were healing as black scabs. Undoubtedly, he had lost weight; his double chin was almost gone and his belly was less plump.

'Didn't I say that we should get you dressed this morning?' the woman shouted at the doctor, as if it was his hearing that was damaged. 'You're ready for your visitor, you see.' She turned to Noula. 'I got him dressed, though he didn't really want to. If you let them lie in bed all day, they get depressed. Though anyone'd be depressed, in his condition. I don't know how you'll cope, the two of you.'

As she left them, the doctor wasn't smiling. He tilted his head back, as if by doing so he could see under his blindfold and identify the visitor in his room.

'Who's there?' he asked.

She hesitated, feeling it wrong to be there.

'It's me,' she said at last. 'It's me, Noula.'

Still he didn't smile.

'Well, come in, Noula, and close the door,' he said. 'And close this window, too, before I die of pneumonia. That woman's mad; she makes my life a misery.'

Noula pushed the door to, and crossed to the window. Close to the doctor, she caught the smells of iodine and sweat.

As she fastened the catch, he said, 'I wasn't expecting you, when she said it was a friend. That's something I'd never have called you: friend.'

She found it disconcerting that, as he spoke to her, his face was turned away, towards the wall.

'I don't know why not,' she said. 'I've always been courteous to you.'

'Courteous, yes. Friendly, no. I suppose you're here on Chrissa's business.'

'Chrissa doesn't know I'm here,' she lied. 'If she knew I'd come, she'd never speak to me again.'

'Would that be a bad thing?'

'What, not speaking to my own sister?'

'You've avoided the question.'

'The question was ridiculous.'

'Why have you come, Noula?' He sighed as he spoke, as though already wearied by her presence.

'Why won't you see her? She has a right to know.'

He gave a bark of humourless laughter, and held out his arms to display himself.

'Look at me! Transformed in a moment, from doctor to lifetime patient! I'm an invalid, Noula!'

'Then let her nurse you.'

'I want no nursing! Nurses are like that damned woman next door! She gets on my nerves so badly, I'd wring her neck if I could get to her.'

'She means well.'

'She means cash. You women can be so naive.'

'You wouldn't feel that way about Chrissa, surely? You were going to marry her.'

'Things have changed. As you can plainly see.'

'But you'll be better in time, surely. Chrissa said there are things they can do.'

'In my case, nothing.'

'But won't you just talk to her?'

'Why are you here, Noula, pleading her case? I'm not such a fool that I don't know you'd be glad to see the back of me. Yet here you are, on your sister's business, confirming my place in the family bosom.'

The silence between them grew long.

'Noula? Are you still there?'

'I'm here,' she said. 'I'm here, for her sake. Because whether I like you or loathe you, she wants to be your wife. And I want her – I don't want her to be unhappy. So I'll tell her she can come and see you, shall I? That's what she wants. And don't trouble yourself about whether she'll leave you high and dry. She wants to be married; and when all's said and done, you're still a doctor, aren't you?'

She was going to say more; but loud in the corridor they heard the fast, heavy footsteps of several men.

Outside the doctor's door, a voice asked, 'Is this it?'

The door was thrown open and a policeman stepped into the room. In the corridor were more people: another policeman, a white-uniformed nurse, three men in suits. Behind them all, the woman from the room next door stood on tiptoe, straining to see what was happening.

With cold eyes, the policeman looked at Noula, then at the doctor in his wheelchair.

'Are you Chabrol?' he asked. 'Louis Chabrol?'

'Yes,' said the doctor. 'Who the hell are you?'

The policeman didn't answer, but rejoined the men in the corridor.

'It's him,' he said to the three men in suits. 'He's all yours.'

'Just a moment!' objected the nurse, placing herself in the doorway. 'This absolutely is not allowed! Mr Chabrol has been very unwell, and the consultant ...'

'Step aside, please, *madame*.' One of the three men moved forward as he spoke. His accent was heavy, and his last word was in French. The nurse hesitated; then she moved out of his way. The man motioned to his colleagues to join him, and all three entered the doctor's room. Their clothes were civilian but similar; on their lapels, they all wore the same badge. Their hair was cut as short as the military's; the tallest of them was scarred under his eye. The first man into the room carried an envelope in his hand; he stood in front of the doctor. The scar-faced man moved behind the wheelchair and put a hand on the doctor's shoulder.

'You can't do this!' said the nurse from the doorway. 'I need to speak to …'

'Please,' said the man with the envelope, in his slow, accented Greek – an accent the same as the doctor's. 'Let us do our business.'

Hearing the men's voices, the doctor's grip on the wheelchair grew tight; below his bandages, his unsmiling mouth was grim.

Now the man holding the envelope spoke to the doctor, in a language Noula didn't know. He spoke at length, and as he spoke, the doctor lowered his head; when he had finished speaking, the man dropped the envelope on to the doctor's lap, on the hospital blanket. Feeling for the envelope, the doctor found it and waved it at the man. The doctor spoke with anger and pointed to his eyes, the wheelchair, the room; but the man just smiled, and turning to his companion, stepped out of the way as handcuffs were snapped on to the doctor's wrists.

The doctor offered no resistance. The scar-faced man grasped the wheelchair's handles.

'This is an outrage!' objected the nurse. 'We cannot allow this treatment of our patient! Please do not move until I fetch …'

But the scar-faced man and the wheelchair had already reached the door.

'Mr Chabrol is a fugitive from French law,' said the scar-faced man, in halting Greek. 'He will stand trial in Marseille, and until that time he will have the best treatment possible, in a prison hospital. Excuse me; I don't wish to run over your foot.'

One of the Greek policemen held the door wide open; with the doctor in his wheelchair at their head, the men marched away, down the ward.

'What's going on, *kalé*?' asked the woman from the room next door. 'Why do those men want your fiancé?'

Ignoring her, Noula turned to the nurse.

'Who were they?' she asked. 'What has he done?'

'They're the French police,' said the nurse, 'with extradition papers.' She looked at Noula and the woman. 'Are you family?'

Noula considered, and shook her head.

'No,' she said. 'No, I'm not.'

'Then I'm afraid I can't discuss the matter,' said the nurse.

Outside the hospital, Noula sat down on the wall, considering. Already, she was late for the office, but there was no question of her going there just yet; her thoughts were all on what she had witnessed and how she would explain it all to Chrissa.

She glanced across to the French café, and as she looked, a man stood up at his table, laid down his newspaper and beckoned to her. She knew him; it was the Athenian who had asked about the doctor. She raised her hand and shook her head, declining, but he beckoned to her again, as if he had some urgent need to speak to her; and so she crossed the street and went into the café.

The fat man offered her the best seat at his table, where the view was of the hospital frontage and the park on its far side. With a gesture, he summoned the waiter; after she requested orange juice, the fat man added pastries to the order.

'Breakfast is important,' he said, 'and sugar is good for you when you've had a shock.'

'Have you had a shock?' she asked.

'I was referring to you,' he said, with a smile. 'I have just seen Dr Chabrol taken away in handcuffs, and I assume,

203

from the timing of your leaving the hospital, that you have seen the same.'

'I went to see him, for Chrissa. They came for him whilst I was there.'

'That was unfortunate,' he said. He held out his cigarettes. 'Do you smoke?'

'No, thank you.'

'Have they arrested him?' he asked, putting the cigarettes away.

'It certainly seemed that way. They were foreigners; I couldn't tell what it was they said to him.'

'They were French, I'm sure.'

'What has he done?'

The waiter brought Danish pastries and Noula's orange juice, and the fat man thanked the waiter as he left. She sipped at the cold juice; the fat man offered her the plate of pastries.

'You must have first pick,' he said. 'Please, take one. The sugar, as I say, will do you good. I cannot make the same excuse for myself, but I shall indulge nonetheless, simply because they are so good here.'

She chose, and so did he; and as she tasted the apricots and sweet vanilla custard, she found he was quite right about the sugar.

The fat man sipped at what was left of his coffee.

'Of course this will be a huge blow to your sister. But he was not the man for her.'

'He was so good to Mama; he used to sit with her to give Chrissa a break. But I couldn't like him, and he seemed to know it. What has he done that is so serious?'

The fat man hesitated.

'I really couldn't say,' he said. 'Sometimes, it's better not to know.'

'But Chrissa will want to know. She might want to follow him where he's gone. Maybe I should make enquiries at the police station.'

The fat man took another bite of his pastry.

'These really are excellent, aren't they?' he said. 'You'll find the cherry ones are very good, too.'

But her mind was troubled at the thought of Chrissa leaving, and the fat man knew she wasn't listening. Her hand was on the table, by her plate; gently, he laid his own hand on her forearm.

'He's gone from your lives, Noula. Now take my advice, and ask no questions. You might find your sister was more in love with the idea of marriage than with the man. And circumstances can always change again – and often for the better, if the Fates are kind.' She raised her eyebrows and looked at him sceptically. 'Sometimes they are kind,' he insisted. 'Trust me.'

When she left him, she walked slowly in the direction of the library. At the florist's on Angelaki, the bouquets for the wedding had been packed up and taken away. She paused a while, admiring the flowers that remained: orange gerberas, white lilies, roses in softest pink. There was a little cash in her handbag, which she counted, and went inside.

A group of youths had gathered by the fountain. As one of them drank from a bottle of Fanta, another slapped him brutally on the back, making the drinker splutter and spray his friends with the lemonade out of his mouth. They laughed, all of them; the others called the drinker a pig, and he, indignant and wiping drink from his clothes and clearing his nose, took a swipe at the boy who had slapped him. This boy skipped away to hide, looking back at his pursuer.

He ran into the fat man.

The fat man grasped him by the shoulders, and held him at arm's length.

'Be careful, son,' he said. 'You'll hurt yourself if you don't look where you're going.'

'I'm sorry,' said the boy. His hair was blond; he had his father's eyes.

'You're the mechanic's son, aren't you?' asked the fat man. 'What do they call you?'

'They call me Christos.'

'Well, Christos,' said the fat man, 'it's fortuitous, us meeting in this way. Do you remember me? You father's done some work for me, on my car.'

The boy gave a single nod of his head.

'I want you to take a message to your mother. I was admiring your grandfather's photographs, and I told her I thought they might be worth a little money. I want you to tell your mother I've been in touch with an expert in the field, and he'd like to see your pictures. Would you let your mother know, and ask her if she could let me have some samples?'

The boy said nothing, but looked across to where his friends were waiting, and curious.

'The problem is, your mother wanted to keep the idea of selling from your father. Just for now, I think; I suppose she wanted to surprise him.' Again the youth said nothing, but his eyes were shrewd, as if he had understood his mother and the fat man exactly. 'I expect she wants to take her time, and choose what's sold and what's kept. They are family documents, after all. So the problem is, where she and I can rendezvous in private – no need, of course, to announce the business to the whole town – but equally there must be no whiff of impropriety. I am all too aware of how people talk in these small places, and I don't want to compromise your mother in any way. Perhaps you could accompany her, as chaperone.'

For a moment, the boy remained silent.

'Tomorrow,' he said at last. 'My father will be away from home. You could come then.'

'Excellent,' said the fat man. 'Shall we say one o'clock? If that isn't suitable, you can bring me a message here. Please let your mother know I shall be looking forward to seeing her.'

Noula found Chrissa seated at the kitchen table, a pen in her hand and a tablet of writing paper under her wrist. Scattered across the table were a number of sheets of paper, half filled with writing or written with only one line; on the floor were several more abandoned letters, screwed up and tossed away. The letter she was writing now was barely begun, just five or six words on a single line. Before Chrissa covered it with her arm, Noula read the salutation. The letter began, 'My Dear Louis'.

The kitchen smelled of fried meat and spices: cumin, cinnamon, cloves. The window was clouded with the steam of boiling pasta.

Chrissa looked up at Noula.

'Roses,' she said. She put out her arm and gathered all the rejected letters towards her. 'Who's been sending you flowers?'

'No one,' said Noula. She held out the glorious bouquet – sugar-pink roses and brilliant-green ferns, glossy, crackling cellophane and a bow of satin ribbon. 'I got them for you.'

A smile came to Chrissa's eyes, and in a moment spread to her lips, lifting some of the tiredness from her face. She held out her arms for the flowers and put her face in them, breathing in their perfume and enjoying the petals' softness on her skin.

'They're beautiful,' she said. 'What's the occasion?'

'No occasion. I thought you'd like them, that's all. A gift, from me to you.'

'I'll find a vase,' said Chrissa.

'I'll tell you which vase to use,' said Noula. She held up a key. 'The cut-glass one from upstairs. It's perfect for them. We'll christen it.'

Chrissa frowned.

'The dowry vase? We can't use that!'

'Why not? Who's to stop us? They're our things, yours and mine, and we can use them if we want to. What's the point, Chrissa? All those lovely things up there, and us two old spinsters living like poor folks down below!'

Chrissa's head dropped.

'I was just writing to Louis. To find out how things stand between us.'

Noula sighed.

'Put the flowers in the vase, Chrissa. You'll arrange them beautifully; you have the knack. And whilst you're doing that, we'll talk. I have something to tell you. I went to the hospital today.'

Twenty-three

The fat man drove again to where the log bridge crossed the stream, and followed the track up to Orfeas's meadow.

But as he crossed the meadow and the cabin came into view, immediately he knew something was wrong. By the outcrop which gave the cabin shelter, something moved. Holding his hand to his eyes to block the glare, he trained his eyes to where the creature had hidden behind the rocks. Unmoving, he waited, until the creature judged it safe to move again, and showed itself.

The fat man knew its long-legged, skinny form. In Orfeas's style, he made a circle of forefinger and thumb, and stuck them under his tongue to give a whistle which came back to him in an echo.

The mistrustful dog was not fooled; though it showed its greying muzzle around the rock, it came no closer. Puzzled by the dog's liberty, the fat man went on towards the cabin, passing the empty stock pen, whose gate stood propped open with a rock. The fat man frowned, and again shielded his eyes from the glare to scan the slopes which ran up to the high mountains. Here and there, enjoying their liberty, were Orfeas's Easter lambs, fattening themselves for slaughter on the grass's new growth.

All at liberty: now the implication struck him. At the cabin, the door was unlocked, and calling Orfeas by name, he went in.

The place was as he expected – empty, and so bleak and sparse it was impossible to believe a man had ever lived here. It was impossible, too, to know whether there had been possessions here of value he would take with him, or whether he intended ever to return.

But he had left something behind. Hanging on a stake of wood driven into the cabin wall was a case of black leather, so thick with dust and cobwebs it seemed to be growing on the wall, attached to it like fungus. The fat man laid down his holdall and lifted down the case, brushing the dirt from it as best he could.

He touched the base of the primus stove and found it warm. Orfeas, like all his countrymen, would set off on no journey without coffee; the warmth of the primus said he was only minutes on his way. Outside, the old tarpaulin had been dragged aside and the doctor's silver Yamaha was gone. He had an advantage, possibly, though the shepherd was no expert in riding motorbikes on rough terrain. And the rough route was the way he must have taken, or the fat man would have passed him on the road.

Without doubt, he must move quickly; so, picking up his holdall and the black case off the wall, he set off at a run towards the mountain.

When the fat man arrived at the chapel of St Paraskevi, no one was there. Despite the speed of his journey and his strenuous run, his breathing quickly slowed to a comfortable rate, and the slight pinkness of exertion which had coloured his cheeks soon left them. Perplexed to find the little church, kitchen and refectory all closed up, he succumbed to a moment of doubt, until, climbing on to the courtyard's stone bench, he looked over the wall to where (according to Adonis Anapodos) the doctor's bike had been left by his attacker.

The silver Yamaha was there, in that same place; though not, this time, thrown carelessly on its side, but placed up on its stand, and close to the wall to shelter it from bad weather or hide it from the sight of passers-by. On the bike's seat was a leather doctor's bag.

But where was Orfeas? Never allowing that his deductions might be wrong, the fat man entered the church. The lamps and the candles were out, their wicks cold. The kitchen door stuck with its swollen wood, and the few leaves that had collected at its foot were undisturbed. And yet, something had changed. Standing at the centre of the courtyard, he lowered his head, and seemed to think, deeply. Then his eyes moved to the bell hanging over the gateway. The bell was there; but the rope looped around the hook in the wall was gone, cut through with a knife.

The fat man left the chapel and followed the track in the direction of Adonis's flock. Around the first bend (and, from the chapel, out of sight), was a broad-limbed beech; amongst the spreading roots was the shepherd's pack; and some feet off the ground where the tree's trunk divided was Orfeas, straddling a crook in the branches, tying one end of the bell rope around the highest branch he could reach.

Staying out of Orfeas's sight, the fat man moved round the tree. Orfeas pulled at the rope ends to make the knot tight, then put in another knot and tightened it again. As he worked, he muttered; his face was red with strain.

As quietly as he was able, the fat man laid down his holdall and the black case he had taken from Orfeas's cabin. Clicking the latches on the case, he opened the lid. Inside lay a violin, its old wood mellow and golden, its strings loose on their pegs; in the case's lid, the horsehair bow was fraying. Lifting out both bow and violin, he stood and positioned the instrument under his chin; putting the bow to the strings, he stepped around the tree into Orfeas's sight, and drew the bow across the violin's strings.

The noise he made was awful, as offensive to the ears as squabbling cats. He scraped the bow across each string in turn, labouring from the instrument the most dreadful sound each string could ever produce; then he looked up at Orfeas's astonished face and smiled.

'Orfeas!' he called. 'Come down and show me how it's done!'

But Orfeas looked back at the rope, where the knot he was working on had grown to double the size of a fist. Tying in one last twist of rope, he pulled hard on the loose end of the coil laid on the branch, and, satisfied it was secure, he tossed down the coil, so it swung from branch to ground with length to spare, and its end landed at the fat man's feet.

The fat man scraped on, drawing more offensive sounds from the violin; but Orfeas ignored him, and, scrambling down from the tree, grasped the dangling rope, pulling on it with all his weight to test its security.

The fat man played and played his dreadful music, until suddenly Orfeas snatched the violin from his hands, and prepared to break its back across his knee.

But the fat man was too quick, and grabbed his wrist. Enraged, Orfeas glared at him. The fat man squeezed his wrist, tighter and tighter, until Orfeas's anger turned to pain, and he gasped. He tried to shake free his wrist, but the fat man's grip could not be loosened.

'Leave me!' he demanded. 'What do you want here? Go!'

'Give me the violin,' said the fat man, 'and I'll release you.'

Orfeas offered up his hand.

'Take the damned thing,' he said. 'Here, take it!'

The fat man did so, and released Orfeas's wrist, which was marked like a Chinese burn where the fat man had held it. Orfeas rubbed at the redness.

The fat man held violin and bow in one hand, and with the other, tugged to test the rope, as Orfeas had done.

'So,' he said, 'your preparations are almost complete. You're hoping for better luck this time, are you? Since your venture didn't go so well last time?'

'What do you want here?' asked Orfeas. 'Go and leave me; just leave me, please.'

'Well, I'll tell you what,' said the fat man. 'You give me a tune, and I'll go.'

'I don't play.'

The fat man raised a finger, and in admonishment waggled it from side to side.

'Now I don't think that's true,' he said, 'and you'll find me a man who has a particular passion for truth. If you mean you haven't played recently, that might be true; but if you're saying you don't know how to play, that isn't true, is it?'

'What do you want?' asked Orfeas again. 'Can't a man find any peace here?'

The fat man plucked at a violin string. The noise it gave was hollow, and quickly died.

'Peace, here?' he asked. 'There seems to be none. So people might ask why you insist on this place for what you intend. In fact, I shall ask the question myself. What is so special about this place, Orfeas, that it must be here you play out this melodrama? By the way, I should warn you that the science of hanging is quite complex, and to break your neck satisfactorily, you need a higher branch.' He moved under the tree's canopy and looked upwards into the leaves, then pointed. 'That one there would do you better, though it's a

213

tricky climb to reach it, and you'd have to do an acrobatic leap from quite a height. What is your plan, to stand on a rock and kick it away? The problem is, if you use this branch here, your neck won't break, and you'll die slowly and painfully from strangulation. Am I right in thinking your original plan was to string yourself up from St Paraskevi's gate? It would have been poetic, I grant you – your body swinging in the wind, framed by that charming archway and the bell ready for tolling overhead – but you would have suffered terribly, my friend.'

The fat man put an arm round Orfeas's shoulder as he had done before when leading him towards the hidden motorbike; but now there was affection in the gesture.

'Listen to me,' he said. 'You are a romantic, a dreamer, a gentle man – but too often, romantic dreamers don't get the girl, because some hard-nosed action man gets there first. Here, let's sit.' He coaxed Orfeas to sit by him at the tree's roots, where the shepherd's bag lay. 'Is that coffee I can smell? Break it open, man, and let's have a cup whilst we talk.'

The shepherd's hands were shaking and his lips trembled; his hands trembled too much to open his bag.

'Allow me,' said the fat man. Stretching out his legs as if they were about to enjoy a country picnic, he took the bag from the shepherd and undid the fastenings to take out the tartan-patterned flask. Unscrewing its cup and the inner cap, he poured warm coffee into the cup.

'May I?' He took a sip, pulled a face, and smiled. 'More alcohol than coffee,' he said. 'What is this, Dutch courage?' He passed the cup to the shepherd, who drank it down. The fat man screwed the flask's cap back in place. 'Enough of that,' he said. 'You need a clear head, whilst we talk. Why don't you tell me what happened when you came up here that day?'

The shepherd didn't speak, and the fat man let him look into his own thoughts, and gather them. Behind the chapel, Adonis's sheep were bleating; one of the year's first bees buzzed past them and crawled amongst the petals of a flower. Still silent, the shepherd reached for his pack, and drew out a photograph whose edges were deformed and scorched from burning. He handed the photograph to the fat man. It showed a woman who was familiar to him: a younger Chrissa Kaligi.

'She was mine,' said the shepherd. His voice was hoarse, with the alcohol or with holding back emotion. 'I asked for her, years ago, and her father said we had to wait. It wasn't right for her to be married before Noula. I didn't mind. I was prepared to wait. I loved her.' He lifted his forearm, and drew his sleeve across his nose. 'I had my mother to take care of, and the sheep. I was biding my time, and I thought she was too. I thought we had an understanding. I saw her often; after her father died, I did odd jobs for them, those things that are too much for women: chopping wood, a bit of painting around the house. Time was going by, I knew that, and we were getting older, but I thought it didn't matter. Noula didn't mean to get in the way; she just never found anyone to ask her. When their mother died, I thought I would wait a while, and go and see them, talk to both of them and see what could be done. But that doctor put paid to all that. He got in quick, wouldn't you say – that French bastard got in quick! Before I knew it, she was marrying him. I never had a chance.'

'So what did you do?'

The shepherd gestured upwards, at the tree branch and the rope.

'What else was there to do? I couldn't live with it; I couldn't live with her being with another man. The night before her wedding, I drank a bit. All right – I drank all night, until

I was the best part of sober again. And I decided I'd had enough, and I came up here to make an end to my sorry self.'

'Why did you choose this place?'

Orfeas pointed to the photograph which the fat man still held.

'That was taken at the chapel,' he said. 'I took it the day she said she'd marry me. We said we'd marry there, because we liked the view. I'd been drinking, and the strangest things seem logical when you're drinking. If I'd done the job at the cabin, I'd be dead now, and what's the betting no one would have found me yet.'

'So what happened?'

'I came here early, with a flask of special coffee, to fortify myself. Dutch courage, as you say. But the drinking had made me thirsty, and I was going to get a drink from the well – though why it mattered being thirsty with my intentions, only God knows. But somebody was coming. I heard a motorbike coming up the track. I thought it would be Adonis, and I wasn't in any mood for conversation. So I decided it was time for me to go. I sneaked out of the kitchen and shinned over the wall at the back.'

'You left your flask behind.'

'I thought I'd come back for it.'

'You saw no one?'

'I wasn't here to see anyone.'

'And when you came back?'

'By then, I knew what had happened to the doctor. His bike was there, and I took it, because – as I saw it – it belonged to Chrissa. I knew if it was left there, the local lads would have it stripped for parts within a week. They'd take everything, down to the smallest bolt. It was a valuable piece of property, and it was hers. So I took it for safe-keeping. That was all. But the time's never been right to take it to her.'

'And now?'

He lowered his head to his knees, and hid his face. The fat man reached out, and in a fatherly gesture, clasped the shepherd's rough hand in his own.

'Is this the truth you have told me?'

Head still down, Orfeas nodded.

'I didn't harm him; I wouldn't harm him. That would have hurt Chrissa. Her happiness – that's what's important.'

The fat man removed his hand.

'So tell me, Orfeas – how will your body swinging from that tree contribute to Chrissa's happiness?'

'How did you know to come after me?'

'The dog loose, amongst your fat lambs? A suicidal move, for a shepherd. You'll have your work cut out, rounding them all up, and the dog will have enjoyed its freedom, too. The dog needs its master, and the sheep need their shepherd. And now she's alone again, don't you think Chrissa might need you too?'

He raised his head.

'She's marrying the doctor; that's what folks say. When he's got his sight back, the wedding's on again.'

'Well, as so often with rumour, folks have got it wrong. The doctor's gone back to his homeland on urgent business. He won't be back for any wedding, take it from me. But the lady's got a dress, and shoes, and a house ready to live in – all that's missing is a bridegroom.'

Derisively, he laughed.

'You can't be thinking of me. Look at me! Why would any woman look at me?'

The fat man raised his eyebrows, and looked Orfeas in the eye.

'So?' he asked. 'What will you do about it? Don't think me unkind, but was it not – just possibly – of your making that

Chrissa forgot she was to marry you? She's a romantic, as you are; so did you put on your best clothes and offer to take her dancing? Did you take her flowers, or send her little notes, or let her know in any way at all she was the most important thing in the world to you? Or did you go there – forgive me, friend, but I told you I deal in truth, and sometimes the truth is hard to hear – dressed as you are now, stinking of sheep and with your hair needing a cut and your boots covered in mud? You must accept the part you played in this, Orfeas – you were careless with the lady's affection. In short, you took her for granted, and made it easy for the Frenchman to step in. Now he's stepped out, you have a second chance. Cut out the *tsipouro*; no woman wants the bottle for a rival. And clean yourself up, and go there, declare yourself again. You made a mistake, assuming she could read your mind. What she read in you was carelessness and indifference. Make it up to her. I suggest you make use of this.'

He held out the violin and bow.

'I told you. I don't play.'

'You do play. You can play. But your finger joints are rusty and the violin needs repair. Make amends to your instrument first, and she'll help you win the lady you are after. And return the motorbike to her, as you had planned. The doctor doesn't need it any more, and the money from its sale will go some way to paying for that wedding.'

'But what about the doctor?' asked Orfeas. 'We still don't know who attacked him. I've heard some people think I did it. What if Chrissa thinks so?'

'Those who need to know, know,' said the fat man, darkly. 'There's somewhere else I have to be in the next day or so, but I have time to pay a visit before I go. You need know nothing, except that it is dealt with, and the doctor's no obstruction to your lady. If you don't win her back, you can only blame yourself. Now let's cut down this rope and restore it to its proper, useful place.'

In the square, workmen – the dregs of the task force – were cutting down the bunting; the electrician was making heavy weather of winding up the cabling, whilst the street-sweeper, leaning on his shovel, gave his advice.

On the fountain rim, a young man sat, watching. Approaching him, the fat man offered him his hand.

'I'm very pleased to see you, Mr Mayor,' he said. 'I wanted to give you my thanks for an excellent day's entertainment. You must feel the minister's visit was a resounding success.'

The mayor stood to take the fat man's hand, but his handshake lacked conviction.

'Thank you,' he said. 'I'm glad you enjoyed it. As you see, this is the tail end of it all – the tidying up, and back to normal life.'

'Do I sense,' asked the fat man, shrewdly, 'that you are missing the drama of a challenge?'

The mayor smiled, a little sadly.

'You might say that,' he said. 'Yes, I think that is probably very true.'

'Yet this town presents a challenge, in itself,' said the fat man. 'To me, as an outsider, it lacks any obvious prosperity – would you agree? Whilst there's money for some in agriculture, don't you think it would be a good idea to diversify?'

'Diversify? But into what?'

From his pocket, the fat man drew out a matchbox and slid it open to show the small object inside. He held the matchbox out to the mayor. The mayor looked in at the object and frowned.

'What is it?' he asked.

With finger and thumb, the fat man picked out the lead scroll he had found in the sands of the ancient ruins.

'It's a curse tablet,' he said. 'Your ancestors were well known for necromancy – for spell casting and ill wishing, in malicious and sometimes highly original ways. I found this example of their work – between you and me, of course – in the ruins on the Platania road. I think, if you could persuade the Department of Archaeology to investigate, there could be more to find.'

'But why would they investigate?' asked the mayor. 'The place is no Ephesus, is it? Their schedules are backed up for years to come. And what do we have, after all? Just a few stones.'

'Just a few stones above ground, maybe; but what if those stones hide something more? You're a man with great powers of persuasion, Angelos. Get them to dig, and who knows what they might find? Perhaps something to put Morfi on the map. Here, take the scroll; use it to bolster your argument. If you have enough faith in yourself, the next time you welcome a visiting dignitary, it could be the President himself.'

Twenty-four

At one o'clock exactly, the fat man pulled up alongside the pumps. Across the garage forecourt, the space usually occupied by the mechanic's truck was empty, its absence marked by a rectangle of dry cement where the remainder was damp. By the workshop door, Christos squatted amongst rags and dusters, applying polish to a moped. As the fat man switched off the Mercedes's engine, the boy raised his eyes, but gave his full attention back to his polishing.

Slamming the car door, the fat man called out, cheerfully.

'*Yassou*, Christos! I see you're hard at work. And I hate to interrupt you, but whilst I'm here, I'm needing petrol. So fill her up, will you? I've a long journey ahead of me, and the old girl drinks more than she should. And could you let your mother know I'm here?'

In imitation of his father, Christos wiped his hands on an oily rag which he dropped to the ground, and passed the fat man in silence. A half-formed man still uncomfortable with what he was becoming, he strode lankily and self-consciously up to the house, and called a single word of summons through the kitchen door. Sullen-faced, and with an air of being grossly inconvenienced, he returned to the

221

pumps, where he was careful to invite no conversation as he removed the car's petrol cap and slotted the pump's nozzle into the tank.

On the road, two girls were going by, walking quickly with their bags of bread and groceries, heads bent together in conversation, their faces covered by their long, luxuriant hair. Christos glanced at them and coloured red, bending low to hide himself behind the Mercedes's body.

The fat man smiled and shook his head; as the gauge on the pumps ticked slowly round, he wandered to the verge where wild flowers grew in the spring-fresh grass, and bent to touch the mauve petals of an anemone.

From the house, the mechanic's wife hurried towards them, glancing back over her shoulder. The hem of her black skirt needed stitching; her slippers had holes at the toes. Under her arm, she carried a leather-bound album, and in her hand, a large and tattered envelope.

She didn't smile, but laid the album and the envelope on the bonnet of the car, holding them there with the palms of both hands as though to stop them from blowing away, though there was no wind.

'*Kali mera sas*,' she said. 'We must be quick. Tassos is away, but he might be back at any time.'

The car's tank was full; as Christos lifted out the nozzle, a splash of petrol fell near the fat man's feet. With a clatter, Christos replaced the nozzle on the pump and turned to leave them, but the fat man wanted him to stay.

'You'll be interested in what I have to say,' he said. He glanced at the dials on the pump. 'Let me pay you what I owe, first of all.' He took out his wallet, and handed over notes to cover the amount shown on the dials. 'Keep the change. Maybe you should buy new brake pads for that moped of yours.'

The boy took the money. The tip was generous, but still he didn't speak or smile, though he inclined his head a little as a thank you before stuffing the cash into his jeans.

'I haven't said anything to Mama about the photographs,' said Litsa. There was regret in her voice for her deception.

She pulled out what was in the envelope. There were ten black and white shots, all taken at the shore: the face of a young fisherman, whose old eyes looked far out to sea; a catch of dying fish, gasping in a dripping net; an upturned boat, long-abandoned and decaying on a winter beach. All captured both a moment and all time, an age already past but never passing in men's consciousness and dreams.

'Extraordinary,' said the fat man, shaking his head as he went through them. 'Simply extraordinary.'

'It would break her heart,' said Litsa, sadly. 'And I don't want Tassos to know. If there's money to be had, it's to spend on a few comforts for Mama and some nice things for the kids, not on truck parts and his card games.'

The fat man handed back the photographs.

'If your mother would be upset at your selling the photographs, perhaps you should wait a while,' he said.

'You mean until she dies.'

The fat man's eyes were kind.

'I do mean that, yes,' he said. 'Perhaps it would be better to wait until then.'

There was silence between them. The boy looked down at his feet and kicked a stone; it rattled across the cement and came to rest close to the anemones the fat man had admired.

'But the money would bring her benefit,' said Litsa, as if thinking aloud. 'I wanted to buy her some nice things. She's never had much; nothing of her own.'

At last, the boy broke his silence.

'What's the point, Mama?' he said, fiercely. 'She doesn't know what day it is, what year it is, even! What's the point in buying her things? She won't know they're there.'

'Because she deserves them,' said his mother, quietly.

'But you said yourself,' said the boy, with logic, 'it'd break her heart to see Grandpa's pictures sold. She wanted us to keep them. You know that.'

'And what's the point of pictures?' She looked directly at the boy; her pale skin was pink with indignation. 'We can't eat pictures, or wear them!'

'What's the point in buying things for someone who can't use them? You're just trying to make it up to her. You're trying to make yourself feel better.' Plainly, the boy was angry, yet there seemed no reason why. Christos's objections seemed out of character; what teenager would object to trading boring photographs for new clothes?

Litsa looked at the boy with tears in her eyes, and with hands made clumsy by emotion, forced the photographs back into their envelope.

'I'm sorry, *kyrie*,' she said, 'but our pictures aren't for sale.'

She and the boy turned to leave him, he heading back to the workshop, she towards the house, clasping the album and envelope to her chest.

But the fat man didn't let them go.

'Just a moment,' he said. 'There's something I'd like to show you.'

The boy kept walking as if he hadn't heard.

'You too, Christos,' said the fat man.

He opened the passenger door of the Mercedes. On the seat lay papers like those he had left at the hospital.

'These,' he said, holding them up, 'are copies of letters sent to Dr Louis.'

Hearing that name, Litsa gave a polite smile. The boy folded his arms across his chest; his expression gave no hint of his thoughts.

'You know Dr Louis, don't you?' asked the fat man. 'I believe you told me he treated your mother.'

'That's right,' said Litsa. 'How is he?'

'Blind,' said the fat man. 'Blind, and unlikely to see again.'

Litsa gave a small *tut* – the kind of insignificant sound appropriate to the misfortunes of a stranger.

'You'll be interested in these.' The fat man offered her the papers.

'I?' She touched her breastbone with her hand; her face was puzzled. 'Why should I be interested in Dr Louis's correspondence?'

'They are translations of letters sent to him by the overseeing medical body of France. There is one from the Courts of Justice, too. Please, read them.'

Placing the photographs back on the car bonnet, she took the papers from him with a show of reluctance. The boy moved close to her, and read over her shoulder. After a while, she looked at the fat man in confusion.

'What do they mean?' she asked.

'They mean,' said the fat man, quietly, 'that your mother wasn't the first.'

She handed the papers to her son, and placed her face in her hands; yet there was no sound from her to suggest she might be crying. The fat man took her arm, and guided her to the open car door, pressing her into the passenger seat.

The boy's mask of indifference had slipped; he crouched down next to his mother and laid a hand on her knee.

'Mama,' he said. 'Mama, are you all right?'

'Run inside, son, and fetch your mother a glass of water.'

'No,' said the boy, firmly. 'I'm not leaving her.'

'Are you ready, then, both of you, to hear what I have to say?'

Her face still hidden, Litsa nodded.

'She wasn't the first, Litsa,' said the fat man. 'But she was certainly the last. You made sure of that.'

Now she took her hands from her face, and the boy grasped them and held them inside his own in her lap, and looked up at the fat man with defiance.

'We had to do something,' she said.

'Don't say anything, Mama!' said Christos. 'Just say nothing!'

'I'm not a policeman, son,' said the fat man. 'Your secrets are safe with me; your consciences are yours to live with.'

'My conscience is clear, in regard to him,' spat Litsa. 'He had to be stopped, and I'd do it again tomorrow.'

'Don't say anything, Mama,' implored the boy again. 'You don't know him! You can't trust him!'

'You can trust me, Christos,' said the fat man. 'You can, and must, trust me. My interest is not in courts and trials, but in justice. The two are often not the same. Persuade me what you did was justified, and I will keep silence with you. You have my word.'

The boy was silent, but the fat man saw the movement of his fingers as he squeezed his mother's hands in assent.

'Tell me,' the fat man insisted.

Litsa gave a sigh, deep and releasing.

'It was Christos who saw,' she said. 'He's such a bright boy, my lad, bright and observant. Dr Louis came to see her regularly, twice a week. Perhaps my husband was right, in that respect; it was too often, for a patient whose condition was unchanging. I took it as his admirable commitment to his work, his interest in geriatric medicine. He pricked her fingers with pins, shone lights in her eyes, all sorts of things

226

to generate some response. He gave her a new medicine he said might stimulate her brain, bring her out of her – what did he call it, Christos?'

'Catatonia.'

'Out of her catatonia. I was pleased he was prepared to spend the time: half an hour, often; more, sometimes. I left him with her. Of course I did! I left her in his care. He was a doctor, so I believed she was in caring hands.'

A tear ran down her cheek, and, reluctant to remove her hands from her son's to dry it, she left it there; but Christos slipped one hand from hers, and with his thumb, brushed it away.

'I took advantage of the time to do the chores,' she went on. 'There are always chores. I made him coffee. I made him welcome, and I left him to it.

'But that day, he didn't bank on Christos being there. He could keep one eye on me, I suppose, through that back window, whatever I was doing. And who knows what I was doing? – hanging out washing, feeding the poultry, picking spinach. He could watch me with one eye and still do what he did. He thought he was safe. But Christos had been unwell, and had the day off school. He'd been asleep in his bedroom. And he got up, for whatever reason, and came looking for me in Mama's room. Barefoot, I suppose he was, so he made no noise. And he saw. He saw what that man was doing, with one eye on me. The doctor was watching me, and Christos watched the doctor.'

The fat man spoke to Christos.

'Do you want to tell me, son, what you saw?'

Violently, Christos shook his head.

'He's not to tell you!' said his mother, vehemently. 'I've told him never to think of it again, never to speak of it! If it were possible, I've told him to wipe it from his mind.'

'Will you tell me, then? One of you must tell me, Litsa.'

'I'll tell you what he saw, to my shame.' She lifted her head, showing her face red with deep blushing. 'He saw the doctor peel back the bed sheets and the blankets, and lift poor Mama's nightdress to show her – parts. He saw him pull her nightdress right over her face, so he had her there, naked and blind to what he was doing. He saw him probe between her legs with his nasty fingers, and touch her poor old breasts. And then he saw him unzip his flies, and with his dirty hand, take himself out and start to play, and rub himself against her, until he satisfied himself. And then Christos came running to me, when he had gone, and told me what he'd seen. And here's the biggest sin of all: I didn't believe him.'

'You believed him in the end; you must have done, to take the action you took.'

'I didn't believe him, though, at first, and that made his burden worse.'

'Why didn't you believe him?'

She gave a short laugh.

'Who would believe such a disgusting tale? And yet that was why in the end I was forced to believe him. He's always been, on the whole, a truthful boy; and he wouldn't, I had to accept, invent such a terrible tale. Why should he, why would he? His tears and his anger made me believe him, though I didn't want to. I set a trap, to prove it to myself. I was still thinking he had misinterpreted what he'd seen, that what he'd seen was some medical examination, and quite legitimate. So I left him with Mama when he came again, and told him I had to go out. He took advantage of it; I saw the self-same thing Christos had witnessed. I watched him from my hiding place, and then I went behind the hen house and I was sick, sicker than I've ever been before. To think, to speak of it now, still turns my stomach over. My mother was – is – one of nature's most modest creatures; to see her abused like this in her final, helpless days ... What can you say? I used to pray, before this happened, that when I spoke, she could hear and understand me; now I pray she's far away, remote from everything. My guilt is more than I can bear.'

'Why didn't you stop him, interrupt him?'

'Because he'd have got away. By the time the police or Tassos were here, he'd be long gone.'

'I think you're right. He'd run before, from his home country. So instead you chose a punishment to fit the crime.'

'We wanted – God forgive us – to kill him, but the risk was too great. If I were locked up, who'd look after my family? And the thought of Christos jailed – no, it couldn't be. More than anything, anyway, we wanted to cause him pain. And Christos said, What about those chemicals of Grandpa's. And I remembered there was one above all we were never to touch, as kids, because it burned so badly. And I thought, that's what we'll do: we'll burn his eyes, so he can't see ever to do his evil deeds again.'

'Sodium hydroxide,' said the fat man. 'A powerful alkali, and it did its work. But how did you get him to the chapel?'

'Quite easily. Christos took him a message, then drove me up there on his moped. We did what we did, and left him there. We knew he wouldn't be found too quickly, there.'

'Those papers,' asked Christos, 'what are they?'

'They tell us he is a predator with some history. Our doctor is a rare and deviant creature, the most despicable of perverts, a gerontophile. In short, a man who desires carnal relations with the elderly.'

'So it wasn't just Mama. It wasn't just here.'

'No.'

Despairing, Litsa shook her head.

'I feel so stupid,' she said. 'I was so taken in.'

'That's not your fault, Litsa. Why should you not have trusted him?'

'Will you turn us in?' The boy's face was pale and worried. The fat man shook his head.

'He's been arrested by French police, and I imagine has already left this country. He faces trial in France, regardless of his blindness. And, whilst I do not normally advocate anyone taking the law – the law of the courts, or the more appropriate law of natural justice – into their own hands, it is my belief that, in this case, the punishment – brutal though it was – so perfectly fits the crimes, it could not be improved on. Dr Louis's crimes were amongst the worst imaginable, and, as you say, by far the worse for the natural, deep modesty of his victims. In your case, it is a sorry thing indeed to hope she wasn't conscious of his attacks, as we must call them, because I know how much you hoped she was still conscious of your care, because the alternative is that you are caring for a living corpse, and I do not want you to feel that. You have cared for her wonderfully in this, her final illness; and I'm sure, on some level, she appreciates all you do for her – all your acts of love.'

Litsa began to weep. The boy pulled her head on to his shoulder and held it there, as though he were the parent and she the child.

'You have a difficult choice to make now, if you believe she may have been conscious of what he did. You could tell her he is caught and punished, and already taken away – in other words, you could make her aware that she is safe. But in doing this, whilst you would satisfy her natural demand for justice, she will realise you know what has been happening. I think it very likely that she would then feel great shame, as victims of sexual assault too often do. You might also tell her what you both have done. It might please her, or trouble her – who could say? Or you might – and on balance, I think this is what I would suggest – you might simply tell her there'll be a new doctor from now on, as Dr Louis has been recalled to his homeland.'

Litsa lifted her head from her son's shoulder, and looked up at the fat man with tear-swollen eyes.

'You'll tell no one, then?'

'I'll tell no one. The doctor himself made no complaint to the police; we understand why, now. But no one will come asking questions, after me.'

Litsa ran the back of her hand across her face to dry her tears.

'I'll leave you to decide which course to take. For now, I think you should keep those photographs. They're something your mother values very highly. And the buyers won't go away. The museums and collectors will still be there, when she's gone.'

Rising from the car, Litsa walked slowly up to the house. Christos carried his grandfather's photographs under one arm; the other, he placed round his mother's shoulders to guide her.

He found a quiet place beside the cotton fields. Applying the flame of his lighter to the papers, he watched the flame consume them, turning them to let them burn evenly, taking care not to burn his fingers. Their smoke dissolved in the wind; their black ashes broke up and floated away, until nothing but a singed corner was left. He hid the last white corner under a stone; and climbing back into the car, drove slowly back to Morfi.

Twenty-five

Storms were forecast, overnight; already clouds were gathering to the north. Towards evening, a motorbike pulled up outside the house. Upstairs, Noula and Chrissa were sitting on the sofa, watching the new TV. The newsmen were predicting localised flooding.

Above the newscaster's voice, they both heard music: a solitary violin played an old Italian tune whose sweet, clear notes were beautiful.

Chrissa crossed to the window and looked out.

A man was playing in the street – a well-dressed man she didn't recognise, who, though not handsome, had an honest face.

As she watched, he finished his tune, and knocked at the door downstairs.

From the top of the steps, she called down to him.

'Can I help you?'

'*Yassou*, Chrissa,' he said.

She thought his voice familiar.

'Orfeas?' she asked. 'Is that you?'

'The same,' he said. He ran a hand over his close-cut hair, and loosened his tie a little. 'May I come up and talk to you?'

She smiled, and lit his world.

'Of course you may,' she said. 'It's good to see you.'

At Evangelia's *kafenion*, the TV was tuned to the lottery draw. At their usual table, Dr Dinos and his friends had been served the evening's first drinks. They seemed somewhat morose, with little to say to each other.

The postmaster stubbed out a cigarette and opened up his packet for another, but the packet was empty.

'Hey, Adonis,' he called, 'run to the *periptero*, will you, and get me some smokes?'

Adonis was seated on a stool at the counter, sipping orangeade through a straw.

'In a minute,' he said. 'I have to see first how much I've won.'

The four men at the table laughed.

'That'll be the day,' said the pharmacist. 'People play for years, and never win.'

Evangelia was cleaning out the bird cage. Old newspaper and soiled sawdust covered the counter, whilst the cockatoo fluttered anxiously over all their heads.

'Leave him be,' she said. 'The lad can dream, can't he?'

'Not when I'm out of cigarettes,' said the postmaster, and they laughed again.

The fat man sat alone at his table, his holdall packed and ready under his chair. He sipped at his Coca-Cola, and made no comment.

The compère gave the word for the draw to start. The first number came up, and Adonis whooped, delighted. The second he didn't have, but on the third ball, he whooped again.

'Two,' he shouted. 'I've got two so far, two!'

The fourth ball he didn't have, but the last two were his again.

'Four!' he shouted. 'I'm a winner! I got four! How much do I win, Evangelia, if I've got four?'

'See,' said Evangelia, pointing at the four men. 'The lad's a winner, no matter what you say. Ten thousand drachmas at least in your pocket, *agori mou*,' she said to Adonis, 'and if you're lucky, maybe as much as twenty.'

The grocer laughed, derisively.

'Ten thousand?' he said. 'What kind of win is ten thousand? Now if you'd got a hundred, or two, or three, that'd be worth winning.'

'But four numbers is still a winner,' said Dr Dinos, knocking the ash from his pipe. 'And it's traditional, in here, for a man to buy his friends a drink with his winnings. Isn't that right, gentlemen?'

'Tradition or not,' said Evangelia, laying fresh newspaper in the bottom of the birdcage, 'the lad'll be buying you lot no drinks. Now take your ticket and get out of here, Adonis. Go and show your mother what you've won.'

Adonis emptied his bottle, and climbing down off his stool, approached the fat man.

'What about you, *kyrie*?' he asked. 'Have you been as lucky as me?'

The fat man's ticket was in his hand. He glanced at it again. Five of its numbers matched the six on the screen.

He looked at Adonis and smiled; folding his ticket, he slipped it into his pocket.

'No, son,' he said, 'I haven't had your luck at all.'

Dr Dinos ordered another round for his friends.

'Will you join us?' he asked the fat man. 'Or are you not drinking tonight?'

'I shall be leaving Morfi shortly,' said the fat man, 'and I face a long and tiring drive. I find, under those circumstances, that soft drinks suit me better.'

'If you're leaving us, you must have solved the mystery surrounding Dr Chabrol,' said Dr Dinos. He struck a match, and put it to the fresh tobacco in his pipe bowl. 'Aren't you going to tell us who the culprit was?'

'No,' said the fat man, 'I'm not.'

The doctor's three companions smiled.

'Perhaps because he doesn't know,' said the postmaster to the grocer. He spoke quietly, but not so quietly that the fat man couldn't hear.

'It would be indiscreet of me to tell you, simply as gossip,' said the fat man, 'as you, as a doctor, will respect. But there is one small mystery you can solve for me, if you would. I'm aware I'll have to trust you to be truthful, though Evangelia here will no doubt tell me if you lie. You told me a tale of Dr Chabrol, of his incompetence and misdiagnosis; I have to tell you he told the same tale against you. Which of you was guilty? Was he the better doctor, or were you?'

Surprised at the question, Dr Dinos raised his eyebrows.

'I would have thought,' he said, 'that an investigator, as you say you are, would do his research, and perhaps check the backgrounds of those he is investigating. But since you haven't, I will show you this.'

He reached inside his tweed jacket, and taking out a small box covered in indigo leather, handed it to the fat man for him to open. The box held a silver medal, stamped with the snake and staff of his profession; on the reverse, it was engraved simply, *Thessaloniki*, and a date some years past.

'It's quite a rare award; they don't give it very often,' said Dr Dinos. 'For services to medicine, the details of which are rather dull. Would the recipient of such a prestigious prize be likely to make such a mistake in a diagnosis? I told the truth. *I* bailed *him* out, not the other way round. And if we never see him here again, it'll be too soon.'

'I think you need have no worries on that score,' said the fat man.

The fat man walked slowly to his car, along town roads he had come to know quite well. The growing dark was being hastened by the storm clouds; under the street-lights, the shadows of the pomegranate trees shifted in the strengthening wind.

Unlocking the Mercedes, he placed his holdall carefully on the passenger seat and walked round to the driver's door.

Around the corner, into the light of a street-lamp, came the old man and the donkey which wore no saddle. The old man walked slowly, with one hand on a painful hip; but the donkey was lively, and kept well ahead of him. The old man saw the fat man, and touched two fingers to the peak of his seaman's cap.

'*Kali spera*!' he called.

As he drew level with the fat man, the old man planted his feet firmly, hauling back on the donkey's halter with both hands. The fat man stepped up to the donkey and, putting a hand on its head-collar, brought the animal to a stop. The donkey jerked its head and tried to shake him loose; but the fat man's grip was immoveable, and in a few moments, the donkey conceded and stood still.

'She's the very devil, this donkey,' said the old man. 'I'm wanting to go to my sister's, but the donkey wants to go home, so that's where we're going. It's a rough night, in any case, to be socialising.' He stopped, and peered closely at the fat man. 'It's you,' he said. 'I know you!'

'Of course you do,' said the fat man. 'You met me in this exact spot, a day or so ago.'

But the old man shook his head.

'Before that,' he said. 'You've been here before.' He dug into the pockets of his trousers and pulled out a photograph.

'Look here,' he said. 'I looked this out; I knew I still had it, somewhere. That's me, over here. And that's you, there.'

The photograph showed a group of men and boys, standing proudly with pitchforks before a wagon-load of hay. The old man pointed himself out, as a youth; standing beside him, relaxed in shirt sleeves, was someone who was the image of the fat man, though the hair was somewhat shorter and a little less grey.

The fat man laughed.

'He's like me, I grant you,' he said, 'but how could he possibly be me?'

'It's you,' insisted the old man. 'You gave me some apples, and I've never eaten better to this day.'

'Well, next time I visit, I'll be sure to bring you more,' said the fat man, laughing again.

'I knew you'd be back,' said the old man. 'You said at the time you'd be back.'

'The donkey has sense, at least; you should get home,' said the fat man. 'When this downpour comes, you'll catch your death of cold.'

He released the donkey's bridle, and the donkey trotted on, leaving the old man no choice but to follow it.

'I remember you, like it or not!' called out the old man.

But the fat man seemed not to hear. As the first drops of rain fell, the Mercedes's engine was running. He threw the switch for the windscreen wipers, and they moved smoothly across the screen; when he switched them off, they stopped.

By the time he reached the coast road, the rain was falling hard, and everyone who was out had run for shelter; and by the time he passed the port and reached the limits of the town, there was no one still around to see him leave.

ACKNOWLEDGEMENTS

My grateful thanks, as always, to the teams at Christopher Little and Bloomsbury. Thanks too to photographer Jonathan Reed for his good-humoured research.

A NOTE ON THE AUTHOR

Anne Zouroudi was born in England and lived for some years in the Greek islands. Her attachment to Greece remains strong, and the country is the inspiration for much of her writing. She now lives in the Derbyshire Peak District with her son.

A NOTE ON THE TYPE

The text of this book is set in Linotype Sabon, named after the type founder, Jacques Sabon. It was designed by Jan Tschichold and jointly developed by Linotype, Monotype and Stempel, in response to a need for a typeface to be available in identical form for mechanical hot metal composition and hand composition using foundry type.

Tschichold based his design for Sabon roman on a font engraved by Garamond, and Sabon italic on a font by Granjon. It was first used in 1966 and has proved an enduring modern classic.